The DIVA Goes Overboard

The DIVA Goes Overboard

KRISTA DAVIS

Kensington Publishing Corp.
www.kensingtonbooks.com

KENSINGTON BOOKS are published by

Kensington Publishing Corp.
900 Third Ave.
New York, NY 10022

All Kensington titles, imprints and distributed lines are available at special quantity discounts for bulk purchases for sales promotion, premiums, fund-raising, educational or institutional use. Special book excerpts or customized printings can also be created to fit specific needs. For details, write or phone the office of the Kensington Special Sales Manager: Kensington Publishing Corp., 900 Third Ave., New York, NY, 10022. Attn. Special Sales Department. Phone: 1-800-221-2647.

KENSINGTON and the KENSINGTON COZIES teapot logo Reg. US Pat. & TM Off.

Library of Congress Control Number: 2023952663

ISBN: 978-1-4967-4342-8

First Kensington Hardcover Edition: June 2024

ISBN: 978-1-4967-4344-2 (e-book)

10 9 8 7 6 5 4 3 2 1

Printed in the United States of America

Dedicated to my editors,
Wendy McCurdy and Elizabeth Trout,
with gratitude.

Acknowledgments

A sincere thank you to my readers. I love that you come back to read about Sophie and her friends. Your emails to me show me how much you care about them. You make me smile when you tell me whether you think Mars, Wolf, or Bernie is the right man for Sophie. And I appreciate the readers who tell me they like reading about a woman who can stand on her own-with a little help from her friends. It is because of you that I have the honor of continuing to write about these characters. And frankly, it's reassuring that they are as real to you as they are to me.

Writing is a solitary endeavor for most authors. But I am lucky to have friends to turn to when *I* need a little help. I know how to pronounce charcuterie, but when it came to writing it phonetically so readers would understand, I turned to Ginger Bolton, Allison Brook, Laurie Cass, Peg Cochran, Kaye George, and Daryl Wood Gerber. Everyone chimed in with suggestions until we were all in agreement! It's wonderful to have writing friends. I'm never alone because they are only an email away.

My non-writing friends are the best, too! They even accompany me to mini-cons. You would think they were my personal publicists! Thanks go to Susan Smith Erba, Betsy Strickland, and Amy Wheeler.

And speaking of publicists, I need to thank Larissa Ackerman, who among other things, sets up mini-cons and makes it look so easy. I know it's not. She's amazing! And a lot of fun, too.

I will never be able to thank my agent enough. Jessica Faust has been through ups and downs with me. Thanks to her, everything seems to come out okay and it's usually a fun ride.

Characters

Sophie Winston

Mars Winston—Sophie's ex-husband

Nina Reid Norwood—Sophie's best friend

Orson Chatsworth
    Stella Chatsworth St. James—Orson's daughter
    Jordan St. James—Stella's husband
    Myra Chatsworth—Orson's ex-wife
    Audrey Evans—Orson's former girlfriend
    Karl Roth—Orson's former business partner

Wanda Smith
    Natasha—Wanda's daughter

Bonnie Shergold

Riley Hooper

Doreen Donahue

Joan Jankowski

Cheryl Mancini

Ian Hogarth

Tripp Fogarty

Colin Warren

Terry Warren—Colin's uncle

Chapter 1

Dear Sophie,
My seventy-five-year-old father is getting married!
The bride and groom have been married before to
other people and have adult children and grand-
children. They're planning a huge wedding and the
bride will wear white. I think this is in poor taste
and they should quietly tie the knot at the court-
house in a civil ceremony by themselves. What do
you think?
                    Tied in Knots in Loveland, Ohio

Dear Tied in Knots,
A wedding is one of life's most significant and
lovely events. If the bride and groom want a big
wedding with all the traditions that accompany
nuptials, I think they should do it and celebrate in
any way that makes them happy. There are no age
limits on joy.
                                        Sophie

On Sunday evening, when other people were settling in and getting ready to start a new workweek, I walked my mixed breed hound, Daisy, to relax after finishing up my busy week. An unpleasant waft of smoke reached me. Most likely from a fire pit in someone's backyard, I supposed.

As an event planner, I often worked when others didn't. I had just finished a major convention for the Federation of Pharmacists. They had been lovely to work with and their exhibits were fascinating. It was a major convention and I was ready for some downtime.

The sun had set in Old Town Alexandria, Virginia, but the temperature was perfect for sleeveless attire. The balmy air made me feel summery and carefree. Lights on porches and front doors gleamed on Federal style homes, many of which had been built in the 1800s. Now and then I caught a glimpse of lights strung over a backyard and the sound of laughter.

We had no destination in mind. Mostly, I needed to stretch and unwind, and Daisy needed to get outside and sniff the world. We ambled along until I saw a blaze. In the seconds that it took me to realize that it arose inside a car, it quadrupled in size.

I reached for my phone and called 911. "A car is on fire!" I gave the operator the name of the street and the closest cross street. "Hurry! The flames have moved from the front seat to the back." I felt completely helpless. There wasn't a thing I could do about it. Although we were a good distance away, Daisy leaned against my legs as if it scared her, too.

Sirens sounded louder than normal in the quiet night. They passed us and clanged to a stop. In minutes, firefighters had the flames under control.

One of the firemen recognized me and strode over. "I hear you called in the fire?"

"Yes. It was small and then *whoosh*, it grew so fast!"

He nodded. "Yeah, car fires will do that. Did you see anyone get out of the car?"

"No!" His question worried me. "I hope there wasn't anyone inside."

"We don't think so. We'll open the trunk and have a look as soon as it cools off."

I shuddered to even imagine that possibility. I thanked him for responding so quickly and said good night. Daisy and I headed for home.

On Monday morning, my best friend and across the street neighbor, Nina Reid Norwood, and I sat in my garden, drinking tea and eating healthy avocado and egg toast for breakfast. Birds sang overhead in the trees, Daisy and Nina's tiny fluff ball, Muppet, followed the trails of squirrels with their noses, and the temperature was a blissful eighty degrees. A perfect summer morning in Old Town.

We both noticed when Daisy's ears perked up and she ran toward the side of my house.

Two minutes later, Natasha Smith, who preferred to be known by her first name, like Martha and Cher, emerged around the corner and collapsed on one of the cast iron chairs at my outdoor table. With all the drama of an old-timey actress, she threw the back of her hand against her forehead and moaned. "Mom is getting married!"

"Wanda? I didn't even know she was seeing anyone," I said.

"Can you believe it? My mother is getting married for the second time while *I* haven't managed to walk down the aisle once. I'm so depressed."

"Who is the lucky guy?" asked Nina.

Natasha sat up straight. "That's the only bright spot in

this whole miserable business. She's marrying Orson Chatsworth."

Nina gasped out loud. "I thought he was seeing Audrey Evans."

"Not anymore." Natasha leaned forward and whispered confidentially, "I hear that Audrey is still chasing him, though. She's trying to win him back."

"That's wonderful! Not about Audrey, but I'm very happy for Wanda. Orson is a really nice man." I knew Orson because he often attended the galas and fund-raising efforts I handled. He was well-off and reportedly a very generous donor. I had even bought a necklace in Orson's store, Chatsworth Antiques.

In a breathy voice Natasha added, "He's loaded. My days of worrying about money are over."

It seemed to me that might not be the case. Just because her mother was marrying a wealthy man didn't mean money would trickle down to her. But I didn't know otherwise, either, so there was no point in saying so. "When is the wedding?"

"That's where you come in."

Uh oh. Why did I think this was about to become my problem?

"They planned to go to the courthouse for a civil ceremony, but I'm not having that. Mother's first wedding was a simple country affair. Seriously, her bouquet was wild daisies that she picked herself. This is a major event and I think it deserves to be celebrated."

For once Natasha and I were in agreement. But what the bride and groom wanted was the most important thing. If they desired a simple ceremony, then perhaps that would be better. It was their decision. Not Natasha's.

"They've agreed to an engagement party. The only day I could book an evening event at Mosby's Gardens is Wednesday. It's not even enough time to send out proper invitations! Apparently, the couple who reserved it a year ago have split up. And now Mother and Orson insist the wedding should be in two months and I can't find any-place that can accommodate it. I tell them who I am, but everyone is booked."

"Natasha, you have to reserve a wedding venue at least a year ahead. Sometimes longer for the coveted places."

"Would you try, Sophie? Please?"

"I can make some calls, but don't expect results. Two to three months is hyper speed for a wedding. Your only hope is that someone found a different venue or called off their wedding entirely. I wonder where that other couple planned to marry."

She heaved a big sigh. "I know you can't wave a magic wand. But Mom thinks you can work wonders, so I promised I would ask you."

"Why are they in such a hurry?" asked Nina.

"They're not exactly spring chickens, Nina." Natasha shot her a look.

It was actually very sweet. I was overjoyed for Wanda. Her first husband had walked out on them when Natasha was seven years old. Wanda had done her best to support Natasha, working all hours at a diner in the small town where Natasha and I had grown up. Wanda's life hadn't been easy, especially with the expenses of the beauty pageants Natasha had loved so much.

Being abandoned by her father had scarred Natasha for life. To this day she continued to look for him. She had even tried searching familial DNA, which had turned up a half sister, Charlene, and their father's second wife, Griselda. Unfortunately, he had left them in the same abrupt manner in which he had jilted Natasha and her mother. He simply walked out the door one day and never returned. The two free-spirited mothers were very much alike. They had bonded and opened a new-age store in Old Town that featured CBD oil products, crystals, and other trendy items.

"Natasha, you have a lovely backyard," Nina hinted.

Natasha winced. "Have you seen it lately?"

Nina shook her head.

"Mom and Griselda have turned it into a farm. I put my foot down and said *absolutely not*, but they ignored me and planted the entire thing with raised garden beds. Corn, peppers, tomatoes, squash, beans, herbs. My beautiful backyard!" she wailed.

Nina's eyes met mine. I knew what she was thinking. I had a nice backyard, too. . . .

"Besides, it would have to be early in the morning or in the evening when it cools off. I'm sure they'll be inviting a lot of their older friends. We can't have everyone collapsing from heat stroke."

"I'll make some phone calls and see if I can find a venue."

"Thank you, Sophie. Um, one other little thing. I need a caterer for the engagement party, but no one is available. I proposed a formal dinner, but Mom insists they want to keep it simple. More of a cocktail thing."

"You could do charcuterie boards."

Natasha finally smiled. "I love those! They're so artistic and pretty when they're done correctly. But I won't have time to make enough."

"Orson's daughter has a charcuterie board business. It would probably make Orson very happy if you threw some business her way." I picked up my phone and called Stella Chatsworth St. James. She had created beautiful boards for a party I had arranged for the Ladies of Interior Design. I thought she might jump on it because she'd told me she needed the money. In the middle of a divorce and saddled with expenses for her three young children, she had confided to me that she could use any business, even if it was last minute. After confirming that she could make the boards on such short notice, I handed the phone to Natasha so she could give Stella details on the number of people and what Natasha might like.

While Natasha spoke to her, she gave us a thumbs-up. When she disconnected the call she asked, "Are you sure you can depend on her? Sounds like it's a new business."

"She hasn't let me down yet. You might have seen her work on Instagram."

"Really?" Natasha's attitude changed. "I have to check it out."

"She's calling her business Style by Stella. I have to admit that she has a good eye. She'll help people decorate their houses and style their outfits, too. But her biggest business at the moment is charcuterie and butter boards."

"But that's exactly what I do!" She thought for a moment before casting a critical eye over my attire of a sleeveless cotton shirt and a skort. "I hope she has better luck convincing you to upgrade your wardrobe."

I had to admit that her sleeveless leopard print dress was very attractive and definitely many steps above my simple clothing. But breakfast in the backyard with Nina didn't exactly call for anything quite so elegant. I let her comment slide.

"Thanks for helping me, Sophie. I keep waiting for the third bad thing to happen. But now I think my luck might be changing. You've given me an idea."

"What were the first two bad things?" asked Nina.

"Not being able to get a venue for the wedding came first. What a nightmare. And then Orson's car burned up."

Chapter 2

Dear Natasha,
How do you pronounce charcuterie and what is it?
Confused in Bacon, New York

Dear Confused,
Charcuterie is pronounced shar-koo-teh-ree. *In French it means a selection of meat products like salami, bacon, ham, and pâté.*

Natasha

I stared at Natasha. "Was that here? In Old Town?"

She nodded. "Just last night. They think it was arson. Can you even imagine? Why would anyone set a car on fire?"

"I saw it. I'm the one who called nine-one-one. I had no idea it belonged to Orson. How odd."

"I know! Trouble comes in threes, so there's bound to be something else. I'm treading carefully."

"That's just nonsense, Natasha. You can find three of anything if you look hard enough." Nina tilted her head and smiled.

"Oh, Nina, you're such an innocent. It's absolutely true. The week my father left, I broke my arm, our roof started leaking, and then he was gone. Trouble always comes in threes."

When they left, I called Daisy inside, poured myself a mug of tea, and retreated to my small home office to work. While I was looking for a caterer for an event in December, I happened upon Colin Warren's card. I had seen him at the fund-raising dinner for the arts and he'd told me about a building he was restoring in Old Town for events. It had an address on Washington Street.

An hour later, I walked over to see how they were coming. It might be just the ticket for Wanda's wedding and they might not be fully booked yet.

I swung open a tall glass door and entered a white marble foyer that needed a little work but was nearly finished. Hammering and occasional shouts came from deeper in the building. Watching my step, I opened another door and peered into an expansive room. The ceiling was two stories high, and a balcony ran all the way around the second floor.

"Hey! You two on the scaffolding," shouted an older man. "What did I tell you about taking shortcuts? You're a bunch of dimwits. Do I have to come up there and do it myself?"

The young men on the scaffolding were red-faced. They glanced in my direction, which caused the man to turn around. "Who are you?" he blasted.

"Is Colin Warren here?"

He pointed toward the door. "Only work crew is allowed back here and I don't see you carrying a hammer."

I was a little taken aback by his hostility. I reached out my hand to shake his. "I'm Sophie Winston. I'm an event planner."

He ignored my hand and grumbled, "Can't you see

we're busy? Unless you're carrying a nail gun in that purse, I'm not interested."

I pulled Colin's business card from my pocket and flashed it at him.

"I don't want your fancy business card. Now scram!"

I didn't know who the old guy was, but he wasn't doing Colin any favors. I would have to phone Colin.

I turned without another word and was leaving the room when Colin spied me from the foyer. "Sophie!"

"Hi, Colin. You're just the man I came to see. The building looks great. It will be a wonderful venue."

"Thanks. We're scheduled to open our doors in two weeks."

"Are you booking events yet?"

"I hope you'll be the first."

"Natasha's mother is getting married and they're having an awful time finding a venue that isn't booked."

"Natasha? Wow! That would be great. Think she would feature it on her TV show?"

"I think that could be arranged. I'll give her your number and the two of you can choose the date and set it up."

"I owe you, Sophie. This is better than I could have hoped for. I've been trying to come up with an opening event that would be incredible, and I think this might be it. Natasha will go all out."

The old man started shouting again in the grand room behind us. Even the closed doors couldn't squelch his hostile rant.

Colin winced. "Sorry about that. My uncle is old school. He knows his stuff better than anyone about building, but he came up the hard way and yelling is how he deals with people."

"That's sad."

"Aw, don't feel sorry for him. This place isn't just *my* dream come true. Uncle Terry moved here to reconstruct this building. I'm saving a ton of money by having him do it. We're trying to preserve the Old Town style that everyone loves so much, and he knows how to build things the old way. No cutting corners or using cheap plastic replicas. The younger guys groan about it, but he hired a slew of old characters to show them how to get it right. He doesn't show it, but he's about the happiest I've ever seen him."

"You're lucky to have him then. It's wonderful when family is supportive."

"If I could only get him to turn it down a little bit." Colin shook his head. "You know what they say about a sow's ear. He doesn't mean anything by it. It's just how he is."

"It looks wonderful. I'll have Natasha call you." I left in haste and hoped his uncle wouldn't be a regular fixture yelling at guests.

I made two people happy that day. When I called Natasha and gave her the information she was overjoyed.

The rest of the day passed calmly. I worked from home, scheduling events, hiring caterers, booking venues, and writing responses to questions for my newspaper column. There was no mention in the paper or on the news about the car that had burned. I guessed that meant they hadn't found anyone in the trunk. That was a relief!

In the late afternoon on Wednesday, I dressed in a soft rose-colored sheath with glitsy sandals that did not have high heels that would poke into the grass. Nina and I met on the sidewalk for the short stroll to Mosby's Gardens, a beautiful event site full of blooms and sprawling lawns. The house that adjoined it had been outfitted for catering. A glamorous gated entrance led to the fenced garden.

The heat had begun to abate, making the outdoors more tolerable, if still quite humid. I thought Orson and

Wanda must have been pleased with Natasha's selection. Annabelle hydrangeas bloomed profusely, their huge white flowers dominating the landscape. Rose-colored hibiscus plants were shorter than the hydrangeas, but bright and cheerful. Tall purple and pink crepe myrtles lined the interior of the fence, and all along the walkways, brown-eyed Susans, petunias, and impatiens added more color. Guests already mingled in the lovely gardens and sat on the benches. A violin quartet played on a knoll.

My ex-husband, Mars Winston, strode up with our friend, Bernie Frei. Mars, a political advisor, had an uncanny ability to look at home wherever he was, equally comfortable on a farmhouse porch as he was with high-powered clients in elegant offices. He'd been blessed with an appealing face and a calm manner about him.

Bernie had been the best man at my wedding to Mars. Born in England, he still spoke with a charming British accent. Bernie had traveled the world footloose and fancy free for a long time. We had never expected him to settle down in Old Town. But our friend with the kink in his nose where it had been broken, and sandy hair that looked like he'd just rolled out of bed, had made The Laughing Hound, a local restaurant, into a popular destination in Old Town. He never flaunted his success and told most people that he only managed the place when he actually owned it. I gave him kudos for remaining the same fun guy he had always been.

Natasha looked fabulous. Her dark hair had been swept back into an elegant chignon. She could have been a model in a gauzy robin's-egg-blue gown that seemed to float around her. Her half sister, Charlene, had dressed in a black fit and flare dress. The resemblance was uncanny. Charlene wasn't as tall or thin as Natasha, but the raven hair, facial shape, and brown eyes were remarkably similar.

I knew most of the people who were present. It was like a who's who of Old Town.

Wanda had never looked happier. She wore a bright blue, floor-length, patchwork print dress in a delicate fabric. It was the first time I had seen Wanda in makeup. I was willing to bet that she and Natasha had squabbled about that. It accentuated Wanda's wrinkles when she smiled, and she was doing a whole lot of smiling. She wore her silver-white hair in a pixie cut, which suited both her face and her personality.

Wanda drifted over to us with Orson in tow. "I'm so glad you came! You kids are like family to me. Have you all met Orson?"

We showered them with congratulations and hugged Wanda.

"Of course, I know Sophie well," said Orson, leaning over to kiss my cheek. "She's tops when it comes to organizing galas. And Bernie runs the best restaurant in town."

Bernie blushed. "Orson is one of our favorite customers."

Orson eyed Nina. "And I know you from the animal shelter where I got Rosebud, my best friend. Next to Wanda, of course," he hastened to add.

"Mars is in politics," said Wanda. "He was married to Sophie and then he"—she stumbled over the next word—"dated my Natasha."

Orson chuckled. "This must be a little bit uncomfortable for you."

Mars grinned. "Not a bit. Besides, I wouldn't have missed a celebration for Wanda."

At that moment, a boisterous man approached Orson and Wanda.

Orson slugged back the drink he held in his hand as if he needed strength to deal with the man.

Bernie cocked his head away from them, and we followed him along a flower-lined path.

"Boy, you beat a hasty exit. Who is that man?" asked Nina.

"Karl Roth. We try to seat him in a nook when he comes to the Laughing Hound. He's obnoxiously loud and opinionated. I've often wondered if he has a hearing issue. He's also a lousy tipper, according to my servers."

I laughed at him. "You know the scoop about everyone."

"You wouldn't believe how my servers gossip about who does and doesn't tip well."

Tripp Fogarty walked by us holding an empty tray. He wore a typical waiter's uniform of black trousers, white shirt, and black vest. I knew him from one of the art galleries in town.

"Sophie!" he said in a surprised tone.

"Hi, Tripp. Have you quit the art gallery?"

"No." He lowered his voice. "But it doesn't pay very well. I moonlight for caterers now and then. Hmm. You folks don't have any drinks. I'll send someone right over."

He hurried on his way, and I saw him direct a server with a tray full of drinks in our direction.

The server approached us. "Lavender lemonade? It's the couple's signature drink, designed by the bride's daughter. We also have a mocktail version for those who would prefer."

"Mocktail? What's that?" asked Mars.

Each of us took a glass.

"Mocktails are alcohol-free," explained the server before he moved on.

"All the flavor but none of the booze," said Bernie. "They're the current rage."

A short time later, Orson sought me out. "Sophie, may I have a word with you?"

"Yes. Of course." I stepped away from my friends. "But

I'm not handling the wedding. Natasha is in charge of that. I wouldn't dare tread on her territory," I joked.

Orson laughed. "Don't I know it! No, no, it has nothing to do with the wedding. That's up to Wanda and Natasha. I'd have been perfectly happy to tie the knot before a judge at the courthouse."

A man in a suit cut so perfectly that I thought it must be custom made for him interrupted. "Orson, old boy! Never thought I'd see you marry again. Congratulations!" He held out his hand to shake.

No sooner had he left, than he was replaced by a young woman with chestnut hair and incredibly blue eyes. "Orson, I'm so happy for you. Have you set a date yet?"

They chatted briefly before she gave him a big hug and wandered away.

Orson took a deep breath. "I've been meaning to give you a call. There's something I would like to discuss privately."

Chapter 3

Dear Sophie,
How do you make a smoked salmon rose?
Rose in Salmon, Idaho

Dear Rose,
Use thinly sliced smoked salmon. You may need to cut the slices into long strips. Take a small piece and roll it. That is the center. Stand it on end. Add seven to nine more slices around it. Bend the tops of the slices outward to resemble a rose.
Sophie

"How about tomorrow at my store?" asked Orson. "Certainly. What time?"

"Is eight thirty too early? The employees arrive at nine forty-five to open the store."

"That would be fine. Do you want to set up an event for a charity?"

Orson looked at me with earnest eyes. "Nothing like that." He lowered his voice. "It's a personal matter." He glanced around. "I'd rather not discuss it in public."

Natasha swept toward us like a goose protecting its nest. "Sophie! We can't have you hogging the groom. I'm going to steal him away from you." She latched onto Orson's arm. "Have you had a chance to try Stella's marvelous charcuterie?"

I watched them walk away, wondering what personal matter I could possibly help Orson with. He was probably mistaken about my job. Many people thought I arranged small, private parties and birthday celebrations. Maybe he hoped to set up something special for Wanda. No matter, Daisy and I would be out walking around that time in the morning anyway. We could easily stop by his store.

I drifted over to Mars, Bernie, and Nina, who were checking out Stella's charcuterie boards.

She had loaded the table with a variety of boards, not only charcuterie. "There's something for everyone!" I exclaimed.

Mars laughed. "A little different for an engagement party." He picked up a slice of salami and nibbled on it. "Mmm. I like this. You can choose what you want. Salami isn't something I eat often. I'd forgotten how delicious it is."

"Not all boards have charcuterie on them. There are butter boards, doughnut boards, dessert boards, cookie boards, breakfast boards, just about everything you can imagine. I'm looking forward to pancake boards in the winter."

"Nice selection, but there's no cake," Nina grumbled.

"It's an engagement," Mars pointed out. "Not a wedding."

"We host a lot of engagement parties and you'd be surprised how many people want a cake," said Bernie. "Sort of a pre-wedding cake with multiple tiers and the works."

"Whatever makes them happy," I said. "There aren't really any rules, you know. I think it's fun."

A shrill scream pierced the murmur of voices, followed by a loud thud. The quartet stopped playing.

We rushed up a path to see Orson writhing on the ground in pain. Beads of sweat clung to his forehead.

A hush fell over the guests, which made Wanda's next scream seem all the louder. She fell to her knees next to him. "Orson, what is it? A heart attack?"

I pulled out my cell phone and punched in 911.

When the dispatcher answered, I said, "We're at Mosby's Gardens. A man has collapsed. Please send an ambulance right away."

"Is he breathing?"

"It appears so. But he's clearly in distress. He's sweating profusely!"

"An ambulance is on the way."

"Thank you." I disconnected the call and knelt next to Wanda, thinking Orson might need CPR, but he was conscious and breathing. I forced a smile at him. "Orson, how can we help? Do you need to sit up?"

Orson raised one hand and pointed at me. "Tell Stella . . ." His voice faded and his body jerked.

Wanda tapped his cheeks gently. "Stay with us, Orson. Help is on the way."

He looked at me and very softly uttered, "Tell Stella . . ."

"Orson!" screamed Wanda. "Talk to me. Talk to me!"

Orson's eyes were open, but his hands shook as if he couldn't control them.

Stella rushed toward us. I moved over to make room for her beside Wanda.

"Dad! Dad! What happened?" Stella cried.

Another woman rushed to the opposite side of Orson.

"Orson, no!" She checked his pulse. "It's his heart. I can feel it. Tachycardia."

"What does that mean?" I asked.

"His heartbeat is very fast," she said. "Too fast."

"No! No, no, no." Wanda clutched Orson's hand. "You'll be all right, Orson. But you have to hang in there. Help will be here any moment. Can you hear me? Orson?"

"Dad!" wailed Stella. "You're going to be fine. An ambulance is coming."

"All this was too much for his heart," said the other woman, who looked very worried.

"What?" Wanda blanched. She stroked his cheek. Then she lay her head on his chest, as if listening for a heartbeat. "I don't hear his heart anymore! Orson, please. It's not your time, honey. Please don't leave me."

The sound of clanking caused me to look up. Emergency medical technicians hurried toward us. But behind them, several people rushed out the gate as if they were trying to make a hasty escape.

I helped Wanda get to her feet and make room for the EMTs. Two of them attended to Orson, while a third asked Stella questions about Orson's health.

One of the EMTs on the ground uttered, "What on earth?"

He had opened Orson's mouth. From my vantage point, I could see the EMT remove something bright yellow.

Stella clutched one hand to her chest. "It's a daffodil! He must have choked on it."

The other woman stared at Stella as if she had said something incredulously stupid. She stood up and straightened her skirt, answering the questions about Orson, apparently more informed about his health.

"Who is that?" I whispered to Bernie.

"Audrey Evans. She was a nurse," he murmured close to my ear. "And she was Orson's girlfriend before Wanda. I was surprised to see her here."

Audrey was the opposite of downhome Wanda. About the same age, she was slightly pudgy with enviable thick hair in waves of carefully shaped loose curls the color of light-brown sugar. She wore a chunky gold necklace that had either been very expensive or was an excellent piece of costume jewelry. Two rows of golden buttons accented her dressy, cream-colored suit jacket. In all, she was dressed simply, but refined. A woman of taste. The sort of woman Natasha wished Wanda were.

Mars frowned at another group of people. "Do you see that? Clusters of people are hurrying out the gate."

After a few minutes, the EMTs lifted Orson onto a gurney and rolled him out to the ambulance. Wanda stayed by his side, holding his hand. Stella followed along with us behind her.

"We can only take one person in the ambulance," said an EMT.

Stella nodded. "You go, Wanda. I'll meet you at the hospital." She ran toward the kitchen.

When the doors closed, it was eerily silent. Voices slowly built up a din again. Within five minutes, more than half the guests had left.

I wandered over to the charcuterie and butter boards Stella had made. They were lovely, despite the fact that a good bit of the food had been consumed. I picked up a smoked salmon rose, unrolled it onto a slice of rustic bread, and bit into it. I eyed a butter board with slices of rustic toasted bread around the edges. The butter in the center had been disturbed, but one could tell that it had been smeared on in delicate swirls. Something had been drizzled across the top. I broke off a piece of the bread and swept it through the lush butter. Yum! Stella had mixed thyme and sage into the butter, drizzled it with honey, and topped it with a sprinkling of flaked salt.

Natasha joined me, looking pale and troubled. "What a nightmare!"

I swallowed, feeling guilty for eating. "Wanda must be worried sick."

"I hosted the party. Everyone will remember that. For years people will be saying, 'Remember Orson, who died at the engagement party Natasha threw?'"

I was horrified. Speaking softly, I said, "He's not dead yet, Natasha. I hope he's just ill and will recover." Not to mention that even if the worst came to pass, I doubted that Natasha's name would come up at all. People would remember that Orson collapsed at his engagement party, but it was highly unlikely that anyone would remember it was Natasha who had made the arrangements.

"Are you kidding? At his age? It's like I'm cursed. I almost had a father again."

Nothing about Wanda and Orson's engagement or pending marriage was about Natasha. Not a single thing. I, who had a wonderful father, hadn't realized how much this meant to Natasha, even though she was an adult. It never occurred to me that she would see this like a child who was getting a new dad. As self-centered as she was, my heart broke for her.

"As soon as someone wonderful or special comes along, some mystical force pulls out a magic wand and says, 'We can't have this. Natasha can't be happy.'"

Griselda overheard her. "Honey, we'll burn some salt and sage tonight. I have a lovely Eye of Horus at the store that you can wear. You'll see. Your luck will improve."

Natasha forced a smile. "It's too late now. The harm has been done. It's the third bad thing."

Griselda patted Natasha's back and plucked something from the board. I caught a glimpse of the orange corona of a daffodil as she bit into it.

"Griselda!" I held out a napkin to her. "Spit that out this instant. Don't swallow it."

Chapter 4

Dear Sophie,
I want to make birthday boards and cookie boards,
so I've been studying pictures of them online. Most
of them have flowers on them, which I love. They
make them so much prettier! But I thought most of
the flowers we grow are poisonous. People will
know not to eat them. Right?
        No Longer Bored Mom in Bloomfield, CT

Dear No Longer Bored Mom,
Never use anything that should not be eaten to gar-
nish a dish or a board, other than utensils. Always
assume that someone will eat it.

        Sophie

Griselda daintily removed the daffodil from her mouth.
"Why? What's wrong with it?"

I inspected the boards on the table. Oh no! Stella had
used daffodils as a colorful garnish. They were toxic and
weren't meant to be eaten. People were still enjoying the
food on the boards. I skipped answering Griselda and col-

lected the daffodils as fast as I could. I rushed into the kitchen and dumped them into a large, open trash can.

Stella held her purse as if she was ready to leave. She stopped to watch me. "What are you doing?"

"Just a minute, please." I pulled out my phone and called Wanda. She didn't answer and my call rolled over to voice mail. I tried again.

This time she answered the phone. "Hello?"

"Wanda! You have to tell the doctor that there were daffodils on the serving boards. Orson had one in his mouth, so there's a chance that he ate some."

"What are you saying? That a daffodil made him sick?"

"Yes. They're toxic."

Stella slapped a hand over her mouth.

"But we sell a narcissus tincture for sinus headaches and persistent coughs at the store," said Wanda. "Daffodils aren't poisonous."

I didn't understand how they could sell something made out of narcissus for people to ingest. I was certain they were toxic. To people as well as to animals. "Just tell the doctor, Wanda. It won't hurt if he knows."

"Okay." I could hear voices in the background and suddenly the line went dead.

"I have to get over to the hospital." Stella took keys out of her purse and looked as if she was on the verge of tears. "Please tell me you're not serious about the daffodils."

"I'm afraid so. I think the bulb is the most poisonous, but the entire flower is toxic. They're so bright and beautiful and I'm sure you meant well, but—"

"What if someone else gets sick? Oh, Sophie!" Her voice dropped to a whisper. "What if I killed him? My own father!" She gripped my arm. "I would go to prison. And Jordan would raise the kids! He would marry someone else, and they would call her Mommy! That can't happen! It can't. I couldn't bear it."

I patted her arm. "Let's hope not. Maybe he had a sensitivity that caused the strong reaction."

Stella's eyes were as wide as if she was watching a horror movie. "I've been trying to stay, to clean up and all. I can't believe I might have poisoned my own father. Do you think the people here will be miffed if I don't tidy up? Oh, never mind. So what if they are? I have to leave!"

"We'll take care of everything. You go ahead." She grabbed the trash bag and pulled the ties to close it. The last I saw of her she was rushing out the gate.

I returned to the boards and glanced around. Everyone who remained seemed to be all right. I didn't know how long it would take for the toxin to kick in. Guests who ate one earlier and felt ill might have left already.

I helped myself to a nugget of delicious Gouda. At room temperature, it had become almost soft, and the flavor seemed stronger than usual.

Nina and Griselda joined me.

"Griselda says they sell lots of products based on flowers." Nina gazed at me with wide eyes.

"Many natural products are used in medicines." Griselda selected a slice of salami and placed it on a cracker. "Paracelsus, the father of toxicology, said, 'All things are poison and nothing is without poison. Solely the dose determines that a thing is not a poison.' That's as true today as it was in the 1440s."

I nodded. Even things we took for everyday pain relief could be toxic when taken too often or in too large a dose. Still, it wasn't wise to eat daffodils!

The crowd had diminished considerably. Only a few of us remained, pecking at the delicacies on the boards. Olives, carrot sticks, breads and crackers, a few cheeses and some salmon roses remained. Most of the meats had been devoured.

Mars sidled up to Nina and me. "Anyone up for Indian food?"

Natasha spoke behind me. "I would love to go with you, Mars. I'm afraid I'll have to take a rain check on that, though. I'd better get over to the hospital. Mom won't have a way to get home if I don't pick her up."

"Should we go with you?" I asked.

Natasha swiped her hand through the air. "That's not necessary. Griselda insists on accompanying me. I don't think she needs to go, but she's as stubborn as my mother." Natasha skirted around me and tried to plant a kiss on Mars. He turned his head just in time for it to land on his cheek.

"Maybe I'll see you later?" asked Natasha.

A red flush crawled up Mars's face. "I think you'd better stay with Wanda tonight. She must be incredibly worried."

"Oh." Natasha didn't hide her disappointment. "That's probably true. Maybe another day?"

Mars seemed uncomfortable. I blurted, "Please keep us posted about Orson and also about Wanda."

"I'll do that." Natasha gave Mars one more look and strode away.

"Okay, then," said Bernie. "Let's go!"

"Hold on there, Bernie," said Mars. "Let's wait a minute."

Nina, Bernie, and I burst out laughing and teased Mars mercilessly for trying to avoid Natasha.

"I promised Stella that I would clean up," I said. "You go ahead and I'll catch up to you."

"No problem. We'll help," said Bernie, taking off his suit jacket and rolling up his sleeves.

We were a melancholy bunch that evening, but we resisted the urge to call Wanda or Natasha for an update on Orson. They were probably inundated with calls.

News spread like wildfire on Thursday morning. Orson had passed away. By afternoon, Wanda's friends began arriving with casseroles in hand. I walked over to Natasha's house and to Stella's house to express my condolences, but decided to wait on bringing food. They had more than they could possibly eat.

The morning after Orson's untimely demise, I sat in my kitchen stroking my cat Mochie, and thinking about how quickly a death could occur and change everything. Poor Wanda must be crushed. Even though the two of them seemed direct opposites, she and Orson must have connected at a deeper level. I could understand that. Sometimes people assessed us incorrectly based on outward appearances.

My landline phone rang, and I picked it up expecting to hear from Nina. A man's voice asked for me.

I hesitated. Probably a pesky spam call. "Who is calling, please?"

"Gerard Philoby from the law office of Ronin Walker. Mr. Walker requests your presence at the reading of Orson Chatsworth's will today at two in the afternoon. He apologizes for the short notice. Will you be able to be present at that time?"

The reading of the will? That was weird. Why on earth would I be involved? "I'm sorry, but I believe you have made a mistake."

I heard papers being shuffled. "Are you Sophie Winston?"

"Yes."

"No, ma'am. There's no mistake. You're on my list. Will we see you at two?"

"Sure. Thank you for your call." I hung up the phone and groaned. This had happened to me before. Many people thought I was a caterer, when the truth was that I hired caterers for events. Orson probably wanted me to cater his funeral. I would just have to delicately and politely explain that there had been a mistake.

I checked to see where the law office of Ronin Walker was located. Like many law offices, it was just around the corner from the courthouse.

At one o'clock, I dressed in a black linen sheath, pearl earrings, and black ballet slipper shoes. I took along a small black clutch. When I stepped outside, I saw Nina, in similar black attire, locking her front door. I crossed the street and met her on the sidewalk. "Are you going to the reading of Orson's will?"

Nina looked perplexed. "You too? What's going on?"

We started walking toward the courthouse. "I thought maybe he wanted me to throw a party or cater his funeral."

"Ohh. That would make sense. But then why am I involved?"

"I can't imagine."

We discussed his sad death on our way there. Ronin Walker's office was marked by a black plaque next to the door denoting it as a historic building. I opened the door and we entered a small reception area. A young man sat behind a circular desk. Brass lamps with black shades gave the room a calm, upscale, traditional look. The walls featured large photographs of Old Town framed in black.

Wanda jumped up from her seat when she saw Nina and me. She hurried toward us and grasped our hands. "What are you doing here? Never mind. I'm just glad to see your friendly faces." She lowered her voice to a whisper. "Orson's family thinks I killed him!"

"I'm sure that's not true." But as the words came out of my mouth, I noticed the angry, sour face of Orson's ex-wife, Myra.

The door opened and Stella's soon-to-be ex-husband, Jordan St. James, entered.

Jordan was a large man, over six feet tall I guessed, and while not lean, he gave the impression of being muscular and athletic. I knew him by sight, but had never engaged in conversation with him. His hair had begun to recede. He looked exhausted, which wasn't terribly surprising. Orson's death had probably come as a shock to all of them.

Stella looked a little intimidated and weepy. She appeared surprised to see me, but remained near her mother.

Nina and I walked over to her.

"Stella, I'm so very sorry," I said. "I thought for sure that he would make it."

Her pretty face wrinkled up as she fought back tears. "Me too! I just can't believe that he's gone."

Nina added, "I'm so sorry for your loss. Is there anything we can do for you?"

"Thank you for offering." Stella's gaze swept past us, and she huffed.

Nina and I stepped aside as Jordan approached her.

He held out his arms for a hug, which revealed a chunky Rolex, with a navy blue face and bezel, but Stella backed away. "What are you doing here?" she asked in a whisper.

Jordan shrugged. "Beats me. I thought the old man hated me. But they phoned and asked me to be present, so I guess he left me something."

Stella and her mom, Myra, exchanged a look.

Chapter 5

Dear Natasha,
Our son is getting married. His fiancée's family
served a wedding cake at the engagement party!
Now her mother has asked us to be sure we don't
serve a cake at the rehearsal dinner. What do we
serve as dessert?
                To Cake or Not to Cake in Old Sugar Load,
                                        Pennsylvania

Dear To Cake or Not to Cake,
Many people now serve a cake worthy of a wed-
ding at the engagement party. If you are not serv-
ing a groom's cake at the wedding, then the
rehearsal dinner is a good time for that. Otherwise
you can serve whatever you like. Pies, cupcakes,
cheesecakes, and crème brûlée are always popular.
                                        Natasha

We were called in to a conference room. The photographs of Old Town continued there on the walls. A mahogany conference table gleamed with a high polish. A television screen was set up at one end of the room.

When we were seated, a handsome man with a strong, defined jawline introduced himself as Ronin Walker. "Thank you for coming today. My heartfelt condolences to all of you. I was very fond of Orson and never imagined that he would leave us so soon. As you know, Orson was a bit of a character. He saw some actor in a movie, I think it might have been Burt Reynolds, record a message to be read to his loved ones upon his death. Orson wanted to do that as well, so in a minute you will hear from Orson. Before we watch this, I feel I should inform you that there is a no contest clause in the will and the trusts, which means that if you contest the will or the trusts, then you will be disinherited."

Jordan huffed. "I knew he'd pull some kind of stunt."

"And now," said Ronin, "I give you Orson Chatsworth." He pressed a remote control.

Orson smiled at us from the screen. He sat in a leather chair and was casually dressed in a turtleneck sweater that appeared to be cashmere, leading me to believe that he had taped this in cold weather, at least several months ago. "Thank you, Ronin. Well, folks, it looks like I bit the dust. I could have left you a stiff, impersonal piece of paper with instructions, but that seemed cold to me. Ronin insisted on it, and he'll do his job when I'm finished here. I want you to understand that I gave this a lot of thought. Lost some sleep over it, actually. I want to be fair, but life has taught me that sometimes it's better to be smart than it is to be generous. I can see you squirming now, Jordan, so I'll begin with you."

Jordan sat up straight, but eyed his soon-to-be former father-in-law's image with suspicion.

"I wanted you to be here so there would be no mistake. You have put my daughter through hellfire with your ridiculous demands on her, not to mention the fuss over custody of your children. I thank you for my wonderful grandchildren, but, son, if you don't knock off that terrible behavior, I swear I will come back to haunt you. You might be laughing about that now, but make no mistake, you will regret it if you don't let my Stella and the children live in peace. Oh"—Orson waved his hand—"and you're not getting one more cent of my money."

Jordan blanched, clearly disturbed.

"Stella, I love you, sweetheart. We've had our disagreements, that's for sure. But you were my biggest concern. And out of fatherly love, I am leaving you one hundred thousand dollars because I figure you probably need a new van and have some bills to pay."

His ex-wife, Myra, stared at the screen, her eyes wide and round.

Stella gasped. She gripped the table so hard that her knuckles turned white.

"Stella, sweetheart, I don't want you to go hungry or to suffer. But, sugar, you need to find your place in this world, doing something you love to do. I don't want you to have so much money that you give up that search. Every person on this earth needs to find their own way. They all need to make a life for themselves doing something they love. That's the only way you will ever take pride in yourself. So I'm giving you enough money to make your life easier, but not enough to support you for very long. Now, before you start complaining, you're getting something else, too. You will receive my home and the two rental properties on Lee Street, which ought to provide you with adequate rental income to make your life easier. From here on out, it gets kind of complicated because of the law. Seems I'm not allowed to run your life for you for years to come. I've done all I could to protect you from men like Jordan. Here's the point. I am looking out for the welfare of my grandchildren. I expect them to live in my house as it's the largest. Stella, if you want, you can rent the smallest of the three to Jordan so he'll have a decent place to take the kids when it's his turn to have visitation. But that's up to you."

Stella's mouth dropped open. She glanced at Jordan, whose face had turned frighteningly red.

"In addition, I have taken care of paying for the education of my three grandchildren all the way through a doctorate if that's what they want. Shoot, they can get two doctorates if any of them is up for it. You raise them, but I'll make sure they get whatever education they need. They also get a little seed money, but not until they're old enough to use it wisely."

Stella and her mother, Myra, were the only ones in the room who were smiling.

"Ronin tells me that I don't have to leave my ex-wife a penny. As far as I'm concerned, you got your share when we divorced, and that was plenty. But that seemed kind of cold, so Myra, I am leaving you one hundred—"

Orson stopped speaking to let the number sink in.

"—pennies."

At that point, Ronin dropped a tiny gauze bag of pennies in front of Myra.

"Spend it more wisely than you spent my money when we were married. Wanda, honey, I wish I had met you sooner. I hope that by now, we've had a grand time together. I'm leaving you a bundle of money in trust. Ronin will fill you in on the details, but it's enough to make sure you're taken care of for the rest of your life." Orson winked at us. Or probably more specifically at Wanda.

"Sophie, you're probably wondering what you're doing here. I hereby leave you my antiques business."

Chapter 6

Dear Sophie,
I have been shopping for an antique chandelier.
The prices vary enormously. How can I tell if it's
really an antique?
                    Loves Antiques in Crystal, Michigan

Dear Loves Antiques,
I am not an expert on this, but I understand one
should look for a maker's mark. Crystal daisy but-
tons were popular in the eighteenth century, so you
might look for those as well. Beware of crystals
that are not cut on both sides. Modern ones are
sometimes cut on only one side to save money.
                                            Sophie

I gasped and I wasn't the only one! Everyone in the room turned to look at me. It was the last thing in the world that I ever expected.

Orson continued, "The store, the inventory, everything on the premises, the bank account, the whole kit and kaboodle. You'll know what to do."

I was painfully aware of the glares coming my way. I had no idea what to do. I snapped my mouth shut. Ronin handed me a key ring full of keys.

"And finally, but most important of all, Rosebud."

A door opened and a white bulldog on a leash waddled into the room. Ronin picked up the leash.

"Rosebud will have enough money to live her life in luxury. She can even pay the person who cares for her. Nina Reid Norwood, you will be Rosebud's fairy dog-mother and make sure she gets the best home possible. And there's a little thank-you for your efforts in that regard.

"Well, folks, that pretty much wraps it up. There are a few charities who will benefit from my demise. Ronin will go over all the legal parts with you and take care of the details. Y'all be good because I'll be watching." He pointed a finger. "Especially you, Jordan. See you on the other side, everyone." Orson smiled and winked again, and then he was gone.

For a long moment, we sat in silence, and then it seemed like everyone except Rosebud started talking.

Jordan stared at me, the flush in his face deepening. "Did you have an affair with Orson? That store belongs to Stella." He stretched out his palm. "Give me those keys."

I would have gladly done that except for one thing. This wasn't an accident. Orson wanted me to have his store for some reason, and I intended to find out what that reason was before I turned the store over to anyone. Maybe Ronin would know. With Jordan watching me, I opened my little clutch and slid the keys inside.

Wanda was weeping.

Myra flung the little bag of pennies across the table, and shouted, "If that old coot weren't dead, I'd do him in myself."

Across the table, Jordan badgered me about the keys to the store in a voice that was way too loud and aggressive.

Ronin's receptionist walked around the room, handing out paperwork.

Ronin held up his palm. "May I have your attention, please?"

The voices died down.

"I'm certain some of you are unhappy with Orson's bequests. I would be glad to explain the details at no cost to you. However, you are free to consult with other attorneys. If you would like to meet with me, please make an appointment with my receptionist before you leave. Wanda and Stella, you, in particular, might want me to go over the trusts with you." He stood up. "Thank you all for coming."

We had been dismissed.

Jordan and Myra descended upon Ronin.

I whispered to Nina, "Let's go." I was eager to get out of there and away from Jordan. I didn't need him shouting at me in the street. It was certainly true that I had no business inheriting the store, but he had left Stella and had no claim to it, either.

We walked out with Rosebud, who took her time. The receptionist scratched behind her ears and said good-bye to her before we left the building.

"Do you have any idea who would offer Rosebud a good home?" I asked.

Nina took a deep breath as we walked along the street. "Not off the top of my head. But there's no rush. She can stay with me, provided she gets along with my little Muppet, which I expect she will. Muppet likes other dogs in general. She can be a little yappy, but I think they'll be fine, and that will give me time to find her a good home. What about you? You were just handed a very successful business! Did you know Orson better than I thought?"

"No! There's something very odd about it. I liked Orson, but I can't imagine why he did this."

"Maybe he wished he had a daughter like you."

I laughed aloud. "He does! Stella. I'm heading over to the store now. Want to come?"

"I'll pass. Rosebud has had a busy day and it's hot outside. I think I'd better get her settled in."

Nina turned toward home, and I walked on to Chatsworth Antiques.

The key ring Ronin had given me was packed with keys. I tried three before I was able to unlock the bolt on the front door of the store. A bell chimed when I swung the door open. I closed it behind me and locked it in case Jordan planned to visit the store when he left Ronin's office.

After the lock clanked into place, the silence was positively spooky.

Someone banged on the glass door behind me, and I shrieked.

A woman cupped her hands against the glass to peer inside.

I unlocked the bolt again.

Before I could say anything, she babbled, "I've been all over town looking for the right chandelier. Do you have any?"

Probably, but I didn't know. "I'm sorry. We're not open today."

"Well, do you have *any* chandeliers? I'm looking for one that's large but not too fussy. It doesn't have to be an antique. I'm okay with new or vintage, though I haven't liked a single new one that I've seen."

I capitulated. "Come in and look around."

She bustled inside and I turned the bolt behind her.

She turned around at the sound of the clank. "Are you locking me in?"

"We're not open. I'm afraid Mr. Chatsworth died yesterday."

"Oh! I'm sorry to hear that. I won't be long."

I nodded and wondered where the light switches were. I found two near the front door. When I flicked them on, it was as if the store came to life. Crystal, porcelain, and silver gleamed. Paintings covered the walls and fancy chandeliers hung from the high ceiling. Beautiful displays filled the show windows on each side of the glass door. A staircase led upward. An ornate jewelry display case with a white base and glass top was nearly empty. Only a few beaded necklaces lay inside.

I headed toward a two-level checkout counter in the back and found more light switches on the wall. I turned them on.

"I see it!" the woman cried. She pointed upward at a crystal chandelier. "It has the daisy buttons I've been looking for."

I gazed up at the light fixtures. The chandelier was connected to power. How on earth was I supposed to get it down?

"Can you tell me the dimensions?" she asked.

I had assumed that she wouldn't find what she wanted. Now what? I didn't even know where I might find a ladder. Unfortunately, I spotted one behind the checkout counter. I toted it over to the light and climbed up the ladder to read the tag on it.

Luckily, it had the dimensions. I rattled them off to her. I turned the tag over. "It says 1886 on it." And then I read the price tag and nearly fell off the ladder.

"Steady," she said ever so helpfully from below.

Telling her the price would probably bring this entire negotiation to an end. "It's eighteen thousand dollars."

As I descended the ladder, the woman said cheerily, "It's like you've never done this before."

"I haven't."

"I'm sure you'll be adept at it soon. I'll tell my husband about it and let you know."

I followed her to the door. She turned back to admire the chandelier. "It really is stunning."

"Just a minute, please." I hurried back to the checkout counter and searched for a business card. They were black, with a gold script that matched the sign in front. Swell. I'd thought I would be able to write on it. I opened a drawer and discovered a gold pen. Hoping it would write in gold or white, I wrote my cell number on it. Thank heaven it worked.

I strode to the front of the store and handed it to her. "We're going to be closed for at least a week. Probably longer. But I'll open the store for you so your husband can see it. Just give me a call."

"Wow. That's great service!" She waved at me and left.

Great service? I might not know why Orson had left the store to me, but I wasn't stupid enough to pass up an eighteen-thousand-dollar sale.

I returned to the counter and looked around for a computer and printer. I discovered a series of doors in the back. The first led to a huge storeroom. It was packed with more furniture and decorative items. The second led to a powder room. The third was an office. I had figured there had to be one somewhere.

I turned on the computer and printer and quickly designed a simple sign for the door.

WITH DEEPEST SORROW, WE ANNOUNCE THE DEATH OF OWNER ORSON CHATSWORTH.

THE STORE WILL BE CLOSED TO HONOR HIM AS WE PAY OUR RESPECTS.

IN CASE OF EMERGENCY, PLEASE CALL 703-555-1212.

I printed it out and taped it to the inside of the glass front door.

When I returned to the office, I looked around for something, anything that Orson might have left for me. Some clue as to why I was there.

I was under the Louis XV rococo desk when I heard someone banging on the door and shouting.

Chapter 7

Dear Natasha,
I thought I would serve a charcuterie board with a
mixture of meats and cheeses garnished with fruits
at my book club meeting. But one member has told
me that you're not supposed to mix cheeses with
meats. Is that true?
Cheese Lover in Colby, Kansas

Dear Cheese Lover,
While charcuterie means a selection of meats, there
are no rules. People even make cookie boards and
dinner boards! Mix whatever you want. I'm sure
you are not the only cheese lover in your book
club.
Natasha

The banging continued. Someone was being very persistent. Probably Jordan.

Crouching, I scuttled out of the office and peered around
the side of the checkout counter. It wasn't Jordan.

I had forgotten about Karl Roth, Orson's previous business partner. It hadn't taken long for word to get out to him about Orson's will.

I crouched on the floor behind the checkout desk and waited for him to go away. It was a chicken-hearted thing to do, but I didn't have to answer to him or anyone else about why Orson left his store to me. Besides, I didn't know why.

When the racket stopped, I stood up and straightened my dress. Studying the key ring, I realized that there was only one key to the front door. That meant someone else probably had a key, too. I needed to change the lock. And I had to change my clothes if I was going to crawl around on the floor.

I left the lights on in spite of the electric bill because it seemed safer. People would think someone was inside. At the front of the store, I examined the lock. I knew I could dash to the hardware store and get a new one, but the plate looked antique, and I was concerned that replacing the lock might be complicated. I retreated to the desk and called a locksmith who said he could be there in two hours.

That worked for me. I left the building and carefully locked the door behind me. How would I know if someone entered while I was gone? The place was large enough for a person to hide and I would be none the wiser. Using an old trick, I found a piece of a dry leaf on the sidewalk and jammed it in the crack between the door and the door frame, very low, where it wouldn't be noticed. If anyone opened the door, the leaf would fall.

I hurried home and changed into a skort, a sleeveless cotton shirt, and pull-on sneakers. The store wasn't dusty, which led me to believe there must be a cleaning service that came in. Maybe if I looked back through recent bank statements, I could figure out who it was. There was way too much to keep clean in that place for one person to do it.

I suited Daisy up in her halter and leash and considered taking Mochie with me. He was remarkably good about not knocking things over. But maybe I should explore the whole place before he found a hole I didn't know about.

I fed him before we left. On our way to the store, I stopped to buy a strawberry milkshake for me and a doggy ice cream cone for Daisy. When we arrived at the store, I checked for my leaf. It was securely in place. I unlocked the door. Daisy and I rushed inside, happy to be out of the afternoon heat.

I removed her leash and crossed my fingers that she wouldn't bump into anything. She sniffed the floor and wandered around contently. I found a dog water bowl that probably belonged to Rosebud. I scrubbed it out, filled it with fresh cold water, and set it behind the checkout desk for Daisy.

Out of curiosity, I walked up the stairs to see what was there. It appeared to be a French country nook. Unlike the downstairs, most of the furniture didn't appear to be antiques. It was packed with tablecloths and pillows in provincial patterns as well as a large selection of French style chairs.

At that moment, I heard a knock on the door and raced downstairs to greet the locksmith.

When he was working, it dawned on me that there must be a second entrance through which they brought large pieces. And where did they load them? I called Daisy, and the two of us explored the stockroom I had found earlier in the day. Sure enough, there was a back door that led to an alleyway large enough to accommodate moving trucks and vans. Nearby, an automatic garage-style door connected to a loading dock.

I returned to the locksmith and asked if he could change the locks on those doors as well. Then I sat down and looked through bank statements. The cleaning company,

Dust Bunnies, Ltd., was easy to identify. It appeared Orson had had several employees. I looked up phone numbers and called each of them. Everyone except the Dust Bunny lady already knew about Orson's passing. I arranged to be present for the next cleaning, so I could give them a key. You couldn't let a place with this many items go without a regular cleaning! I told the employees we would be closed for at least a week. They were sad but understanding and relieved to hear they were still employed.

By the time the locksmith was done, I had had enough for one day. I locked up and walked Daisy home.

I fed Mochie and Daisy their dinners, then made my own little charcuterie board from leftover salami, morsels of Gouda and Havarti, a hard-boiled egg, a slice of lovely whole grain bread, a little butter, and a fresh pineapple tomato from the garden, mostly golden on the outside with beautiful red stripes inside.

After checking e-mail and phone messages, I went up to bed. It had been a strange day. I still didn't know what to make of Orson leaving me his antiques store. Nothing about it made any sense at all.

In the morning, I spent a couple of hours writing my advice column and taking care of business. I couldn't afford to let that slide.

Apologizing to Mochie for leaving him alone, I pocketed the new keys, harnessed and leashed Daisy, and headed back to Orson's store, dressed again in a skort and sleeveless top, ready for any eventuality, like dusty parts of the storeroom.

But this time, we cut through the alley behind the store to the loading dock and back door. I stood there for a few minutes, studying the rear of the building. The back door had only a peephole. It didn't need a window. Still, I wondered if Orson had been concerned about burglaries. Next to the door was the loading dock with the garage door. It had high windows to let in the light, and mock handles and hinges, as if it opened like two doors. And next to that was a window.

For a moment, I thought it must belong to the adjoining building, but the brick was different on the place next door. Both buildings had red brick, but the brick on the neighboring store appeared a little lighter in color.

On the second floor, there were four large windows. On top of that was an attic.

If I considered the building as whole, then the extra window on the main floor seemed to belong. But where was it? I hadn't noticed any rear windows on the main floor.

I unlocked the back door. Daisy bounded inside, dragging her leash behind her. I took care to lock up, in case Jordan thought he would pull a fast one and enter that way.

I hadn't given him much thought, actually. Probably because I was so stunned by Orson's bequest to me. Why hadn't he left the store to Stella? He must have had a reason.

Entering the main part of Chatsworth Antiques was like walking into a different world. Most of the street sounds disappeared inside. Beautiful statuettes and assorted porcelain, dogs, cats, birds, and bulls watched as I walked around turning on the lights until I noticed broken glass on the front door. My first thought was that someone had been unhappy that their key no longer worked and had broken the glass to enter the store. But it could easily have been someone without a key who intended to steal something. With so much inventory, how would I ever know what was missing?

I shooed Daisy away, worried that glass shards might cut her feet.

I started toward a broom and dustpan when it dawned on me that the person could still be in the store. I stopped dead and listened.

I didn't hear anything except Daisy. Still, to be on the safe side, I pulled out my phone and pressed 911 to report the break-in.

While I waited for Officer Wong, I called the glass store to have someone replace the glass. How annoying it all was! Then I fetched the broom and dustbin and began the tedious cleanup.

As I swept, I noticed a small piece of fabric snagged on a shard that was still in the door frame. No more than an inch at its longest part, it was light blue and somewhat plush. I didn't dare touch it. While I knew the culprit would never be found and arrested, Wong didn't need me messing up the crime scene.

By the time Wong arrived, I was on my knees, going over the floor with a soft cloth to be sure I hadn't missed any tiny shards.

"What happened here?"

I looked up to see Wong on the outside of the door looking in at me. "Your guess is better than mine. Were any other stores broken into last night?"

"None have been reported." She tried the door handle. "It's still locked."

Silly me. I fetched the key and unlocked the door for her.

Daisy came running, eager to see her friend. Wong had been assigned to the Old Town beat some years ago. I loved to see her arrive at the scene of a crime because Wong was sharp. She didn't miss anything. She could read people well and noticed details that others might overlook. Wong had kept her husband's name when they divorced, but she had told me he was the wrong man for her by a mile. She wore her hair in a sleek bob that framed her face and suited her. Wong battled her weight like I did. We were pushovers for sweets, especially cupcakes.

Wong pointed at the blue tuft of fabric. "Is that yours?"

"Nope. I noticed that. It's just the way I found it. I came in through the back."

Wong sighed. She pulled on a glove, plucked the fabric off the glass, and deposited it in an envelope. "I hate to break the sad news to you, but we won't be sending anyone to dust for fingerprints or collect evidence."

I pointed toward the dustbin and asked facetiously, "What? Are you sure you don't want all the shards of glass?"

She smiled at me. "At least it will be on file if you make an insurance claim."

"Insurance." I hadn't given it a single thought. "Thanks, Wong. I've called someone to replace the glass."

"Is it true that Orson left you his store?"

I nodded. "I'm more shocked than anyone. A short time before he collapsed, he asked me to come by the store. He said he wanted to discuss something personal."

"Oh no! And now you'll never know what it was he wanted to tell you."

"Exactly. Do you know his previous business partner, Karl Roth?"

Wong nodded. "I'm afraid I do. He's as much a character as Orson was."

"He came by yesterday afternoon and banged on the door and shouted. Is he the type who might have broken into the store?"

"As far as I know he has never been in trouble with the law. He prides himself on being southern. He acts like a gentleman, though I'm not sure that he is if he's banging on the door and shouting. I'll go by and have a chat with him."

"Go by where?"

"He has an antiques shop"—she made air quotation marks with her fingers when she said "antiques shop"— "on the other end of town."

"Let me know if he says anything interesting."

"Will do. Good luck with the store!"

I dragged a sofa over to the door to block Daisy from wandering out and to prevent someone else from slipping inside through the gap left by the missing glass.

That done, I faced the rear of the store. The door on the far right led to the storeroom and the back door. Nearing the middle was the powder room. Had I missed seeing a window there? I opened the door to have a look.

Orson couldn't help decorating everything in style, even the powder room. What appeared to be an inlaid antique dresser had been repurposed as a vanity topped by cream marble with a sink. A black and gold chinoiserie mirror flanked by double sconces with black shades on both sides hung over the sink. There was even a clawfoot tub with a curtain in case anyone needed a bath!

But there was no window. I stepped out and continued my search.

Close by was the door to the store office. The room was a good size with two gorgeous desks. Several desk-height, burled wood filing cabinets lined the wall on the right.

The missing window should have been in the rear wall, but it contained built-in bookshelves.

Confused, I went upstairs and counted windows. There were four, as I expected. I opened the window on the far left, leaned out and looked down. There was the missing window. It had to be downstairs in the building.

After closing the window, I returned to the main floor and walked to the front door, which appeared, as far as I could tell, to be approximately in the middle of the store. To my far left in the back was the door to the office.

Could the window have been boarded up for some reason? These old buildings had been through countless renovations over the centuries. Maybe it had been covered from the inside, but left looking like a window for aesthetic balance on the outside.

I returned to the office one more time. The bookcases at the end wall could be covering the window for some reason. I tapped on the wood, but that wasn't particularly helpful. I removed some of the books for a better look, but that didn't prove helpful, either. I would simply have to accept that the window had been blocked for some reason. Maybe Stella knew why.

But as I replaced the books, I heard a click and the bookcases swung open into a hidden room. And there, against the back wall, was the missing window.

Chapter 8

Dear Sophie,
Do you have to use salted butter to make a butter
board?

Not Salty in Salt Lake City, Utah

Dear Not Salty,
Not at all. You can certainly use unsalted butter. In
fact, that leaves you open to decide how much salt
you want on your butter board, if any at all. You
can also use smoked salt, Bourbon smoked salt,
black Truffle salt, and other flavored salts to in-
dulge your taste.

Sophie

Sunlight flooded the hidden room. It contained an elegant desk and a daybed with plush cushions. Like the
rest of the store, assorted decorative pieces, including
some that looked to my untrained eyes like priceless antiquities, lay about.

I blew air out of my mouth. Had Orson collected antiquities that he wasn't supposed to have? I gazed at the paintings on the walls. Had they been stolen from museums? I would have to look them up to know for sure.

Things began to fall into place for me. He gave me the store because he knew I would do the right thing and return them to where they belonged. I had to assume he thought Stella wouldn't have done that.

For just a moment, fury welled within me. Why didn't Orson do it himself? Was he so weak that he had chosen to surround himself with these items? Did he find some pleasure in knowing he was the only person who had access to them? "Oh, Orson! What have you done?"

Corkboard in an elaborate gilt frame served as a bulletin board. The photographs of five women were pinned to it. Their names were tacked on beneath their photos. I knew three of them—Bonnie Shergold, Joan Jankowski, and Riley Hooper. Why would he have these pictures? They appeared to have been taken when the women didn't know they were being photographed. All of them had chestnut hair and blue eyes. He had a type. My skin crawled. There was something very creepy about taking pictures of women without their knowledge and posting them where he could see them every day. I had thought Orson was a decent and honorable man. This was a side of him that I never imagined. I turned away, sorry that I had seen his bulletin board.

The desk was neatly organized and didn't look like a desk that had received much use. I walked behind it and pulled open the top drawer. That was when I saw the envelope. *Sophie Winston* was written on it in a steady, ornate script.

I flipped it over, tore open the flap, and withdrew a sheet of stationery. The name Orson Chatsworth had been embossed across the top.

Dear Sophie,

If you are reading this, then the worst has come to pass. I have feared this eventuality for some time. No one knows about this letter to you or about the contents. You may share them with your sleuthing friends if they are sworn to secrecy and if you can trust them to keep mum.

I have been murdered.

Lest you think I am an old man who is confused or teetering on the edge of dementia, please allow me to assure you that is not the case. I have a clean bill of health from my doctor. My ticker isn't young anymore, but there isn't any medical reason for me to die.

The suspects are plenty. Someone has been following me in recent months. I spoke about it with Sergeant Wolf Fleischman. Feel free to check with him so you will know I am not making this up. He recommended hiring a bodyguard or a private investigator. I have done neither, depending instead on my own wits to carry me through as I have done my whole life.

I credit my wealth to luck, pure and simple. Somehow, I was blessed with an uncanny wisdom about buying antiques and real estate at low prices, only to see them skyrocket in a few years' time. But money carries its own price—jealousy and avarice. Too many people think they are entitled to other people's money and are determined to obtain it through deadly means.

In short, then, there are four people who top my list of suspects. My former wife, Myra Chatsworth, and my former companion, Audrey Evans, believe they are entitled to my money. To avoid their scheming, I have allowed them to believe that they will receive substantial sums upon my death by natural means. As that was not the case, I imagine they are put out and furious with you. My apologies for that.

It fills me with sorrow and regret that my soon-to-be-former son-in-law, Jordan, may have taken my life. He needs money and I'm quite certain from various comments he has made that Jordan expects my daughter, Stella, to inherit my estate in its entirety. If only that could have been the case. But Jordan spent my money as if he thought it would multiply exponentially. He always thought there would be more, more, more, and conducted himself accordingly, living the life of a spoiled and entitled brat. It is the sole reason that he pursued Stella and led her to believe that he loved her. I pray that you will not find that he is the one who ended my life. I leave this world imagining that my daughter held me in some esteem and that she loved me. But I must face facts. Jordan needs money and he sees Stella as a direct conduit. Mark my word. As soon as I kick the bucket, Jordan will be in pursuit of Stella once again. It is my duty as a father to protect Stella and ensure that even if Jordan manages to reconcile with her or convinces her to remarry him in the future, he will not be able to access the assets I leave to Stella and their children.

As for Stella, she may be shocked by the way I have structured the funds she will receive. I am very proud of her, but she needs to pursue that which she loves, thereby allowing her to find herself and to evolve into a happy individual, secure in her own abilities and achievements. Because ultimately, happiness is the most important thing in this life. It does not come from cars, big houses, or bank accounts. The ability to be happy lives within each of us. No matter what Jordan might think, it won't come from squandering my money. It can only arise within my dear Stella. She deserves to know the satisfaction of a job well done and the eagerness to continue on a path because she yearns to do so.

My fourth and final suspect is my former partner, Karl Roth. I cannot fathom any situation in which he could imagine that he would inherit anything from me. But jealousy and anger are powerful motivators. At one time, we split our business and each of us received a half share. At that moment, we were equal in every way. But he chose a different road and soon frittered away his share. He came to me years later, insisting that I owed him more, unable to grasp that I had made efforts to see my money grow. I had built upon it and none of my hard work and long hours were owed to him. He could have done the same had he so chosen. Beware of Karl, for he is crafty and has no morals. Had he been a better and honest man, we would still be partners today.

If I have any other enemies, they are long in my past. You, with your uncanny ability to solve murder, may find someone else.

I apologize for hiding this letter in my secret room. I trust your natural curiosity will draw you to it. I'm sure you can see, given all this information, why it couldn't be left anywhere else. Any of the above-named persons would have burned it, and unless my death was very clearly murder, you might never have gotten involved. My will and associated trusts might have raised suspicion, but this

is much more clear. You may imagine me dancing a
little jig as I watch the squirming ensue.
            With my appreciation and fondest regards,
                        Orson Chatsworth

I sat back in the soft leather chair, one of the few things
in the store that wasn't an antique. I gazed at the letter,
looking for a date, but there wasn't one. He had lived with
this fear in his head for some time. I shuddered to imagine
it. No wonder he loved Wanda so much. She hadn't had
any designs on his money. When he was with her, he could
relax and enjoy life.

A bell rang in the store and Daisy barked. I could hear
her claws tapping against the hardwood floor as she ran
through the cavernous showroom toward the door. I
hastily jammed the letter into my pocket and exited the
hidden room, pausing briefly to carefully close the book-
shelf doors behind me.

In the showroom, I recognized the shape of the man
standing at the door even before I was close enough to
make out his face.

I had dated Sergeant Wolf Fleischman of the Alexandria
Police Department and knew him very well. I shoved the
sofa away to open the door.

"Good morning. You must be the newest millionaire in
town."

I laughed at him. "Not exactly."

He frowned at me. "Did someone break in?"

He walked inside and I explained what happened while
I shoved the sofa back in place.

Daisy wound around his legs seeking attention from her
old friend. He handed me two lattes, then reached down
and massaged her ears. "I haven't seen you in a while,
Miss Daisy. Have you been a good girl?"

Her tail wagged wildly.

"I was about to call you. Do you have a cause of death yet for Orson?"

Wolf had the best poker face of anyone I had ever met. It drove me crazy when we dated because it was hard to read his emotions and reactions.

He turned his attention away from Daisy and reached out for one of the lattes. "Why do you ask?"

I handed the drink to him. "He was murdered, wasn't he?"

"How did you know?"

I ignored his question. "What killed him?"

"Respiratory failure. More specifically, respiratory paralysis, most likely from neurotoxins."

"So he was poisoned?"

"Possibly. The lab results aren't back yet. Did you know Orson well?" He asked it ever so casually, but I understood what he was getting at.

"Not well enough to inherit anything." I handed him the letter.

Wolf settled on a lush, green, velvet sofa and read.

I sat on a Louis XV Bergère chair. A little wider than a dining chair, it was very comfortable.

When he finished, Wolf asked, "When did you receive this?"

"I found it about an hour ago. Wolf, he didn't leave me the business out of any love for me. He simply didn't want to take the chance that he was bequeathing it to his killer. It's all a little crazy, but I knew there had to be a reason he left the store to me."

"How will you know to whom you should pass it along?"

"Good question. I'm hoping his lawyer, Ronin, will have a directive for me. I haven't had a chance to speak with him yet and now it's the weekend."

"Got any idea which one did him in?"

"I was hoping you might have a lead."

Wolf ran his hand over the seat of the sofa. "This is really comfortable." He flipped over the price tag. "Good grief! I believe I'll stick with what I've got."

"Are you evading my question?"

"No."

I sipped my latte.

"Obviously, I wouldn't be here asking questions if the coroner hadn't been suspicious about Orson's death. His letter seals that deal pretty well. Poor guy. I would hate to think that the people closest to me were planning to kill me. Now I wish I had followed up on the person he thought was stalking him. Have you spoken to Wanda yet?"

I shook my head. "Only to express my condolences. She's swamped with friends dropping by. I've been over here trying to figure out why he left me the store. Until you walked in, I didn't know for certain that Orson had been murdered. Do you know Karl Roth?" I asked. "He was present at the party where Orson collapsed. Come to think of it, all of Orson's suspects were present, except possibly Stella's husband, Jordan. But it was a good crowd. I might have missed him."

"Good to know. Roth is eccentric. Be careful. He'll probably be dropping by here to make a fuss."

"Are you saying he's dangerous?"

"I don't know, but you should be cautious. He's loud. I'd like to think he's all hot air, but I'm not sure about that."

Mars had once told me that Wolf only gave me information that he wanted me to know. I suspected that was true. Like warning me about Karl. So I knew he wouldn't tell me everything. I tried anyway. "Do you know of anyone who had a grudge against Orson outside the four in his letter to me?"

Wolf's eyes met mine. "One has to think that a businessman like Orson has probably ruffled a few feathers in his life. But I don't know about them. Not yet, anyway. How did he seem at the party?"

"Fine. I thought he and Wanda were enjoying themselves. He did pull me aside and ask if I would meet with him here the following morning. But then he died, so I don't know what he planned to discuss." I gulped part of the latte. "I assume that neurotoxins work fairly fast?"

"I think that's a safe bet."

"So it's likely that he was poisoned at the party?"

Wolf nodded. "Or shortly before. But he would have been feeling sick and you're telling me he seemed to be fine, so I'm inclined to believe that it was slipped to him at the party. I'm told that cheeses can contain some neurotoxins, but no one else has reported feeling ill, so we don't think it came from anything that was served to other guests."

Swell. It could have been any one of them. "Did you get a guest list from Natasha?"

"Not yet. We didn't have a final autopsy report until this morning. I wanted to see you first."

I laughed. "Am I a suspect because Orson left me his store?"

"I can't discount you. Though I do find it reassuring that you thought Orson must have had an ulterior reason for his unusual bequest." He stood up. "Keep me posted. And if you see my wife in here, please escort her out." He gazed around. "She loves antiques, but I can't afford Orson's prices."

Daisy and I followed him to the door.

"Does this place have a security system?" he asked.

Chapter 9

Dear Sophie,
My husband wants to bring a pizza to the family of
a friend who passed. I think that's tacky. I would
be so embarrassed! Help me convince him that's
wrong.
                Pizza Nut's Wife in New Rome, Georgia

Dear Pizza Nut's Wife,
Bake a nice casserole to bring to them. He may de-
cide to forgo the pizza. If he continues to insist on
the pizza, then bring both because it sounds like it's
important to your husband and might help him feel
better.

                                            Sophie

I hadn't even considered an alarm system. I looked around
for cameras or a keypad. "Ronin gave me a fistful of
keys. If there's an alarm, I don't know about it."

Wolf nodded. "Given the prices, I would imagine there
must be one. If not, I think you'd be wise to install one."

"Thanks. And thanks for the latte." I moved the sofa again and shoved it back when he left.

The first thing I needed to do was talk to Wanda. Maybe Orson had confided in her, and she knew about someone who had it in for him. The second thing was to have an alarm system installed. And then I would find time to bake something for Wanda.

I was thrilled when the glass replacement guy arrived. While he worked, I phoned Ian Hogarth, one of Orson's employees. He had sounded insightful when we spoke the day before.

"Ian, hi! It's Sophie Winston again. I hate to bother you, but I wondered if there's an alarm system in the store." I could hear laughter in the background.

"Sophie! Just a second, let me get to a quieter place. There's a very old system and I'm not at all certain that it works. Orson told us he was planning to install something modern, with cameras, but I don't think anything was ever installed."

"Thank you. That's very helpful. Is there anything else I should know?"

"I'd be happy to show you how to run the cash register. I guess I shouldn't give you the code for the safe over the phone."

I smiled. "Probably not."

"I've been wondering what happened to Rosebud."

"My friend, Nina Reid Norwood, is looking for a home for her."

"Oh. Okay. She used to come to work with Orson, and I was worried about her. Do you have a date for the funeral yet? I'm at Sandbridge Beach with friends. I know that sounds just awful of me, but it's not often I get a week off. I plan to come back for the service, though. To pay my respects. Orson was very good to me. I still can't believe that he's gone."

"I'm not aware of a date yet, but I promise I'll let you know."

We said good-bye and I called a local security company to come by the store and tell me what it needed in terms of a security system.

The man on the other end of the line said, "I'm glad you called. I read about Mr. Chatsworth's demise and didn't know if we should come out on Monday as planned."

"I'm sorry, I don't understand. You were supposed to come to the store?"

"Yes. Mr. Chatsworth said his store had a very old alarm system that didn't work. I was under the impression that he was eager to get the new one installed as soon as possible, but then I read about his death and didn't know what to do. I've been calling the store, but no one ever answers."

"I apologize. The store has been closed, but I would like to keep the appointment if you can still come."

"That would be great. I'll be there as scheduled on Monday afternoon."

I locked up the store. Daisy and I walked to my favorite florist. A bell rang when I opened the door and Bonnie Shergold emerged from the back.

"Hi, Sophie!" She reached into a treat jar on a shelf and offered Daisy a tiny cookie in the shape of a dog bone. "Hi, Daisy. These are blueberry!"

Daisy wagged her tail approvingly and delicately took the cookie from Bonnie's hand.

"Thanks, Bonnie."

"What can I do for you today?"

"I'd like to bring Wanda some flowers."

"That was the saddest thing. I was shocked when I heard about Orson. Did you have anything special in mind?"

"You probably know better than I do what's suitable for bereavement."

"No problem. How about some white lilies, coral roses, daisies, salmon ranunculus, purple gladiolus, and some of Wanda's favorite, lilies of the valley?"

"That sounds great! Thanks." I watched as she artfully gathered the flowers together. The photo of Bonnie on Orson's bulletin board couldn't have been very old. She was slim and pretty, without much makeup or fuss. She wore her chestnut hair pulled back into a ponytail with what appeared to be a real daisy adorning the place where it was bound. "Did you know Orson well?"

"I wouldn't say that. He dropped by once in a while for a bouquet or to send an arrangement to someone. Mostly, though, I thought he seemed lonely. Sort of wistful, and he just wanted to chat."

"What did you talk about?"

"Nothing special. I asked him questions about antiques." She pointed at a demilune console table with gilt legs and a white marble top. She had artfully displayed vases and flowers on it. "He gave me a terrific price on that table. It's a little bit over the top, I think, but it gives the shop an upscale look."

"I didn't know you were interested in antiques."

"My mother was crazy about antiques. When I was growing up, she would drag me to flea markets on weekends. That's how she furnished our house. We weren't wealthy by any means, but my mom could bargain better than anyone I have ever met. It didn't hurt that she had a charming way about her. Somewhere along the line, I guess I caught the antiques bug, too. Here you go. What do you think?"

"The lilies of the valley make it. Without them, it would be too plain. I'd never have thought it."

She wrapped them in paper, and I paid her for the flowers.

"Daisy," she said, "no nipping or tasting the flowers now. Lilies of the valley and the other lilies are poisonous. They are not for eating."

Daisy listened attentively and received pats for her good behavior in the store.

We left the store and walked home. The whole way, I wondered why Orson had a picture of Bonnie in his secret room.

At home, I placed the flowers in my office and closed the door to keep them out of Mochie's and Daisy's reach. Then I headed upstairs to dress a little bit better.

It was another hot summer afternoon, so I stepped into a sleeveless black dress with white trim around the neckline and armholes. I pulled my hair up into a loose twist and pinned it, then slid my feet into black patent sandals.

"I'll be back soon," I assured Daisy and Mochie.

They didn't seem concerned. Daisy had stretched out on the cool kitchen floor and appeared quite content to remain in the air-conditioned house. Mochie curled up in his favorite spot, the bay window in the kitchen where he could watch squirrels and people.

I didn't bother taking a purse. After all, I was only going to the end of the block. I collected the bouquet, locked the door behind me, and crossed the street.

A couple left Natasha's house as I walked up the stairs. The door opened before I had a chance to knock. A woman stepped out and forced a sad smile at me.

If it hadn't been for the somber mood, it would have looked like a party. But the hushed voices conveyed the melancholy atmosphere.

I caught a glimpse of Wanda in the center of a group of people, so I headed for the kitchen to retrieve a vase for the flowers.

Natasha saw me coming and plucked them out of my hands, holding them carefully away from her sleeveless, black, knit sheath. "Thank you for coming. I thought you would be here yesterday. Did you have too much fun playing in your new store?"

There was no mistaking the jealousy in her tone. "I was here yesterday. Natasha, you hate antiques." I thought about telling the truth—that there was a reason he'd left it to me. But I decided she might blab too much or spread weird rumors. Maybe I would tell her later.

"Did you know that he cut me out of his will?" she asked.

"Why would you have been *in* his will?" I followed her into the kitchen. With stainless steel counters and cabinets, it looked like a restaurant kitchen, spotless but cold. "I thought you were changing the kitchen."

"As you well know, money has been tight for me. I can't afford major revisions at the moment. Besides, stainless steel is all the rage. It just took a little longer for everyone else to appreciate it."

"I hate it," said Griselda, who overheard as she entered from a different door. "I've tried to dress it up with some country pieces, but Natasha will not have it. No sooner do I put something up than she takes it down."

"Hi, Griselda." I gave her a hug. "Natasha, why did you expect to inherit from Orson?"

"He was marrying my mother," she said in a haughty tone, as if that said it all.

"So you thought he would treat you like a daughter?" I found that unrealistic, but I tried to cut her some slack. Maybe she yearned for a father figure.

"I thought he would leave everything to my mother, which I would inherit from her. But that rotten man double-crossed me by leaving her share in a trust. I won't inherit one penny of it."

Griselda groaned. "Natasha, the man your mother loved, the man who made her happy and brought joy into her life, has died. This is not about you."

I flashed a little smile at Griselda. She was no nonsense and brought us back to where we should be.

Natasha poured a few drops of vodka in the water to keep it fresh. "Sophie is my best friend. I can say anything I want to her."

Griselda winked at me. "Lucky you. Perhaps you could be a little bit more considerate of your mother's feelings, Natasha." She left the room.

"You should be very grateful to only have one mother bossing you around. I still can't believe that Orson did that to me. I thought he liked me, but that was a slap in the face."

I hadn't seen the trust, so I had no idea who would receive anything that remained at the time of Wanda's demise. Some charity, most likely. Frankly, I couldn't see a reason in the world for him to include a bequest to Natasha, but she was clearly put out about it, so I simply said, "I'm sorry, Natasha."

She smiled at me. "I knew you would understand. You're always there for me, Sophie. Except yesterday. But I still don't understand why he left his store to you. Were you . . . you know?"

"I don't know," I said firmly, to dispel any notion of impropriety. "If you're suggesting I had some sort of relationship with him, you would be incorrect."

"There must be some reason."

"I certainly didn't expect it."

"I heard someone broke into your store."

News traveled fast in Old Town. "You heard right. I can't imagine what they wanted."

"People steal all sorts of things, I suppose. Maybe he promised someone something and when he didn't inherit it, the person went and got it himself." She looked out the window with her back to me.

Wanda rushed into the kitchen and collapsed into a chair. Her cheeks blazed pink and contrasted with the dark aubergine background of her dress. It was simple, with long sleeves and a round neckline. She wore no jewelry except for an antique engagement ring containing one substantial European cut diamond and two smaller sapphires. "Sophie, honey! You came! How thoughtful of you."

I reached out and gave her a hug, murmuring, "I'm so very sorry."

"I know you are, sweetheart. Your parents sent the loveliest flowers."

Griselda poked her head in. "People are asking for you, Wanda."

"All I want is a quiet front porch where I can sit by myself with a straight bourbon, none of that fancy modern stuff. Just the good old-fashioned kind. Why don't you have a front porch, Natasha?"

Before Natasha could respond, Wanda's eyes opened wide. "I forgot you inherited Orson's store, Sophie! He must have loved you a lot, darlin'."

It was the wrong thing to say in front of Natasha. A dark cloud of jealousy crossed her face.

Thankfully, Griselda took note of Wanda's exhaustion. "Is it okay if I tell everybody that you're resting and send them home?"

"I wish you would," Wanda said softly.

"Then that's what I'll do." Griselda disappeared again.

"Natasha," said Wanda, "would you be a love and go help Griselda? Please tell everyone how very much I appreciate that they came to visit."

"Certainly, Mother."

The second Natasha was out of earshot, Wanda bolted out of the chair, her wan countenance gone. "Orson was murdered."

Chapter 10

Dear Natasha,
I always thought pesto was made with pine nuts.
But now I'm seeing recipes with walnuts. Which
one is correct?
>   *Getting It Right in Big Pine Key, Florida*

Dear Getting It Right,
Pine nuts and Parmesan cheese are traditional in-
gredients for pesto. That doesn't stop people from
trying other ingredients. But it begs the question, is
it really pesto then?
>   *Natasha*

I knew Orson had been murdered and yet the breath caught in my throat. Had Wolf told her? "Why do you think that?"

"Someone was spying on him. Following him. Also, Orson wasn't in the best shape. You know, he needed to trim down and get more exercise. I was helping him with that. But I made sure he got a clean bill of health from his doctor first. Herbs and potions seem innocent, but they are more powerful than many people think. I didn't want to recommend anything that might conflict with existing health issues. He had high cholesterol, and we were working on that. But I was with him. I saw his expression. That was no heart attack. Something happened to him. Something that made his body give out. I talked to the doctors. I was there with him in the hospital to his very last breath. Somebody killed him."

"Do you have any idea who might have wanted him dead?"

Wanda lowered her voice. "I don't want to cast aspersions on his family, but I know for a fact that Stella's former husband, Jordan, needed money. I was there when he came by Orson's house and begged him for funds to pay off a debt. Harsh words were exchanged. I . . . I think Orson might have paid it off, but he died too soon to do it." She lowered her voice to a whisper. "I suspect that slimeball Jordan is going to try to reconcile with Stella so he can mooch it off her."

She was probably right, and Orson had expected as much as well. If Jordan killed Orson in the belief his former wife would be loaded, he miscalculated. She might have enough money to pay off his debt, but not enough to keep doing that for long.

"What do you know about Orson's former business partner?"

"Orson didn't mention him much. We saw him once on the street and Orson introduced me. They exchanged pleasantries like people do, but Orson rarely talked about him. I can tell you this, though. I think Orson had a premonition. He woke up one night chilled to the bone and said he'd had the most awful dream. He wouldn't tell me what it was, but he made an appointment with Ronin and seemed much more relaxed after that."

"No one else threatened him?"

"Not that I know about. Orson was a good man, Sophie."

Her words hit me hard. She probably had no idea that he had a collection of photographs of attractive younger women. I didn't see the point in telling her. She might as well remember him as the wonderful guy she thought he was.

"At my age, I never thought I would find someone to love." Wanda grasped my arm. "The only thing I can do for him now is find his killer. Please, Sophie. You have to help me!"

"I'll do my best, Wanda." I patted her hand. "If you think of anything, no matter how insignificant, I want you to tell me. Okay?"

I debated informing her that the police were already on the case. But I decided that news would be best coming from Wolf.

"Do you think everyone is gone?" she whispered.

"I'll check."

I poked my head into the dining room and the living room. The house was still and silent.

"Looks like they've cleared out."

"Thank goodness for that."

"Wanda, if it's ever too much for you, you're welcome to come over to my house to get away from it all."

"You are just as sweet as you were when you and Natasha were youngsters. Thank you, Sophie."

"Take care, Wanda." I left the house through the front door. I had no idea where Griselda and Natasha had gone, but it didn't matter. The door clicked shut behind me and I strolled home in the afternoon heat.

As I entered my house, the phone rang.

Nina's voice asked, "What's up for dinner tonight?"

Orson's store would be nice and cool with the high ceiling. And it was time to bring my friends up to date on the developments. "How about meeting me at the antiques store? You can bring Muppet and Rosebud can meet Daisy. I'll call Mars and Bernie to see if they're available."

"Sounds like fun. Will we eat after?"

"We'll eat there!"

"That sounds intriguing. Can I help?"

"You could bring cocktails or whatever you want to drink."

That settled, I phoned Mars and Bernie, both of whom were up for something a little bit different. I walked to my favorite grocery store for the makings of an easy dinner. It was fun strolling through the aisles and picking out delicious finger foods like black and green olives, adorable little cornichons, a cucumber, endive, a package of sliced dry salami, roasted red peppers, blackberries, dates, strawberries, grapes, salted peanuts, a rotisserie chicken, a couple of baguettes, sliced smoked Gouda, mozzarella balls, and Brie.

I toted my purchases home and set to work arranging a fun dinner board. I didn't plan to do much cooking, but a few spreads and sauces were called for. I minced three garlic cloves, then mashed two avocados and blended everything together with lemon juice. A touch of salt and it was a tasty spread. I stored it in the refrigerator while I prepared Mars's favorite pesto. It would add just the right tang to a sandwich or to the chicken. The food processor made quick work of walnuts, basil leaves, garlic, and olive oil.

Daisy and I made a trip to the garden for bright red cherry tomatoes, and sprigs of rosemary to use as a garnish.

Back inside, I loaded my serving board with all the fun foods for our dinner. I removed the chicken breasts and sliced them into rounds that could be eaten plain or used on a sandwich. They went on the board first, then the wings and the legs. I wrapped the remaining bits in aluminum foil and stashed them in the refrigerator to make a chicken broth.

The cheeses and salami were next. The mozzarella balls went next to the roasted peppers, for color contrast and so they wouldn't move out of place. I rolled the slices of smoked Gouda and laid them out like a fan. The salami slices added a nice touch in a semicircle around the end of the Gouda fan. I added two small bowls, one red and one orange, for the onion confit and the pesto. From there on out, it was easy to place the fruits and nuts in small piles.

I scooped the pesto into the red bowl and covered it for the trip to the store. The refrigerated avocado spread went into the orange bowl with a cover. Then I wrapped the whole board with plastic wrap to keep everything in place. And for good measure, topped that with aluminum foil. I would drive slowly and make sure I didn't brake suddenly!

Mochie had watched carefully after he caught a whiff of the rotisserie chicken. I fed him something called Spring Chicken Pâté, which he ate with gusto. I packed three dog bowls along with three servings of Daisy's preferred food. Paper plates and napkins would make for a quick cleanup. I added a few little party picks and some silverware.

Loading sparkling water and the board in the car was easier than I had expected. I had transported a lot of things to events in the rear of my hybrid SUV, so the board wasn't too big a challenge.

Mochie retreated to the sunroom to wash his paws and his face. I promised we wouldn't be late coming home.

Daisy, dressed in her halter, hopped up on the passenger seat in front, where I clipped her harness to a seat belt connector.

Minutes later, I parked behind Orson's store and carried the board inside. I had been right about the high ceiling. The store was blissfully cool.

I retrieved a French tablecloth from the selection upstairs and threw it over a rustic farmhouse table downstairs. The table sat near a fireplace that had surely once
been used for heat. Orson had hung a large carved French
rococo style mirror over the mantel. The gold arms and
dangling crystals of a chandelier reflected in it. Matching
chinoiserie vases with a blue-on-white motif decorated the
mantel. The faux blue and white hydrangeas in them looked
real.

I moved the board to the middle of the table, set out the
plates and napkins, and uncovered the bowls. It looked
like a feast.

No sooner had I finished, than I heard knocking at the
front door and hurried to open it. "Welcome!"

Rosebud, the bulldog, was the first one through the
door. Nina's dog, Muppet, followed and ran toward her
friend, Daisy.

Rosebud sniffed the floor and followed a scent in a dizzying pattern. I worried that she was looking for Orson. His
scent must be all over the store.

"Poor Rosebud," said Nina. "I wish I could explain
what happened to Orson and that she'll be okay."

"How's she doing otherwise?" I asked.

"She has a great appetite and gets along with everyone.
But I can tell she misses Orson."

Bernie and Mars arrived at the same time.

"Wow. Nice store, Sophie." Mars gave me a peck on my
cheek.

"Very nice, indeed," added Bernie, looking around. "I
had no idea you were so close with Orson."

Mars turned toward me. "Neither did I. What's up with
that?"

"Give me a minute and all will become clear."

I locked the door so no one would think we were open
for business, then unpacked the blackberry vodka spritzers

Nina had brought with her, while my friends poked around the store.

"This is much larger than I imagined." Mars picked up a spritzer and sipped it.

"It's an impressive store. Did you look at the price tags?" asked Nina. "Yikes!"

Bernie joined us. "I noticed that. Pretty pricy. The sort of place my mum favors."

Done with the table and the drinks, I joined their conversation. "So, like you, I also wondered why Orson would leave his store to me. We were not particularly close. I thought there had to be some reason behind his generosity." I motioned to them to follow me and led them to the office that contained the hidden entrance to the secret room. "See anything unusual?"

Bernie picked up a statuette of a woman. One arm had broken off. "He's dealing in illegal antiquities?"

"Exactly what I thought. Do you think that's real or just a knockoff?"

Bernie shook his head. "You'd have to ask an expert. The people who make the fake ones are pros. I have no idea."

"Does anything else stand out to you?"

They gazed around. I walked over to the hidden doors, removed the books that had triggered the lock before, and pulled them open.

Chapter 11

Dear Sophie,
Am I a bad mother if I make "dinner boards" instead of cooking?
Too Tired to Cook in Ten Sleep, Wyoming

Dear Too Tired to Cook,
Not at all! Your little ones will probably love eating food they can pick up with their fingers. Just be sure there are plenty of veggie and fruit options.
Sophie

"Well done, Orson!" said Bernie.

Nina had already entered the hidden room and was gazing at the photos of the five women. "Eww. Please don't tell me Orson was some kind of sicko."

Mars peered over her shoulder. "Definitely odd, but it could be worse. At least they're not nude."

"This is why he left you the store? Do you think he wanted you to clean up his bizarre stalker room so his family wouldn't know?" asked Nina.

"Those pictures came as a surprise to me, too. Maybe

you're right, Nina." I removed Orson's letter from the desk. "But he left me this. It's long, so I suggest we start eating."

We exited the hidden room, and I took care to close the doors behind us. We settled at the table.

Mars frowned. "Appetizers?"

"It's a dinner board, silly." Nina speared a piece of chicken and sliced a baguette. "They're all the latest. You get to choose what you feel like eating."

Mars wrinkled his nose. "It's like a picnic, except you have to make your own sandwiches."

"Sort of," I said. "You love rotisserie chicken and I know you like avocado spread on sandwiches."

Mars relented. "I think I like it better when my food is preassembled and arrives on one plate."

"You're turning into an old grouch!" I laughed. I pointed at Bernie, who had already helped himself and was carefully layering salami and roasted red peppers on a baguette. "Loosen up, Mars. Bernie is into it."

Mars grumbled under his breath.

While they ate, I read Orson's letter to them. When I finished, they had stopped eating and all three of them stared at me.

"Does Wolf know about this?" asked Mars.

"I saw him earlier today and gave him the letter to read. Unfortunately, the autopsy indicates that Orson was poisoned. He had a neurotoxin in his system."

"A neurotoxin?" asked Bernie. "Where would one get something like that?"

"I looked it up. All kinds of things. Chemicals, solvents, pesticides, radiation, even some snake venom and plants."

Nina nibbled on a grape. "Poor Orson. What a horrible way to go. I do love the secret room, though. How cool is that?"

"Do you think the women in the photos had reason to

murder Orson?" asked Mars, making himself a second chicken sandwich.

"I have no idea. I stopped in to talk with Bonnie Shergold today and brought up Orson's name to see her reaction. She spoke fondly of him. She didn't flinch or act creeped out at all. The only other ones I know by name are Joan Jankowski and Riley Hooper. Did any of you recognize the other two?"

Bernie nodded. "Doreen Donahue and Cheryl Mancini."

"You know a lot of women," said Mars.

Bernie shot him a look. "I know who they are, but that doesn't mean I know much about them."

"Would any of them kill Orson?" asked Nina.

Bernie shrugged.

"What about Wanda? Have you told her about the letter?" Mars sipped his blackberry spritzer.

"She was broken up and tired. I didn't mention anything about the letter. But she rushed Natasha out of the room and told me privately that she thinks Orson was murdered."

"The letter said you have to swear us to secrecy," said Nina.

"Consider yourself sworn. I'm trusting you not to blab about this to anyone."

Bernie and Mars nodded agreeably.

"Nina?" I asked.

"Of course. I wouldn't dream of talking about this. Orson went to lengths to get this message to you. He obviously gave it a lot of thought and it weighed heavily on him. He deserves to have us figure out what happened to him."

I picked up a black olive and savored the briny flavor. "We're all in then."

At that moment, in the quiet of the cavernous store, something rattled.

"Do you hear that?" Mars whispered.

"Sounds like keys," Nina hissed.

The display in the nearest window blocked us from view of passersby, but I could see that twilight had fallen on Old Town.

Bernie and I rose from our seats quietly. We were to the far side of the door and couldn't see it.

Bernie held out his palm in front of me. He crouched and inched forward. I did the same and waddled behind him.

The person jiggled the door handle as if he was frustrated and hoped it would give. But the man who had changed the locks for me had done a good job. Everything held tight.

Bernie and I scooted closer to the door just in time to see him smash his nose against the glass door, distorting his face.

Nina, who had snuck around behind us, screamed as if she had seen a ghost.

At the sound of her voice, the shady outline of a person in a baggy coat fled, reminiscent of old horror movies.

"Did you see who it was?" asked Mars.

I didn't realize he was behind me and let out an involuntary squeal. "I didn't hear you sneak up on us."

Bernie stood up and stretched. "I couldn't make out much. But it was definitely a man. Good thing you had the locks changed, Sophie."

"Who would have a key?" asked Nina.

I stretched as well. "Employees, for sure. Could be anyone who worked here in the last twenty or more years."

Mars scowled. "Or a thief who read about Orson's death in the newspaper."

"Are you saying that to scare me?" I asked.

"Yeah, a little bit. You need to be careful when you're in here alone. Don't thieves go to the homes of people who died and break in during the funeral services?"

"That's horrible! I can't imagine anyone being so despicable."

"Well, they are." Mars smiled at me fondly. "You always expect the best of people, Sophie. Meanwhile, they're scheming with no regard for others."

"Who would come to a store at night?" asked Nina. "That was intentional. Someone must want something that's in here."

She had a point. Why not come during the day when it would likely be open? And if it were an employee, what would he have left inside the store that would be so important now, days later? He could have phoned me and told me he had left something in the store.

We all glanced around.

"It's impossible to know what he might have wanted." Mars studied a painting. "You'd have to have an expert tell you if anything was particularly valuable. It could be anything we would think of as just another painting or bust."

It wasn't a bad idea. Maybe I should have someone come in to have a look around. "So where do we start on finding Orson's murderer?"

We settled at the table again. "I'm no expert," said Bernie, "but perhaps we should speak to the rest of the women on the corkboard. If Orson was poisoned at the party, we can probably eliminate the women who weren't in attendance."

"Good point. Especially because we know for certain that Orson's family members were present, as was Karl." Following Mars's lead, I made myself an open-faced sandwich with a halved baguette, some of the pesto, and sliced chicken. "Did any of you notice Jordan St. James or Myra Chatsworth there?"

"There were so any people in attendance," said Nina,

"it could have been anyone. Myra was definitely there. I remember being surprised because, well, who would want to go to their ex-husband's engagement party?"

"How well do you know her?" I asked.

"Myra? At the time of the divorce, rumor had it that she was seeing someone else. I understand their home was beautifully furnished, mostly with antiques from the store. We should pay her a visit if only to see the inside of the house."

Mars found a pad and pen at the checkout desk and made a list of Orson's suspects and the five women whose photos were on the wall. We divided them up among us and the topic of conversation soon turned to our lives and lighter themes.

On Sunday morning, Nina phoned Myra and asked if she and I might drop by Myra's house. She was surprised, but readily agreed to see us at ten.

I pulled on a peach dress with a loose skirt and roomy pockets. Cool, casual, and comfortable. Most importantly, acceptable to someone like Myra.

I left Daisy at home in the cool kitchen with Mochie because the temperature would be getting very hot soon and I didn't know how Myra felt about dogs. I had a feeling she wasn't keen on them. Otherwise, Orson might have left Rosebud to her.

Nina and I met on the sidewalk.

"Can we stop for lattes and croissants?" she asked. "I'm famished."

"Sure. I haven't eaten breakfast yet, either."

On the way toward King Street, we saw Wanda and Griselda standing on the sidewalk. As we drew closer, it appeared they were looking at the lock on the door to their store.

"Wanda! What happened?"

"Someone broke in during the night. Can you believe this?"

"I can! Orson's store was broken into the night before." But there was no gaping hole in the glass. "Did they pick the lock?"

"That's what we're thinking," said Griselda. "I'm certain I locked it."

Nina gasped. "Someone is definitely looking for something! Wanda, did Orson give you anything valuable? Something priceless?"

Wanda tapped her hand. "My engagement ring." She still wore it.

I couldn't blame her. I would keep wearing it, too, in her circumstances. "But no one would expect to find that in the store."

"Whoever it was took merchandise," said Griselda. "Otherwise, we wouldn't have known about it."

"What kind of merchandise?" My mind went straight to the CBD products they sold.

"Various things. We haven't had time to do an inventory yet. I did notice that our narcissus for cough and cold is wiped out. We were just wondering how easy it is to pick a lock. That's the only way someone could have gotten in."

"Do you have a back door?" I asked.

Wanda and Griselda looked at each other, their eyes wide.

"We'd better check that," said Griselda.

"You go," said Wanda. "I'll wait here for Wong. I hope she's working today."

Griselda pointed at a camera. "We think we might have caught our burglar on video."

"I hope so!" I doubted there was any connection between the break-ins. The merchandise was very different, and the modus operandi wasn't the same. But you never knew. "Keep me posted on this? It's unlikely, but it could be the same person who broke into Orson's store."

Nina and I hurried to a favorite café where we could enjoy breakfast outside in the shade of umbrellas. I ordered a mocha latte and a chocolate croissant and carried them out to a table. We weren't the only ones who were enjoying the summer weather. At the table next to us, two women were talking over their lattes.

When Nina joined me, I placed a finger across my lips in a signal to not speak so we could listen.

"You didn't hear?" asked the honey blonde in oversized sunglasses. "Jordan just sank to the bottom of the pool of eligible men."

"Did they get back together? I can't say I'm surprised. I thought there was still a spark between Jordan and Stella. And she's so nice. I wouldn't have gone out with him anyway until I was certain they wouldn't reconcile."

"You'd have been too late. The minute he moved out of the house, women descended upon him like bees to nectar. There was simply no shame. Rumor has it that Joan Jankowski is his favorite, but we'll see if he has any interest in her now that Stella has inherited some money."

Chapter 12

Dear Sophie,
My mom says if I refinish the antique sideboard
that I inherited from my grandmother that it won't
be worth anything. Is that true?
  Afraid to Touch It Now in Paint, Pennsylvania

Dear Afraid to Touch It Now,
Your mom is right. You may restore an antique by
carefully cleaning it. Consult an expert regarding
repairs. But anything that changes the finish may
cause it to diminish in value.
                                        Sophie

The other woman sighed. "So Stella is loaded now?"

"No! Apparently, the kids got most of it in trust. He was generous with Stella, but she didn't even get the store!"

"That's horrible! Who would do that to their child? I'm, well, just aghast! Poor Stella. Who did he leave it to? That woman who was going to marry him?"

"Partly. I heard a rumor that he had a mistress on the side who got the store."

Nina jabbed me with her elbow.

"That's not ironic! It's cruel. A slap in the face from the grave. Lordy, if my daddy did that to me, I'd never recuperate. I always thought so highly of Orson. He was very kind to me when I needed a dining room table because my folks were coming for the holidays. I was scraping by, but I had my heart set on an antique. I would go by his store and dream of the day I could afford what I wanted. One day, he saw me there and said he might have something that would work for me. It was an English table that had probably been beautiful once, but someone had ruined the top with water marks. It was ghastly, and you know me, I'm not the handiest person. But the price was right, and Orson said I could pay for it in installments, and he even threw in a tablecloth to cover the top. I still have that table. A tablecloth covered it for years until I had the top refinished."

"You refinished an antique? I thought that ruined the value."

"Believe me, the marks on the top had already done that. Besides, it's the right size for my dining room and I love the design. Have you heard when the funeral will be? I'd like to go to pay my respects."

"I haven't heard a thing. Remember when funerals took place within three days? Now there's always some excuse about kids who are in school or family members who can't fly in on a moment's notice. They'll probably have it a month from now."

The women tossed their cups and napkins in the trash and walked along King Street.

"Interesting," said Nina. "Now I wish I had shopped there. I didn't know Orson would let a person pay over time."

"Really? That's what you took away from that conversation? What about Jordan dating Joan Jankowski?"

"That was interesting, too." Nina lowered her voice. "She's on Orson's bulletin board, isn't she?"

"It might be interesting to talk with her." I finished my latte. "On the way back from Myra's house?"

Nina nodded. We cleaned up the table and headed to Myra's place.

I had walked by hundreds of times, but had never been inside. The exterior had been painted once upon a time, but the white paint had chipped and faded until the red bricks underneath took on a pinkish color. An oval medallion designating her home as historical was mounted on the brick. Black shutters flanked the windows, and a matching black door was slightly recessed.

"Aw, look!" Nina pointed at the door knocker in the shape of a cat's head with a ring in its mouth. It appeared to be antique or at least vintage. She clanked the ring.

Myra opened the door with a kitten clutched to her chest. "Hi. Come in fast before anyone escapes."

We scuttled inside and she quickly closed the door behind us. Five cats sat on the stairs in the small foyer.

"I had no idea you were such a cat lover," said Nina.

"Most of them have come from the shelter," said Myra. She held tight to the orange and white kitten, even though it was sinking its tiny little claws into Myra's caftan. Turquoise with a museum-worthy, purple, floral toile print, it screamed expensive, not to mention the jangling gold bracelets on her arm and the chunky statement necklace of turquoise and pearls.

"It's a scorcher again." Myra smiled at Nina, but when she glanced my way, her hospitable smile stiffened. She led us into a large living room.

Myra clearly had an eye for decorating. As one might have expected of the former wife of an antiques dealer, she had gorgeous furniture and exquisite paintings. The room was painfully formal. The kind where you instinctively knew to sit up straight even if it killed your back.

We sat down on blue velvet chairs that matched the leopard print and blue pillows on two white sofas.

"How can I help you?" Myra asked, unhooking the tiny claws and moving the kitten to her lap.

"First, allow me to say how very sorry we are for your loss," I said.

"Are you really? It seems to me that you of all people would be thrilled. I know you're divorced, Sophia, but Orson was much older than you are. I was married to him for a long time and I know he was bullheaded. I can't imagine what you saw in him"—she paused for emphasis—"unless it was money."

I started to correct my name, but Nina snorted as if stifling laughter. "Myra, it wasn't like that at all. Sophie is as astonished as you must have been. We think there's some reason he left the store to her. She's quite the sleuth, you know. And as it turns out—" Nina became very solemn. "Have the police talked with you yet?"

"If you're getting around to telling me that Orson was murdered, I am aware of that. That policeman—" She snapped her fingers in the air.

"Wolf Fleischman?" I asked.

She pointed at me. "That's him. Thank you. Yes, he came by for a rather ugly interview. He thinks *I* killed Orson. Can you imagine? I spent years married to the cantankerous old coot. If I had intended to kill him, I'd have done it then. Not that the thought didn't cross my mind. In any event, why would I knock him off now when I'm rid of him? Granted, I was forced to see him once in a while. Grandchildren complicate things. Birthday parties, recitals, and such. But for the most part, I avoided him and that suited me just fine. Old Town was plenty big for both of us."

"That's why we're here," I said, having decided not to correct my name. It was more important to keep her talking. "Is there anyone who would want to kill Orson?"

"I think you'd be better off asking the tart he planned to marry."

I desperately wanted to defend Wanda, though a few memories came to mind where she had chased men and been a bit bawdy about it, but right now we needed information from this woman, and she was already miffed about me getting the store.

"Why, Myra!" Nina cooed. "Spoken like a woman who still loves her ex-husband."

A red wave rose up Myra's face. "Nonsense! Orson will always be special to me. He is the father of my only child, and while our marriage was far from perfect, I also have many happy memories. In spite of his shortcomings, Orson has a tiny place in my heart, though true to form, he exited this world in a way that made me so angry all the hatred I felt for him came flooding back. I am furious with him for not leaving his estate to Stella in its entirety. What kind of man skips a generation?"

"One who worries that the second generation might use it all up?" I suggested.

Myra shot an ugly look at me. "I'll tell you what kind of person does that—one who turns every penny and nickel over twice before parting with it." She gave a mirthless laugh. "If Wanda was looking for money, she'd have soon found out that he didn't willingly part with a penny."

Myra scowled at me. "Stella deserves every cent of his estate"—she jabbed a finger in my direction—"including the store. Tight as he was, Orson was the most devoted father I have ever seen. He watched Stella like she was a

Rembrandt. I used to tell him that he needed to loosen up and let her be a kid. But he couldn't do it. No sleepovers unless he knew the parents. Sleepaway camp? Out of the question. He showed up for all her activities. Soccer, volleyball, school projects, you name it. She didn't have a single teacher that he did not meet personally."

"It's a wonder Stella ever married," Nina joked.

"You jest, but it was even tough convincing him that she should live in the dorm at college. She needed some room and the space to make her own mistakes. That's how kids learn. She met Jordan there, which Orson always blamed on me. Orson hated him from the get-go. I told Orson there wasn't a man on this earth he would think worthy of Stella. But between us, I wasn't too keen on him myself. I'd rather she had married a man who was more mature. I don't mean older. I mean one who knew what he wanted to do with his life and was working toward something. Not someone like Jordan, who has no ambition. He has certainly had a lot of misfortune in his efforts to become a restaurateur. Not every business runs smoothly. I recognize that, but I don't think he tries hard. I can't help comparing Jordan's lackadaisical attitude to how much effort Orson put into getting the store off the ground. Of course, Stella made us very happy grandparents, but she had her hands full taking care of babies and toddlers and is just now getting around to her own ambitions."

"When was the last time you saw Orson before the engagement party?"

Myra paused and met my eyes. "Good heavens. I barely remember where I was yesterday. Let's see. Oh! Of course. It was little Lili's birthday party. Divorce doesn't stop doting grandparents from spoiling their grandchildren."

"When was that?"

"About two weeks ago."

"Do you know of anyone who might have wanted

to kill Orson? Anyone who threatened him, perhaps?" I watched her carefully.

Myra's eyes shifted to the fireplace. "Karl Roth, Orson's former business partner. He hated Orson. I'm told he lifted a glass of champagne upon hearing of Orson's demise."

"He was at the party, wasn't he?" I asked.

"I saw him there, though I would be surprised if he was on the guest list."

"Why do you say that?" Nina stroked a tuxedo cat who had sneaked onto her lap.

"Who invites a bitter, angry, archenemy to a party?"

"Archenemy?" Those were strong words.

"Oh yes. Karl used to go to auctions and bid against Orson just to raise the price. It infuriated Orson. But then Orson decided to give Karl a taste of his own medicine. He would bid on a piece until the price was absurdly high and when Karl bid a ridiculous amount, Orson would stop bidding." Myra chuckled at the memory. "Karl didn't have Orson's eye for fine furniture and art. Sometimes Orson would find a piece that was worthless and place a bid on it. When Karl bid higher, Orson let him win the piece of junk." She was laughing so hard that tears rolled down her cheeks. "Oh my. They were definitely adversaries."

"Does Karl have a shop somewhere?" asked Nina.

"Last I heard he had a place on North Saint Asaph Street. I've never been there."

"Did you expect Orson to leave something to you?" I asked.

The red in her cheeks flared. "And why not? He could have trusted me to leave it to our daughter. It would have been a much better solution than the chaos he has created with that bizarre will. There's a marvelous painting in the store of a mother cat watching her kittens at play. It's not a Renoir or anything, but it would have been nice if he had left it to me, just because he knew it would have made me happy. Did you tell him to make that video?" She glared at me.

"No. Ronin said he saw it in a movie."

She exhaled loudly. "What an idiot. I'm furious with him for creating such a mess of things. At the very least he could have created a foundation for Stella to run. That's what sane people do."

"Myra, did you see anyone acting strange at the party? Doctoring a drink or anything like that?"

"The only person who was close to him, and by that I mean practically attached to him, was the not-at-all-blushing bride. If anyone murdered him, it was Wanda. She knew he had changed his will in her favor, and I think she murdered him before he woke up to reality and altered his will to Stella's benefit as he should have."

She was bitter, there was no question about that. I couldn't blame her for feeling the way she did. Part of me wanted to explain that Orson thought he was doing Stella a favor by encouraging her to work and make her own way in life. But Myra would surely argue with me about that, so it was best left unsaid. I wasn't family and she was highly annoyed with me anyway because of the store.

Nina blathered with her about the kitten, which she had found the previous evening.

"Honestly. How does one kitten end up alone? No sight of mama or other kittens. She was mewing in the doorway of Fleur Couture. Poor baby. I couldn't just leave her there. She's a sweet little girl. I like to think these things happen for a reason. That I was meant to find her."

When we departed and were walking away, Nina said, "Don't hold it against Myra. You would be miffed, too, if your ex-husband left your daughter part of his estate and gave his successful business to a virtual stranger."

"I totally agree. I would be highly suspicious. I would think someone had forced him to do that. Or that he had been duped."

"A lot of people are suspicious."

"What does that mean?"

"It means a lot of people in town are asking why he would have left the store to you if there was nothing going on between you."

"Gossip. There's nothing I can do about that. Hopefully, we'll identify Orson's killer, and all the gossipy nonsense will be put to rest."

Nina checked her watch. "Are you still up to paying Joan Jankowski a visit? Maybe grab a real lunch after?"

"Sure. The art gallery where Joan works is on the next block anyway. Might as well pop in."

We were one store away from the Brickhouse Gallery when we heard a scream.

Chapter 13

Dear Natasha,
I would love to use boards to entertain. Do they
have to be wood?
                    Buying Boards in Marble, Arkansas

Dear Buying Boards,
Marble and stone boards are very popular. It can
be fun to mix them up with wood boards to give
interest to your tablescape.
                                        Natasha

Nina and I looked at one another.
   "Where did that come from?" she asked.
   We were gazing around when we heard the next scream.
   Nina pulled open the door to the gallery and we stepped
inside.
   Stella held her hands over her mouth and nose. The
floor was littered with slices of cheese, salami, ham, colorful fruits, olives, and crackers. The mess almost looked
like some kind of artsy display, except that Joan Jankowski lay on the floor in the middle of it. Her shiny chestnut

hair covered part of her face, and her arms were splayed as if she had held them out in an effort to stop herself from falling. But the worst part was the trickle of blood that was oozing down her cheek.

I kneeled beside her. "Joan?" I felt for a pulse. Her heart was still beating. That was a relief. "Nina, call nine-one-one for an ambulance."

"Joan," I said in a loud voice near her ear. "An ambulance will be on the way soon. Hang in there." I was afraid to move her in case she had sustained a neck injury. I certainly didn't want to make anything worse for her.

Nina removed the charcuterie board from Stella's feet and placed it on a table. She wrapped an arm around Stella.

"What happened?" I asked.

Stella pointed a shaking finger toward the table that had been set up for a party. A long cherry charcuterie board laden with goodies sat atop a white linen tablecloth. Two boards lay on the floor. Food had slid off one of them in a long mound in front of her.

"I . . . I was setting up the boards Joan asked me to bring. They're having a lunchtime gallery event. It . . . it's something new they're trying to bring people in." Stella babbled mindlessly. "My van is parked out back. I was carrying in the third charcuterie board when I heard a thump. That's when I saw Joan on the floor."

"Did you see anyone else in here?" I asked.

The pitch of her voice grew higher as sirens sounded in the distance. "No. No, not at all! Only Joan and Tripp."

I looked around, but didn't see anyone else. "Tripp?"

Stella nodded. She gazed around the gallery. "Tripp Fogarty. He was here when I arrived. I heard Joan remind him to pick up the flowers. Maybe he left?"

"Why is that charcuterie board on the floor?" I pointed toward the one that had fallen.

"I don't know. I placed it on the table right next to the first one."

The door swung open and EMTs entered the store, followed by Officer Wong.

From time to time, I wanted to call her Rosa, which I thought such a pretty name, but she had gotten used to being Wong, and I tried to respect that.

I stood up and backed away from Joan to give the EMTs room. They stabilized her neck with a brace and lifted her onto a gurney.

For Wong's benefit, Stella repeated everything she had just told us.

"What are you two doing here?" Wong asked Nina and me.

"We didn't know about the lunchtime event. Sophie and I were in the neighborhood, and we thought we'd stop by to see Joan."

Wong's eyes narrowed and she gazed from Nina to me with suspicion. "By any chance is your presence here related to Orson's death?"

I hesitated to lie, but I couldn't exactly blurt out that we'd heard Stella's husband was having an affair with Joan. And now that I thought about it, if that was true, why would Joan hire Stella to provide charcuterie boards for an event?

"Don't be silly," snapped Nina.

We watched as they loaded Joan into the ambulance.

Tripp Fogarty walked up holding a huge bouquet of flowers in a vase. "What's going on? Good heavens! Is that Joan?"

I was glad to see him because someone would have to man the store or lock it up.

Wong looked him in the eyes. "Where have you been?"

He held out the flowers. "Clearly, I've been at the florist. What happened? Is Joan all right?"

"Stella, I'd like to speak with you alone, please." Wong entered the store and held the door for Stella.

That left Nina and me to explain to Tripp. "We don't really know what happened. Joan was on the floor, along with a charcuterie board. She appears to have a head wound."

The ambulance slowly pulled into traffic and drove away with the siren bleating.

"Noooo!" Tripp dragged the word out breathlessly. "Do you think Stella found out about Joan and Jordan and bonked her?"

"Then it's true?" Nina shot me a look.

Tripp cocked his head. "Are you kidding? Jordan this, and Jordan that. Joan talked about him all the time. I'm surprised more people didn't know. I realize that Jordan and Stella are separated but—man, these flowers are heavy."

I opened the door for him.

He hurried inside and placed them on the checkout desk. "What a mess! There's food everywhere." Tripp checked his watch. "People will be arriving any minute." He stared at the table and the only tray with dismay. "This will never do! Ugh! There are three hundred sixty-five days in a year, why did they have to choose this day to squabble over Jordan? Who, if you ask me, isn't such a spectacular catch anyway."

"I'll see if there are any more trays in the van," I offered.

"Don't bother. We only ordered three. Unless she made an extra one, I think we're looking at all of them. Would you two mind helping me?"

"Of course not," I said. "Where's the broom?"

Tripp disappeared in the back and returned with a broom, a dustpan, and a mop. "Nina, would you call The

Laughing Hound and tell them we need ten pizzas? I don't care what they have on them. You choose."

Stella had just returned with Wong. "No! I can have replacement boards here in half an hour. It would take any pizza shop in town that long to get pizzas here. Not to mention how much more chic and trendy the boards are. They're far better suited to an elegant store like this. Do you really want people walking around with slices of greasy pizza?"

Tripp gazed at her. "Half an hour? Are you sure?"

Stella picked up a board she had brought in. "Absolutely." But she didn't sound confident.

"Maybe Nina and I could give you a hand?" Making a charcuterie board beat sweeping or mopping any day. I hustled over to the board that had landed on the floor and picked it up.

Stella paused. "Maybe just Nina?"

Nina snorted. "Oh, Stella! You need Sophie. Trust me on this."

Stella took a deep breath. "I don't know what you had going on with my father, Sophie."

I started to protest, but Stella held up a hand. "Please! I do not want to know! I'm also devastated to realize that you were ordering food boards from me to make my father happy. I stupidly thought we were friends and you liked what I do with charcuterie boards. Make no mistake, I am in dire need of assistance right now, or else I would turn you down in a hot minute." She glared at me. "Just so we all understand that."

I felt terrible as I followed Stella to her van. Part of me desperately wanted to explain to her what her father had feared. But much as I liked her, Stella was a suspect and I had to keep that in mind. I would tell her one day. Just not today.

Nina and I hopped into Stella's van. Her house was less than five minutes away by car and only a couple of blocks from my house. She pulled into the alley and backed the van into a brick driveway. Unlike other homes, hers didn't have a fenced garden in the back.

She quickly unlocked the back door and tossed her keys on a tiny table that appeared to serve as a catch-all. The kitchen was painfully cramped to accommodate a long, narrow island.

Through a corridor that led to a family room, I could see packing boxes. "You're already moving?"

Stella hastened to wash her hands. "This is a rental. The sooner I get out and move into Dad's house, the more money I'll have for other things. I can hardly believe that I won't have to pay rent anymore. It's such a blessing!"

While Nina and I washed up, Stella placed two long trays on the island and loaded packages of meats, cheeses, and assorted delicacies between them.

Stella checked her watch. "We have fifteen minutes. You two take that board." She sliced a hard cheese in triangles and handed us a stack. "Kids have so much gear," said Stella. "It's a huge project to move their stuff. I'm trying so hard to be organized, but moving is a headache."

I rolled slices of ham and set them on the board in a pretty spray while Nina arranged the cheese. We worked quickly. The boards wouldn't be as lovely as they would have been if we had more time, but we had to deal with the time constraint. I filled in a gap with a bowl of olives that Stella handed me and plopped red and green grapes on the board as fillers.

Nina stacked round crackers in a long tight row. "I love doing this. It's fun! Sort of like a puzzle. The next time my in-laws come for a visit, I might just do this for a dinner."

"I do that all the time. You can imagine how many little

bits and pieces I have left over. The kids think it's fun to pick up food with their fingers. Some days I worry they'll forget how to use forks and knives!"

Stella covered her board with plastic wrap and handed me the box. I did the same, hoping the items wouldn't move. Nina held the door for Stella and me as we carried the boards out to the van.

Nina locked the door and handed the keys to Stella, who said, "Wow. That went very well. Now let's hope traffic isn't stalled somewhere."

Happily, we were at the back door of the art gallery with four minutes to spare. I carried in one board, Nina carried the other one, and Stella helped position them.

People who had come to see the art on display wasted no time at all helping themselves. During our absence, Tripp had lined up glasses of white wine and no one would ever have imagined that food had been splayed all over the floor less than an hour before.

"I honestly didn't think you could do it. This is fantastic, Stella. You're a magician." Tripp pecked her on the cheek.

Considering how little time we'd had to put them together, I thought the boards looked beautiful. Besides, as people removed items, the boards began to look a little less gorgeous, so our ultra-fast creations no longer mattered. Cheese was eaten, salami was placed on crackers, olives and grapes disappeared.

Stella heaved a great sigh. "I owe the two of you big time. Something like this could ruin my reputation and kill my business very fast. Thanks for pitching in."

"We were glad to help."

"Sophie, could I have a word with you, please?" asked Stella.

"Sure." I followed her out to her van.

Stella looked me in the eyes. "I have to know. Were you seeing my father?"

"No." I said it firmly. I considered telling her why I thought he had set up his will the way he did. But I quickly reminded myself that she could have been the one who killed him. The hurt in her eyes pained me to the core.

"I just don't understand. I thought he loved me. He was such a doting dad."

"Stella, he did love you. More than anything. I don't quite understand it myself yet, but when I figure it out, I promise I'll let you know."

"We will never know. I will have to live with this the rest of my life. I don't believe you, Sophie. I think you know exactly why he left you the store, but you can't come out and admit to your relationship with my father because you're trying to protect Wanda. Well! You can forget the butter boards I agreed to prepare for your meeting."

"Stella." I tried very hard not to sound snippy. "We have a contract."

"Contract? You can tear it up, Sophie. I want nothing to do with you." She hurried to her van.

"Good luck with the move," I called out to her.

She drove away in a huff, and I returned to the gallery. I propelled Nina through the store and out to the sidewalk. "Whew! It was getting crowded in there."

"What do you think happened?" Nina asked as we headed home under the sweltering sun.

"Good question. Stella seemed to be in shock when we arrived. I think I buy the idea that someone else was there."

"I don't know," said Nina slowly. "Stella could have thrown one of the boards at Joan, then rushed out to the van and carried the other one inside to make it look like she hadn't done it."

"But she recovered fast. If I had whacked someone with a charcuterie board, and she wound up severely injured, I don't think I'd have had my act together sufficiently to rush home and recreate two more boards."

"You think someone whacked Joan with one of those boards and then ran out of the store?"

"Can you think of a better explanation?"

"It could have been Jordan. Maybe he wants to reconcile with Stella now that she has some money. Maybe Joan threatened to tell Stella about their affair, so Jordan hit her with the charcuterie board. Or with something else, for that matter. Did you notice any statuettes or artsy objects that he might have put back in place?"

"You're saying he dumped the charcuterie board, then when she didn't agree to keep quiet, he grabbed a display item and whacked her over the head?"

"It's possible. Should we check on Joan?"

Nina's Jaguar was closest, so we hopped in, and she drove to the hospital. We headed straight to the emergency room, under the assumption Joan was probably still there.

Unfortunately, she had been sent to surgery and they anticipated it would be hours before anyone could see her. Probably not until the following day.

Nina met my gaze as we left the hospital. "That sounds a whole lot worse than I thought. Did you get that impression, too?"

I nodded. "Those big boards are heavy."

"She might have been hit with the edge of a board."

I cringed at the thought. "Let's hope the surgery goes well."

Nina drove us back to her house, and I walked on to mine. After letting Daisy out for a few minutes, I contemplated what to bake for Wanda. Other people were probably making savory casseroles to bring over. Then I remembered one of Wanda's favorites—banana pudding.

It didn't hold up very long, but with friends and family eating it, that probably didn't matter. I thought Wanda would be delighted.

I did a quick scan of my kitchen for the ingredients. Luck was with me. I even had heavy cream and a fresh box of vanilla wafer cookies.

Two hours later, I had just mixed vanilla and a little butter into the pudding when I heard a timid knock at the kitchen door.

Chapter 14

Dear Sophie,
My daughter is having a slumber party. Would it be
wrong to make a cookie board?
                    Preteen Mom in Sugar City, Idaho

Dear Preteen Mom,
You can make a board of anything you like. I think
it would be a wonderful way to serve a selection of
cookies.

                                        Sophie

Three slightly sweaty, rosy-cheeked children stood at
my door. The tallest, a blond girl, held the hand of a
little boy who couldn't have been older than three. A second girl, whom I gauged to be around eight, gazed up at
me with inquisitive eyes.

"Are you Sophie?" asked the tallest girl.

"Yes." Daisy poked her nose outside and wagged her
tail happily.

"Oh, good. It's really hot out here." The tall girl gave
the boy a gentle nudge. "Go on in, Olly!"

I stood aside as the three of them entered my kitchen. What in the world was going on? Who were these children and why did they think they were supposed to be in my house? Was there another Sophie living close by?

When I closed the door, all three of them sat down on the floor to pat Daisy. With typical feline curiosity and caution, Mochie circled them from a distance before getting closer.

"What's your dog's name?" asked the girl.

"Daisy. What is your name?"

"Oh, sorry. I'm Julie, this"—she said, pointing to the smaller girl—"is Lili, and that's Olly."

"It's very nice to meet you."

The smile on Julie's face vanished abruptly, as if Daisy's presence had caused her to forget her troubles, but now they had returned. "Mom sent us so the cops wouldn't take us away, split us up, and lose us in the system."

Uh oh. That sounded terrible! But who would send their children to me?

"She was arrested," said Lili solemnly.

"I'm so sorry. Who is your mom?"

"Stella," said Julie. "Stella St. James. She said maybe you would give us a ride to our nana's house and then help her find out who hit the lady in the art store because she didn't do it."

"She was arrested for hitting the lady with one of her big food boards," explained Lili.

"Did the police come to your house?"

Lili nodded. "We saw them on the street. Mommy sent us out the back door and told us to come here."

Julie gazed at me with the confidence of a child who assumed everything would be fine because they had done as they were told.

I couldn't see the harm in taking them over to their grandmother's house. As far as I knew, Myra was a responsible person. Unless, of course, she murdered her ex-husband. But that didn't mean she wouldn't be good to her grandchildren.

"Do you have fun at Nana's house?"

Lili nodded. "She has a new kitten!"

"All right, then. You must visit Nana! Do you want some warm pudding?"

Lili screeched, "Yes!"

I scooped a little bit of the warm pudding into three bowls. Hoping Daisy would behave, I handed them to the children, who still sat on the floor because I wasn't sure Olly could sit at the table without sliding to the floor. Only then did it dawn on me that I didn't have any child seats in my car.

While they ate, I looked up Myra's phone number and called her.

I walked into the sunroom so they wouldn't hear my conversation in case their nana said no. "Hi, Myra. This is Sophie Winston calling."

"Good grief. Am I not done with you yet?"

"Stella's children just showed up at my house. Julie and Lili told me that Stella has been arrested and that I'm supposed to deliver them to you."

"Arrested?" she screamed. "For murdering Orson?"

"No." But it was interesting that she jumped to that conclusion. "A woman was accosted in an art gallery today. I can only guess that they think Stella is the one who hit her."

"That's ridiculous. They can't just blame Stella. She probably wasn't even there."

"I'm afraid she was. They had hired her to bring food boards."

"Let me talk to Julie."

I walked into the kitchen and handed the phone to Julie. "Nana?" she said timidly.

I collected the empty bowls. They were polished clean, which led me to suspect that Daisy might have had a taste when they were done eating.

"She can drive us over to your house," said Julie into the phone.

I crouched in front of Julie. "Actually, I can't because I don't have any car safety seats."

Julie relayed what I had said. She nodded her head. "Okay. She wants your address."

I told her my address on Duchess Street.

Julie relayed it. "See you soon, Nana." She handed me the phone. "She's coming to pick us up."

"Would you like some juice or milk?" I asked.

Lili shook her head. "Will Mommy be okay? Do you think she can come to Nana's house, too?"

"Julie, tell me again what happened."

"We saw a police car drive up and park outside our house. A man and a woman wearing police uniforms came to the door. Before Mom opened the door, she told us that if she gave the signal, I should pick up Olly and run out the back way with Lili. And we were supposed to come here to get a ride to Nana's house. Because if we didn't, the police would take us, split us up, and we would get lost in the system. We would be safe with Nana."

"What was the signal?"

Lili raised her hand and made a circle with her fore-finger and her thumb.

I copied her gesture and she nodded. "If you didn't know my address, how did you know which house to come to?"

"Because this is the house where I'm going to live when I grow up," said Lili.

I couldn't help smiling. "Did you hear the police say anything to your mom before that?"

Julie took a deep breath. "They said she had to come

with them for questioning for assaulting Joan somebody and then Mom gave us the signal, so we ran."

"The police didn't try to stop you?"

"A lady cop chased us!" said Lili.

"We hid behind a shed a few houses down and waited until she gave up and went back," Julie explained.

The door knocker on my front door *thunked*. I hurried into the foyer and opened it.

Myra, who still wore her stunning caftan, stepped inside and gazed around. "This is a lovely home." She sounded surprised.

"Thank you."

"I had you pegged as one of those minimalists with ultramodern taste, but this is quite charming."

At that moment, Lili ran into the foyer. "Nana!" She hugged her grandmother in a way that broke my heart. She had seemed so comfortable in the kitchen that I hadn't appreciated just how frightened she was.

"Julie and Olly are in the kitchen."

Myra ran a hand over Lili's hair and whispered, "Nana's here. Everything will be all right." She took Lili's hand and they walked into the kitchen.

Julie got to her feet and hugged her grandmother. Only Olly ignored his nana, perfectly content to watch Daisy's tail swish when he grabbed fistfuls of her fur.

"Thank you for taking care of my little darlings." Myra made a big display of looking at her watch. "Oh my! I think it's ice cream time! Who would like to come with Nana?"

Julie, who had acted like a brave big sister, finally broke into a smile. "I would!"

"Me too! Me too!" cried Lili.

Olly looked up at his nana. "Ice cweam?"

Myra picked him up. "What do you think? Chocolate or vanilla?"

"Bubba gum."

"Do you need help getting them in the car?" I asked.

"Heavens no. I'm an old pro at this. Come along, girls."

They skipped ahead and out the door toward her car.

Daisy and I watched as Myra made sure they were all safely fastened in, and the car slowly drove away.

Exhausted, Daisy returned to the kitchen and stretched out for a nap.

Meanwhile, I thought I had better check on Stella. I doubted that I would get much information by calling the police. I called Wolf instead. He was probably my best bet.

"Fleischman."

"Wolf, hi! I'm sorry to bother you, but do you know anything about Stella St. James being arrested?"

There was a pause. It was so long that I wondered if we had been disconnected. "Wolf?"

"She wasn't arrested. But she was brought in for questioning. How could you know about that already?"

Something was up. I considered playing coy and brushing off his question, but something about that long pause made me wonder if Stella was in deeper trouble than I had thought. "Her children told me."

"Oh, man. She has kids? Are they little?"

"Two daughters and a baby boy. The girls are elementary school age. Why are you asking? What's going on?"

"We got a tip that she's the one who assaulted Joan Jankowski. But the assault charges just changed to murder."

Chapter 15

I gasped. "Joan is dead?"

"Do you know all these people?"

"Not super well, but yes, I know them."

"Is it true that Joan was having an affair with Stella's ex-husband?"

"That's the scuttlebutt, but I can't verify it. I have no personal knowledge about that. Do you know if Stella has a lawyer?"

"Mmm, I don't see anything on file yet. But it's early."

"That's what I needed to know. Thanks!" I ended the call and pressed in Alex German's number. He was a much-respected attorney in Old Town. But it was Sunday and the recording said to call tomorrow.

Oh no! Fretting about Stella, I made myself a cup of tea and for no particular reason, Ronin Walker came to mind. I phoned his office.

"Ronin Walker."

"Hi. This is Sophie Winston."

"Hello, Sophie! What can I do for you?"

"Do you practice criminal law?"

"I do." He sounded cautious. "Is this about Orson's murder, because that might be a conflict of interest."

"Actually, I'm calling about Stella St. James." I told him what had happened in the art gallery. "Wolf says she's only being questioned, but I think she needs someone to help her. Especially now that Joan has died. I feel certain that her mother, Myra, would be willing to pay for the bond if they charge her."

"No problem. I'll head over to the police station right now and find out what's going on."

"Thanks, Ronin. I hate to press my luck, but would you have time to see me tomorrow?"

"Sure. How's ten in the morning?"

"Sounds great. See you then."

I thanked him and hoped for the best. Poor Stella!

I measured sugar and cornstarch and added them to a thick-bottomed pot to make more pudding. As I stirred in the milk, I wondered why Stella had been taken in for questioning. Had Joan been revived long enough to identify Stella as the person who bonked her on the head? That had to be it.

As I cracked an egg, someone knocked at the kitchen door. Daisy whined as the door opened and Wolf walked in. She turned in happy circles as he petted her. Jealous

Mochie sprang from the window to the floor and mewed at Wolf, who picked him up.

"What's cooking?"

I whisked the egg and added a bit of the hot pudding to temper it. "Banana Pudding with Salted Caramel."

"Wow! That sounds great. Will there be bowls to lick?"

"Maybe. If you answer some questions."

"You drive a tough bargain. Depends on what the questions are."

I knew I had to phrase them carefully. If I blurted what I wanted to know, Wolf would clam up and even banana pudding wouldn't convince him to answer me.

"I should be mad at you, you know," he said.

"At me? What on earth for?"

"You should have told me that you're a witness to Joan's murder."

"A witness? Hardly. Nina and I arrived after the act was a fait accompli."

Wolf set Mochie down and walked around the island to face me. I stirred the pudding.

"Tell me what happened."

"Okay. If you tell me what evidence you have against Stella."

If I hadn't known him very well, I might not have noticed the very faint moment of surprise in his eyes. The man was so hard to read. But I caught it. Something was up.

"You first."

I capitulated. "Nina and I walked into the gallery. The first thing I noticed was Stella. It appeared that all the food had slid off a food board and landed around her feet with the food board on top of it. Then I realized that Joan was sprawled on the floor. There was a food board about a yard away from her feet on the ground and bits of food were scattered all over. A real mess."

"Where was Tripp Fogarty?"

"He wasn't there."

Wolf studied me. "Are you sure?"

"I suppose he could have been in the back of the store. I didn't see Tripp until he arrived with flowers from a florist while they were loading Joan into the ambulance."

Wolf's eyes studied me. "Can Nina confirm that?"

"You bet. I can do you one better. Wong was there by then."

Wolf sucked in a deep breath. "Excuse me." He walked outside and made a phone call.

When he returned, I asked, "Did you spring Stella?"

"She wasn't under arrest, Sophie. Apparently she stopped talking when her lawyer, Ronin Walker, arrived. She's still a suspect, but Tripp is, too."

"Oh?"

"Tripp claims he wasn't there when Stella hit Joan with a food board. What do you think? Is it possible that he hit Joan and ran out of the gallery?"

I poured the pudding into a bowl to cool and handed Wolf the pot and a silicone spatula. "Absolutely."

Wolf licked pudding off the spatula. "We need to interview Tripp again. You entered through the front door. Right? Did you see anyone running away?"

"I heard someone scream. Twice. I assumed it was Stella. She seemed to be in shock. It's possible someone ran out the front way and we didn't notice, but I can't say that I recall anything like that. The timing would have been very tight. Stella was in the process of carrying the boards in from her van, which was parked in the alley. The first board was still on the table intact. The second one must have been used to hit Joan. And Stella was holding the third one. So the killer would have had mere minutes to do it."

Wolf nodded. "It only takes mere minutes."

"And Stella would have been focused on the board,

making sure she didn't knock it around and shift the contents. Who gave you the tip that Stella did it?"

"Someone called it in to our anonymous tip line."

Rats. That meant someone didn't want to testify about what he or she saw. "I heard you dropped by to see Myra Chatsworth."

Wolf groaned. "She doesn't like you much."

"I can't blame her. I think I'd feel the same way. The store belongs in their family. I'm an outsider. Does she think I killed Orson for it?"

Wolf simply tilted his head, which I took to mean *yes*.

I used the microwave to make a quick batch of caramel. While it cooked, I took out a nice serving dish and flaked salt.

"I didn't know you could make caramel like that." Wolf peered into the container.

"Careful. It's bubbling hot."

I began to assemble the dish while Wolf looked on. He snitched a vanilla wafer. "You really had no idea that he was leaving the store to you?"

"Not a clue. At the engagement party, he pulled me aside and said there was something he wanted to talk with me about. I assumed it was some kind of charity event, but now I wonder if it didn't have something to do with the store. Have you dealt with Ronin Walker?"

"Yeah. Seems like a nice guy."

"And very good looking. What do you think about Ronin and Wong?"

Wolf snorted. "One of the rules I go by in my life is no fix-ups. They never work out and both of the people hate you forever."

"It doesn't have to be obvious. I could host a little party in my backyard and invite both of them."

"In case you didn't understand my previous objection—no, Sophie. Just no!"

"I could ask her to meet me at his office for some reason."

"Changing the location does not make a difference. Don't do it!"

I finished layering the components in the dish and beat sweetened whipping cream in my mixer, which ended that line of conversation. I took out a small bowl and layered in the leftover pudding, cookies, caramel sauce, and salt. After adding a dollop of whipped cream on the top, I added a spoon and handed it to Wolf.

He dug into it while I piped the whipped cream on the top on the banana pudding I had made for Wanda.

"Mmm, mmm." Wolf licked his spoon. "Tastes like my childhood, only better."

"I'm glad you like it. Maybe I'll make some to serve to Ronin and Wong."

"I want nothing to do with that. And I will say 'I told you so.'"

"Maybe I'll be the one saying that."

He waved as he left.

I placed a lid on the serving dish, grabbed my keys, and left the house, taking care to lock the door behind me. I carried the bowl over to the house where Wanda lived with Natasha, Griselda, and Charlene.

I shifted the dish to balance it on my left arm so I could rap the door knocker.

Wanda opened the door. "Sophie!" She lowered her voice so much that it was barely understandable. "Am I glad to see you."

I stepped inside. "I brought—"

A man appeared behind her. It took me a second to realize that he was Orson's former business partner, Karl Roth.

Standing in front of him, Wanda appeared almost petite, even though she wasn't a small woman. She seemed flustered as she took my dish into her hands.

His fluffy white hair was parted on the side. He wore glasses with a black frame and displayed a mouthful of white teeth when he smiled. In true old South fashion, he had donned a blue and white seersucker jacket to battle the heat and sported a yellow bow tie and matching pocket square. No one could accuse him of not being dapper.

"Sophie!" he said with a big grin that worried me. He reached out as though he meant to shake my hand, so I extended it. He took it into both of his rather soft and fleshy hands. "What a delight. I have heard marvelous things about your parties. You simply must host one for me sometime."

As politely as possible, I said, "I rarely host parties as part of my business. I'm more in the line of arranging conventions."

"Surely you would do *me* that courtesy. What have you brought?" He lifted the top and peered inside. "Whipped cream? Hmm. Chocolate Delight?"

"I'm afraid not. It's Banana Pudding with Salted Caramel."

Reminiscent of Fred Sanford when he feigned a heart attack, Karl placed a hand over his heart. His eyes wide, he declared, "Be still, my heart! I *must* eat some of that. I didn't think banana pudding could be improved upon, but it appears you may have achieved it!"

Wanda watched him with a horrified expression. She turned to me. "I'll just put this on the dining table. Thank you for bringing it, dear. I do love banana pudding."

"That's something else we have in common, Wanda! C'mon, let's try it." Karl snaked his arm under hers in what was probably intended as a gentlemanly manner, but poor Wanda still held the big dish I had brought.

"Maybe you could carry the dish for Wanda," I said. "It's rather heavy."

"How thoughtless of me." Karl showed his pearly whites again as he took it from her.

When his back was to us, Wanda seized my hand and looked at me with desperation in her eyes.

Poor Wanda. He wasn't her type at all. But he certainly was trying to win her over.

"Don't leave me alone," she breathed. "I can't shake him!"

"All right. I'll stick by you for a while."

We walked over to the table that was laden with food. I could hear voices in the living room.

Karl had already filled a bowl with my pudding and was savoring it.

Wanda helped herself and said, "Let's go to the living room where we can sit down."

I followed her, and promptly sat down beside her on a love seat.

Karl shot me a confused look. But he still had a spoon in one hand and the bowl in the other, so he sat in a chair. "Y'all," he announced to the others in the room, "there's a delicious banana pudding in the dining room." He continued eating until he was finished. "That was wonderful, Sophie. My mama was the best cook I ever met, and I thought no one could improve on her banana pudding, but that salty caramel sure is tasty. I'm fairly handy in the kitchen myself. I'm tryin' to talk Wanda into letting me cook her a special dinner over here. We can share stories about Orson, drink some wine, and toast our old friend."

Wanda, who was anything but prim or proper, said in a cautious voice, "Natasha doesn't like anyone else in her kitchen."

"Nonsense! I don't believe that," he said with a laugh. "I tape her show and watch it at night. Natasha is a sweetheart! She would love to have me show her a dish or two."

I shook my head. "Wanda is right. Natasha is very"—I

tried to choose a kind word—"*particular* about her kitchen." I tried to swing him to the subject of Orson. "You knew Orson for a very long time. This must be difficult for you."

"I sure did. We had some good times."

"Excuse me," said Wanda. "I need to say good-bye to someone."

"Of course," I said.

As soon as she was engaged with someone else, Karl dropped his cheery facade. His eyes narrowed ominously. He leaned toward me. "I don't know what kind of game you played with Orson, but I do know that he was a low-down, dirty, conniving sneak, and the fact that he gave you his store tells me you are just like him. My dear, you best watch out or you will soon come to the same painful end."

Chapter 16

Dear Sophie,
I wanted my sister to make a butter board for a party, but she said it's way too hard. Am I missing something? You smear butter on a board. How hard can that be?
Annoyed Sister in Sister Lakes, Michigan

Dear Annoyed Sister,
The difficulty in making a butter board is letting the butter soften. There are several methods, but one must take care not to melt the butter.
Sophie

That was a threat if ever I heard one! Karl's dark expression, not to mention his foreboding words, took my breath away.

He turned and, suddenly all sweetness and cheer again, he smiled and wiggled his fingers at Wanda, who looked like she might throw up.

Chills ran through me. What had Orson said about Karl?

Beware of him. Good advice. He was clearly able to play all sorts of parts. I would come to the same end? But why?

I figured I had two choices at that moment. I could stand up and leave or I could take advantage of being in a room where people mingled so I could engage Karl the snake to see what I could learn. He wouldn't harm me in front of everyone.

Pretending that I didn't care one whit about what he had just said and that I hadn't noticed his chameleonlike ability to change in a heartbeat from Mr. Nice Guy to a devil, I asked, "What happened between you two to make you and Orson divide the store and go your own ways?"

He eyed me with surprise. "We disagreed on how to run the business."

"Oh?"

"Orson was a silver-tongued con artist. I've never met anyone else with his ability to convince people that a worthless piece of junk was a precious antique. They believed him and came back for more. I knew it would catch up with him one day."

"Really? Who had it in for him?"

He raised his eyebrows. "So you *are* concerned for your own well-being." A sinister grin crept across his lips. "They do say the rotten apple doesn't fall far from a slick tree. And I'll tell you something else. That man had secrets. Deep, dark secrets."

"What kind of secrets?"

He raised his palms and pretended to be innocent. "I'll be doggoned if I know. He took them all to his grave."

He stood and walked away, ending my little interview. All I knew now was that Karl had two faces, maybe more. And that instead of causing me to doubt Orson, I believed him even more. Beware of Karl.

Wanda was busy listening to someone tell a tale about Orson.

I was a little unnerved by his proclamation of my end. I wandered into the kitchen where I found Natasha looking much happier than I had seen her in a while.

"Sophie! I have had a eureka moment. For years I have been trying to find the right thing for me. But my talents are varied and plentiful. I finally realized that I shouldn't be focusing on just one thing. That's where I've been going wrong. There's a word that encompasses it all—style! I'm a fashionista, I decorate houses, I invent elegant dishes to serve, I am a trendsetter! It all fits together under the word 'style.' I have style and my goal is to bring it to other people. Like you." She eyed me. "I could do a before and after segment on you for my TV show."

I nearly choked at the thought. When I caught my breath after a coughing fit, I rasped, "I'm not photogenic. You really should use someone else."

"Why, Sophie. I had no idea you were so self-conscious." Natasha handed me a glass of water.

I gulped half of it. "Thank you." In an effort to move the conversation away from a public makeover for me, I said, "Your show will undoubtedly be even more popular than it is now. Good luck with it!"

"There's much more to it. I need you to keep next Friday and Saturday open. I'm not sure which day it will be yet, but it will be amazing, and you simply must come."

"Come to what?" It had better not involve a makeover.

"I'm not at liberty to say yet. I don't want rumors to take over. It all has to be carefully planned, you see. Don't worry. I'll keep you in the loop."

The sound of something crashing in the other room sent Natasha flying in that direction.

I quietly let myself out and went home.

Chapter 17

Dear Natasha,
My daughter-in-law makes pancakes for my son
from a mix! How do I let her know that's not ac-
ceptable?
    Appalled Mom in Egg Harbor City, New Jersey

Dear Appalled Mom,
Put together a gift basket with everything she needs
to make pancakes. And then show her how to
make them. While you're there, surreptitiously
throw out her mix. Now she won't have an excuse
not to cook fresh pancakes.
    Natasha

I wasn't worried that Wanda would succumb to Karl's de-vious southern charms. He had clearly turned her off. Or maybe Orson had told her things about Karl. Remem-bering his unpleasant prognostication, I double checked to be sure all my doors were locked that night before I went to bed. Nevertheless, his words kept me from sleeping. He had uttered them in a way that precluded witnesses. Had he made similar threats to Orson? Perhaps beginning way back when they were in business together? I would leave a partner like that. Did he have a dark side? Dark enough to murder? Or did he like to scare other people to get his way? I had encountered that before. I hoped it was the latter and drifted off to a fitful sleep.

On Monday morning, I walked Daisy early to avoid the heat that would blast us later in the day. Wanda was outside, planting a rosebush beside Natasha's garden gate.

"Good morning!"

Wanda jerked and looked around. "Oh, it's you, Sophie. I swear I have been on edge ever since Orson's death. Griselda says I have nothing to worry about. The way Orson left me money, in a trust, means nobody will benefit from my death. Do you think that's true?"

I assumed that the remainder of the money would go to someone. Probably a charity. If that were the case, someone at the charity might want to do her in, but that was unlikely. To ease her mind, I said, "I don't think you have anything to worry about."

She took a deep breath. "That Karl is a real number. I thought I'd never get rid of him. I can't imagine what he thinks he'll get from me."

"He told me Orson had secrets. Do you know anything about that?"

"I imagine we all have secrets, honey. I have a few of my own. Nothing that would interest anyone else, I guess."

"Why, Wanda!" I said in a teasing tone. "You're such an open person that I never pegged you for secrets."

She giggled. "Everybody has got some. If you promise not to tell Natasha, I'll share one with you."

How could I pass up an offer like that? "Okay. It's a deal."

Wanda grinned. "I cannot abide Pineapple Upside-Down Cake. Somewhere along the way, Natasha got the notion that it's my favorite and she bakes it for my birthday every year."

"You never told her?"

"Well, when she was little, I thought it was the sweetest thing that she baked me a cake and I didn't want to discourage her. Then she moved up here and I got a break for many years. Now she's back to baking them again. She just made one to comfort me after Orson's death. I'm not going to say a word. You know how sensitive she is. I'm trusting you not to tell her!"

I laughed. "Such a dark secret!"

Wanda's shoulders shook with mirth.

At that exact moment, Natasha joined us in full makeup and beautifully dressed. "What's going on out here?"

Wanda gazed at me with wide eyes.

"I was just asking Wanda if Orson had any secrets."

Natasha looked at her mother. "Did he?"

"I imagine so. You don't get to our age without a thing or two you'd rather keep under wraps."

Natasha eyed her mother suspiciously.

I spoke quickly to avoid an argument between them. "It's just that Karl mentioned something about deep, dark secrets. I don't know if he was full of hot air or if there's something Orson was hiding."

"Ohhh, that Karl! I believe he likes to agitate people." Natasha appeared to be relieved. "Do you think Orson had another woman on the side?"

"Natasha! What a terrible thing to say. Don't go around telling people that. They'll think it's true." Wanda shook her forefinger at her daughter. "Not to mention that it's bad luck to speak ill of the dead."

I had a feeling Wanda might chance some bad luck if she knew about the photographs of the five young women in Orson's secret room. Maybe that was what Karl was talking about. Could he know about the secret room in the antiques store?

"If you think of anything, Wanda, let me know. It could be an important lead in finding his killer."

Daisy and I headed home. I suspected that I should have oatmeal for breakfast, but it seemed like a wintery thing to me. Pancakes were good any time of year and I had just bought fresh strawberries.

Mars jogged toward Daisy and me. "You're up early."

"It's going to be a scorcher. Coffee?"

"I would love a cup."

I unlocked the door as Bernie strode up. He ran a hand through his unkempt hair. "Mars, Senator Petrony is trying to reach you." He handed Mars a cell phone. "I thought I might find you here. Morning, Sophie."

Mars took the phone and excused himself.

"I think he forgets his phone intentionally when he runs in the morning."

"That would be like Mars." I mimicked his voice, "Sometimes I need to turn everything off."

"Pancakes?" I asked.

"Sounds good." Bernie opened the fridge and took out eggs while I boiled water for coffee.

By the time Mars returned from the sunroom, pancakes were sizzling, and the scent of coffee filled the air from my French press.

"Problems?" I set the table with Roy Kirkham oversize china coffee cups in the Alpine Strawberry pattern and matching plates.

"Always," he grumbled as he poured coffee for the three of us. "I guess I shouldn't complain. It means they need me. If there weren't problems, I'd be out of a job."

Daisy stood next to a counter and looked from Mars to the counter repeatedly.

Mars chuckled and opened a cookie jar. "Would you like a cookie, Daisy?"

Her tail swished across the floor, and she raised her right paw to shake.

"She has us so well trained." I fixed her breakfast and set it on the floor. Mochie waited by his empty bowl. I opened a can of Savory Salmon and spooned some into the bowl. "I'm glad you two came by this morning. I was wondering if you made any progress with the women in the pictures."

We sat down to eat our pancakes with maple syrup and fresh berries.

Bernie swallowed a bite of his pancakes, nodding his head. "Riley Hooper was waiting for someone in the restaurant bar last night. I mentioned how sad it was that Orson had passed away. She agreed, but she didn't seem particularly sad about it. She told me a little story, though. Apparently, one of her nephews was in hot water with Riley's mother. He and his brother were roughhousing and broke one of Grandma's antique chairs. She was furious. You know the drill. 'How many times do I have to tell you not to wrestle in the house?' Riley found an old picture of the chair and took it to Orson to see if he had one like it. He didn't, but about six months later, he called and asked if she was still looking for a replacement. He had spotted one at an auction and bought it with Riley in mind. It turned out to be a perfect match, so everyone lived happily ever after."

Mars sipped his coffee. "He had a reputation for being a sharp businessman. A lot of people wouldn't have bothered to look beyond their current inventory for that chair. That's the kind of service that brings people back."

Bernie nodded. "She had no complaints. Only good things to say about him."

"What does she do?" I asked.

"She works at the Social Security Administration. Her mom struggled to raise her on her own and pressured Riley to get a government job because you can't beat the benefits."

"I was supposed to talk with Cheryl Mancini." Mars helped himself to another pancake. "Can I get anyone a pancake while I'm up?"

Bernie handed Mars his plate.

When Mars sat down, he said, "Turns out Cheryl was Stella's best friend growing up. She lived across the street from the Chatsworths, so the girls often slept over at each other's houses. Orson was the kind of dad who brought home surprises like puppies and kittens. He took them for ice cream, drove them to the mall and waited for them while they shopped, and, get this, got them tickets to concerts where he discreetly watched over them without being the embarrassing dad. Cheryl didn't have a dad and thought that was how all dads were."

"No wonder people are surprised that he left the store to Sophie." Bernie popped a strawberry in his mouth.

"It's not the first time I've heard about him being a doting dad. But none of this explains why he had their photographs." I studied Mars and Bernie. "Under what circumstances would you two make a little board like that with women's photos on it?"

"Eww. Ick. What kind of heathens do you think we are?" asked Bernie.

"That's my point. I know you wouldn't do that for revolting reasons. So what kind of *good* reason would there be to do that?"

"One of them committed a crime?" Mars said in a tentative tone. "Maybe one of them fit the description of a criminal?"

Bernie perked up. "That could be true. Maybe someone stole something from the store, and they all match the description."

"So far, it appears that he knew them. He would have recognized the thief," I said.

"Not if he wasn't there. What if that was the description one of his employees gave him?" said Mars.

"Okay. Maybe. I can see how that might happen." But I wasn't at all confident that was the case. "I thought I might see if I can talk to Doreen Donahue today."

Bernie grinned. "Want me to come with you?"

I shot him a quizzical look. "Is there something I should know about her?"

"She's . . . different."

"You're welcome to come along. Do you know where she lives?"

"I suspect so."

"What does that mean?"

"She moves around. One o'clock?"

"That works for me."

I cleared the table, Bernie washed the dishes, and Mars dried them. The kitchen was clean in no time. When they left, I watered the flowers in my flower boxes and the veggies in the garden. After a shower, I changed into a sleeveless periwinkle linen dress and walked over to Ronin's office.

When I opened the door, Ronin's receptionist said, "Good morning, Ms. Winston. How is Rosebud doing?"

"She's great. Nina is still working on a home for her, but Rosebud has settled into Nina's household nicely."

Ronin appeared in a doorway. "Right on time. I like that in a person. Come on in."

Ronin's office was nicely furnished with leather furniture. A tall window overlooked a garden. I took a seat across from him.

"Do you have questions about Orson's will?"

"Sort of. What I'd really like to know is whether he left me any instructions."

Ronin rubbed his chin. "Orson was an unusual client. I won't pretend that I was surprised when he told me you would receive the store. I imagine he had his reasons."

I nodded. That was for sure. He hoped I would find his killer. I wasn't sure I could reveal anything to Ronin. Orson hadn't mentioned him in the letter that he left me. "Did he say anything about *why* he left the store to me?"

"He did not, and I didn't question him. It didn't seem like it was any of my business. But he did tell me one thing. And I remember it as clear as if it were yesterday. He said, 'Sophie will know what to do.' And he repeated that in the video he made."

"I appreciate his faith in me."

"Are you here because you don't know what to do?"

"I understand part of it but not the whole picture. He wanted to speak to me the next day, but then he died. Did he indicate what that might have been about?"

"No, I'm afraid not."

"Thank you for taking the time to see me."

"I don't think I've been much help."

"If anything comes to mind, if you recall him saying anything unusual, would you give me a call?"

"Of course."

I said good-bye and left Ronin's office wondering what I was overlooking. I felt as if Orson had left me a puzzle with pieces missing.

Chapter 18

Dear Sophie,
My brother gave his wife all their furniture when they divorced. He's living like an eighteen-year-old again. His house looks like a dorm room. How can I help him without being too pushy?
Big Sis in Fort Couch, Pennsylvania

Dear Big Sis,
You could offer to throw a painting party at his house. Buy fun hats for everyone, set out snack boards, and make fun drinks for your guests. You could also offer to go shopping with him. Whether it's in a furniture store or a flea market, it's always more fun with a friend or a sibling.
Sophie

I worked in my home office for a few hours, but thoughts of Orson and the store were never far away.

At five minutes to one, Bernie appeared at my kitchen door. I locked it behind me and slid the keys into a mini cross-body bag that contained a little cash and my phone.

"Where does Doreen live?" I asked.

"Only a few blocks from here."

"You'd think I would know her. Has she lived in Old Town long?"

He nodded as we walked up to a gray house.

"Wait a minute," I said. "Isn't this Graham Nye's house?"

Bernie shot me a sly look. "Indeed, it is." He tapped the golf club door knocker.

I recognized Doreen Donovan from her photograph when she opened the door. She was pretty, but she appeared tired, and more worn out than the other women in the photos.

"Bernie!" She wrapped her arms around his neck and kissed him on the cheek. "What are you doing here?" She wore a halter top of bright blue colors and white short shorts that couldn't possibly have been any shorter. High-heeled, leopard print ankle boots covered her feet in spite of the heat.

"Doreen, this is my friend, Sophie Winston."

I held out my hand to her.

She barely touched my hand with her bony fingers, as though she wasn't quite sure what to do. Long fingernails glittered in the sun. "I've heard of you. You throw all those grand parties, don't you?"

"I organize some galas, yes."

"We wanted to talk with you," said Bernie. "Do you have a minute?"

"Oh, sure! Y'all come on in."

I'd heard that Graham Nye and his wife had divorced, and his house certainly looked like a bachelor lived there. The living room was sparsely furnished with white walls. A dark brown leather sofa and a giant TV dominated the room. A collection of black-framed golf tournament flags decorated an otherwise empty wall. On a small side table, a resin Santa statuette was putting a golf ball.

"Have a seat. Can I get you anything?" Doreen asked.

"Don't go to any trouble for us," I said. "But thanks for asking. I guess you heard about Orson Chatsworth?"

"That was so sad. I was just crushed. I mean, I didn't know him super well, but he seemed like a nice man."

"Did you ever buy anything from him?" I asked.

Her eyes fixated on me. "I love that store!"

There was something odd about the way she looked at me when she said it. Because he had left it to me? Or maybe because of the high prices? It didn't worry me much. There were stores I had browsed in without buying anything, usually because they were out of my price range. Orson's prices were steep and not affordable for everyone.

Her eyes narrowed. "That's right! You own it now, don't you? I should drop by sometime and have a look around."

"It's closed right now. In respect of Orson's passing."

She nodded.

Remembering what some of the other women had said, I asked, "Did he ever give you a special deal on something you wanted?"

She seemed to hold her breath. "No."

Why did I get the feeling that she was holding back information? "Where did you meet Orson?"

Wrinkles appeared between her eyebrows. "Why are you asking me that?"

Bernie looked at me, tense.

"Maybe I have you confused with someone else," I said. "I was told you were friends with Orson."

"Oh, I was! Let's see, how did I meet him? I think it was through Joe Bulfin. Yes, I'm sure of it. I was having dinner with Joe when Orson stopped by our table and then joined us for a drink."

Joe Bulfin had to be thirty years older than Doreen. I supposed it would be rude to ask what on earth she was doing having dinner with Joe Bulfin. But, since I happened to know Joe, I knew how to find out.

"So you became friends with Orson?"

Honestly, the poor woman looked confused. It wasn't as though I had asked her a difficult question.

She looked to Bernie for help, but I didn't want him to guide her responses. "Did you work for Orson?"

"No," she said tentatively.

I smiled at her, hoping she would feel reassured. "What do you do?"

"I'm a model."

I hadn't expected that. She *was* attractive, but her face seemed lined and her eyes tired. "That must be a lot of fun."

"It's harder than people think."

"Have I seen you in advertisements?"

The clueless expression returned. She flicked the fingers of her right hand near her face and then touched them to her shoulder. "Um, maybe?"

She hadn't worked for Orson, and I had a very strong suspicion that she wasn't a model. "Did you go out with Orson?"

"No. But he was always real nice to me. Real friendly-like. You know? Some people aren't nice, but Orson wasn't like that."

Bernie made a little production of looking at his watch and tapping it. "Look at the time. I have to get back to the restaurant. Thank you for your help."

Doreen smiled at him and held his arm possessively as we walked out. She chattered at him, but I was thinking that she had gone around in a quiet arc from not knowing Orson *super well* to thinking he was a *nice man*.

When the door had closed behind us and Bernie and I

were well away from the house, I asked, "Okay. What's the deal with Doreen?"

"She had a rough upbringing. I'm told she was raised by her mother. An only child, sort of like Natasha, actually. Except Doreen's mom was what one might call a shady lady, as opposed to Wanda, who is the salt of the earth. Wanda might believe in crystals and the magic of nature, but she's as good and honest as they come. Now, mind you, none of this information came from Doreen. People who know her have confirmed that her mom made a living as a scammer and a thief. Little Doreen learned at her feet. It's just rumor, but some claim that her mother once stole a city bus full of people!"

"What? That's crazy! Why would anyone do that? Her mother must have a screw loose. I can't imagine being brought up like that. But I can see how Doreen might have gotten irrational ideas. We all look to our parents for guidance when we're kids. If that's all she knew growing up, then I can see why she might take the same path in life. Do you think she conned Orson?"

Bernie shrugged. "She was evasive about how she knew him and what her connection was to him."

"You must hate seeing her at the Laughing Hound."

"We don't have much to steal. It's not like we use sterling silver flatware. And, I have to admit, she's generally in the company of a well-heeled gentleman who picks up the tab."

"That's what she's doing at Graham Nye's house?"

"Yup. She mooches off them."

"I see. So basically she's a hooker?"

"I wouldn't put it quite that way. I don't think she hangs out on streets or gets paid for sex. I guess in the old days we'd have called her a companion."

"They don't bring her to the galas and such or I would have seen her around. What a sad life."

Bernie wrapped an arm around me and gave me a squeeze.

"Some people have it hard. I'm off to the restaurant. Feel like some lunch?"

"I think I'll pass today. Thanks for the offer, though. And thanks for taking me to see Doreen."

"Always glad to help. See you later!"

Bernie turned left and headed toward the Laughing Hound. I checked my watch. I had two hours before I was supposed to meet the alarm installer at the store. I kept walking toward Joe Bulfin's house.

His brick home had been painted a greenish gray. The forest green door shone in the sunlight as did the matching shutters. I could hear the TV on inside and what I thought might be a blender.

I rapped the anchor-shaped door knocker.

Suddenly the sound of the TV died. I waited, assuming he had heard my knock.

When he didn't open the door, I tried again.

This time, he shouted from inside, "Go away!"

Now I was in a quandary. Did he want to be alone or was something wrong inside his house?

"Joe? Are you all right? It's Sophie Winston."

The door swung open. Joe's pale, fleshy face was flushed and contrasted with his silvery hair. He had the body of a man who worked a lot and didn't get much exercise. He was nicely dressed in white shorts and a light blue golf shirt. "Sophie! I am so sorry. I, uh, thought you were someone else. Come on in."

I stepped inside. His home was a bit of a mess, but in a nice, comfortable, lived-in kind of way. As might be expected of a professor at a nearby university, his living room had two walls of floor-to-ceiling bookshelves. A rolltop desk was piled with papers and a few had been stacked on the hardwood floor.

"I was just making myself a smoothie. Would you care for one?"

"I'm fine, thanks. But don't let me stop you." I followed him into a small kitchen. A pizza box protruded from the trash can and an open box of doughnuts rested on the countertop.

As if he realized how it looked, he said, "I try to make healthy smoothies once in a while. Can't eat doughnuts and pizza all the time. Right? To what do I owe the honor of a visit?"

"I hear you know Doreen Donahue."

Joe promptly spilled the smoothie he was pouring into a glass. He grabbed a paper towel and wiped it up with a nervous hand. "What has she done now?"

Chapter 19

Dear Sophie,
My neighbor gave me a jar of onion confit. It
smells great but how do I use it?
                    Curious in Vidalia, Georgia

Dear Curious,
Onion confit adds a savory and sweet zing to
foods. Serve it with meat or fish or use it on sand-
wiches for delightful flavor. Mix it with vegetables
or, for a change of pace, put it on your pizza!
                    Sophie

"Are you okay?" I asked.

Joe slugged back way too much smoothie. "Just hearing her name makes me nervous. She was here earlier today. That's why I yelled 'Go away.' I apologize for that. I wouldn't have done it otherwise, but Doreen can be very persistent."

I followed him into the living room. He gestured toward a comfortable club chair, and I sat down. "She said you introduced her to Orson."

"Orson." He shook his head sadly. "I'm going to miss that man. We played poker together every other weekend. A whole group of guys. We've been together for years. Orson was the first to leave us. He was a good friend." His voice trailed off. "A really good friend."

"Do you recall introducing him to Doreen?"

Joe tweaked the bridge of his nose, then looked at me with tired eyes. "The *Doreen time*, as my daughter puts it, was a nightmare. Something I'd just as soon forget. That woman wreaked havoc in my life. She comes across as fun and"—he glanced at me with sad blue eyes— "pretty young women don't often take an interest in an old guy like me."

"What happened?"

He drank more of his smoothie. "I admit, I was a fool. A remarkably stupid old fool. How I did not see it coming is now a mystery to me. Let's see, what was first? I suppose in the beginning, she came around asking if I would give her a ride to various places where she could shop. The catch, of course, was that I wasn't only her chauffeur. She considered my wallet to be her wallet and expected me to pay for the things she wanted. She started out small. Reasonable. Except there was no reason I should be buying her anything now that I look back on it. At the time, I didn't think it would hurt to help out a young woman who didn't have much money. But once she got started, there was no amount of *my* money that she wasn't willing to spend. It made her so happy to have all those clothes, and in the beginning, I guess she made me feel special. Now, don't go thinking salacious thoughts. There was no carnal knowledge going on. I think that's what people find the most surprising about it all. But then she helped herself to the key to my house. I didn't even know she had a key until I came home from work one day intending to drive over to Maryland for a meeting only to find my car was gone. Just plain gone. Of course, I called the police and reported it stolen. They found it in Georgetown near a nightclub. Fortunately, nothing was damaged. I told her all about it and she acted surprised, as if it was all news to her. But when it happened a third time, I discovered a key chain wedged into the little space between the driver's seat and the console in the middle. And I was pretty sure it was her keychain because of the letter *D* in rhinestones, and it had my house key on it. She searched all over my home for it. It's hanging right there, on that little knob on my desk drawer." He pointed toward a dangling letter *D*.

"I keep it just so I won't forget what an idiot I was. I had the car fob reprogrammed and changed the locks on my doors. I told her we were through." He waved his hands as he spoke. "That I couldn't afford her anymore and I was done with her. But she kept coming over anyway like it had all been a joke that floated right over her head. You know, I am not a rich man. Comfortable, for sure, and maybe that looks wealthy to Doreen. I had a few little knickknacks that were worth something. Not a lot of money, like Orson's paintings and antique furniture, but a few pieces I had picked up along the way. And some family heirlooms. One day, it dawned on me that some were missing. I confronted Doreen and she broke into tears." He massaged his forehead and took a deep breath. "She needed money for food. She needed money to pay a doctor's bill. That woman can lie as easily as most of us breathe. Well, I had had enough. I demanded to know to whom she had sold them. When she finally coughed up their names, I escorted her to the front door and told her she was no longer welcome in my house. I thought she would understand that it was the end of the story."

He slid his hands against each other as if he were dusting them off. "I have to tell you, it was an enormous relief. I was so glad to be rid of her."

"But you said she came back today?"

"She knows no bounds. She comes by all the time. But this place is like a fortress now. She's not getting in unless she breaks a window, which I wouldn't put past her."

"I can see why you might not open the door to her."

He took a deep breath. "I'm not through yet. I *thought* I was done with her. And then the bank began to call. That, that"—his face flushed a deeper red—"*scoundrel* had made off with my checkbook and was writing bad checks all over town! I was embarrassed and ashamed. I'd like to think I have a pretty good reputation around town, and she was wrecking it. She hadn't even done a decent job at forging my signature. Employees at a lot of the stores had seen me with her and they accepted the checks because they thought I had given them to her. Orson said I shouldn't press charges, but I did. Not that it helped much. I have to tell you, I felt guilty about it. Just thinking about her in jail was upsetting to me. Even after all she had done! But she was out of jail in no time, and do you know she had the moxie to come right back to my house and knock on the door asking for money? Who does that?"

"A person without a conscience."

He gazed at me as though I'd said something shocking. "Of course! You're so right. Like the children who never bond with their mothers and grow up with emotional neglect. That leads to a lack of empathy for others. They can't understand it."

Now he was worrying me. Could she have killed Orson? "Did she have a similar relationship with Orson?"

"No. I'm certain of it. He didn't know all the details that I've just shared with you. I was too embarrassed to tell him."

"Were you at Orson's engagement party?"

"Yes. When he fell to the ground, I felt like a part of me had gone with him. It was wrenching."

"I can imagine. Especially since you were so close to him. Was Doreen there?"

Joe rolled his eyes. "I seriously doubt that she was on the guest list, but I saw her at the party."

It would have been easy enough for anyone to join the party. Nina and I had walked right in. It dawned on me that Doreen had been feeling me out earlier and had given me answers that she thought I wanted to hear. It was in her nature. "Did Doreen have any reason to dislike Orson?"

"Not that I know of. What are you getting at?"

I couldn't exactly come right out and say that Doreen had just landed on my list of suspects who might have poisoned Orson. I forced a smile and tried to dodge the question. "He must have liked something about her if he thought you shouldn't press charges after all she had put you through."

"He didn't know the half of it. He had a soft heart. He was a kind person."

"So are you. By the way, did you hear him saying, 'Tell Stella . . .' when he lay on the ground?"

"I did. Do you know what that was about?"

"I was hoping maybe you knew." I thanked him for sharing his story with me and left with new suspicions. Something must have happened with one of the women whose pictures he had pinned on his corkboard. Something that Orson felt he must keep secret for some reason.

I walked toward the store thinking Orson was either ashamed or fearful. There were a lot of reasons he might have wanted to keep a secret, but most of them seemed to fall into those two categories.

In light of all that had happened, I couldn't help wondering if Joan had been killed by someone desperate to keep Orson's secret, whatever it was.

I had just turned the key in the lock on the front door of the store, when I heard a vaguely familiar voice ask, "Are you Sophie?"

A young, slender, sunburned man stood behind me.

I took a guess. "Ian Hogarth?"

"Yes!" He wore khaki shorts and a colorful, Hawaiian style, short-sleeved shirt. His wavy blond hair was neatly cut.

I reached out and shook his hand. "I didn't expect you back from the beach this soon."

"I didn't think I would be back. My friends had to return early, and as much as I love the beach, I didn't feel like staying there by myself, so I drove back, too."

"Come on in." I left the door unlocked, but closed it behind him. "How are you holding up?"

Ian looked at the floor. "I've never had anyone close to me die before."

"I'm so sorry but, in a way, I guess that's a lucky thing."

"Orson was kind of like a second dad to me. It's inconceivable that he won't be around anymore. I didn't just lose a boss. I lost a friend and a confidant, and"—he wiped his eyes, sniffled, and looked up at the ceiling—"he was the best. He took a chance on me, and I will be forever grateful for that."

"I'm sure he loved you, too."

"Do you know what you're going to do with the store yet?"

"No. But I am having an alarm system installed. Someone is coming to tell me what I need in just a few minutes. Hey, do you know how to lower the chandeliers?"

Ian grinned. "They're on lifts. Orson had a local electrician rig up the lifts for him. They're all controlled from the loft."

I followed him up the stairs.

Ian removed a painting and opened a small door behind it. "There are five of these across the store. You just select the chandelier you want and pull the lever for up or down."

"That's amazing! I've never seen anything like that."

"Me either. Who'd have thought it? Apparently, they make them for home use, too. Some people have really high ceilings, like two stories high."

"Makes sense. They have to be cleaned."

"That's what Orson said."

The bell downstairs jingled, and we returned to the main floor.

When Ian saw who it was, he groaned. "I'll take care of her."

Doreen Donahue wandered through the store, running her hand over statuettes, furniture, and decorative pieces. She was dressed in the same outfit as earlier, but carried a giant leather purse shaped like a round sack and imprinted with a designer logo.

"Wait!" I whispered. "Is she a friend of yours?"

His eyes went wide. "Good grief, no. I should hope not. She pockets something every time she comes into the store. We follow her and keep an eye on her. Don't worry, I'll be nice."

He sauntered toward her. "Hi, Ms. Donahue. I'm sorry, but we're not open. Perhaps you heard about the death of Mr. Chatsworth?"

"I was crushed. He was always so nice to me."

"We're all very sad. Anyway, we're not open."

"The door was open."

"We're expecting someone to do some work."

"Oh. Well then . . ." She eyed a vase and picked it up.

For a long moment, I thought she was going to put it in her purse. I was certain she contemplated it. But she placed it back on the table, and said, "See you around."

She sauntered out with Ian right behind her every step of the way.

When she left, he let out a breath and returned to the cash register where I stood. "She's bad news. Ask anyone with a store."

The bell rang when the door opened again. A man stepped inside carrying a case that said *Hubert's Alarms*.

For the next hours, I was immersed in system installation. As it turned out, it was fortunate that Ian had dropped by. His knowledge of the store proved very helpful.

After Ian and the alarm guy departed, I locked the front door and returned to Orson's secret office. One at a time, I unpinned the photos of the five women and looked for writing on the back sides. They were all blank. Except for their approximate ages and general appearance, I still hadn't found any common threads between them.

Doreen had clearly been known to the store staff as a thief. And yet, even though she had caused terrible problems for Orson's friend, Joe, for some reason, Orson had discouraged him from pressing charges against her. Why? What had Orson known that Joe didn't?

And why hadn't Orson left an explanation for me? He had expected me to find this office and knew I would see the photos. I wondered again if that was what he had wanted to talk to me about. Orson had died too soon and left several questions in his wake.

I lowered the lights and locked the door. As I walked

home, I felt I had been so absorbed in the connection between the women on the corkboard that I had lost sight of
Orson's murder. Unless, of course, one of those five women
had reason to kill Orson. Which led me to the thought
that maybe Joan had murdered him and that was the reason Stella had killed Joan.

Chapter 20

Dear Natasha,
I'm eager to make a butter board. Do I have to do it on a board? My boards are so big.
                    Hungry in Big Bend, South Dakota

Dear Hungry,
There isn't a reason in the world that you have to use a board. If you're like me, you probably have loads of cute, small, serving dishes that would be perfect to serve softened butter with beautiful toppings.

                                        Natasha

I stopped in my tracks. Could that be what happened? Had Joan been at the party? I hurried along the street, planning to stop by Natasha's house to see if Joan had been on the guest list, but when I passed my own home, I heard a woman call my name.

"Sophie!" Stella waved at me from the stoop at my kitchen door.

I turned and walked toward her. "Hi, Stella."

"I hope you don't mind my stopping by like this."

I unlocked the door, grateful for the cool air inside my house. "Of course not. Come on in. Could I offer you some iced tea?"

"Yes, please! I'm parched."

While Daisy and Mochie introduced themselves to Stella, I pulled a pitcher from the fridge, added ice to two tall glasses, and poured the tea.

Handing her a glass, I asked, "How are you?"

She gulped tea, then said, "Everything considered, I'm okay. I'm still breathing, the kids are healthy, and—" She burst into tears.

I steered her to one of the chairs by the fireplace and handed her a box of tissues.

"You have a lot going on. Losing your dad must be overwhelming."

She gulped tea, sniffled, and then hiccupped. "I'm a wreck. I was so ugly to you and then I sent my children to you! And you took care of them in spite of what I said," she wailed, tears coursing down her face.

"It's okay. You're under a lot of stress. They were darling! Your mom was over here in no time to pick them up."

"I didn't want them walking all the way to Mom's house. They might have disappeared. Been kidnapped or something. I was so desperate to keep them out of the system. I knew that Lili and Julie would know which one was your house because it's Lili's favorite, and it wasn't nearly as far for them to walk."

She sniffled and held a tissue to her nose. "I'b going to lose custody!" She sobbed so hard that Daisy laid her head in Stella's lap.

"You don't know that," I said in what I hoped was a soothing voice.

She nodded her head. "Yes, I do. They think I'b a criminal. And now, the way Dad set up the trusts for the kids,

Jordan is determined to get custody so he can use their money."

I frowned at her. "But doesn't Ronin have to okay expenditures? Neither of you can just take the money meant for the children."

"Jordan says he can. My lawyer said Jordan's lawyer has already been in touch with her about custody. He didn't care about it before! He only wants them now because the money is tied to them."

She was in a pickle. I had a bad feeling that Jordan might try to do exactly what she claimed.

"Sophie." She sniffled again and looked me in the eyes. "I need your help. You have to find the person who murdered Dad and Joan. I can't have this hanging over my head. Can you imagine what a judge would say about a mom who might have killed someone?" She twisted the tissue in her hands. "I'll tell you who I'd like to kill—that rotten Tripp Fogarty! Why would he say he saw me hit Joan with a charcuterie board? Why? I don't understand."

My first thought was that Tripp must have done it himself. It wasn't impossible. He could have grabbed the board and hit Joan from behind in two minutes. Then all he had to do was flee the store and pretend to be picking up flowers. "Do you think Tripp had a reason to kill Joan?"

"I hadn't thought about that." She brightened up. "Maybe! Can you ask around? Apparently, I was the only one who didn't know that Jordan was seeing Joan! Did you know that?" She didn't wait for an answer. "Why didn't anyone tell me? I was hoping he would reconsider and come back to me." She wailed again. "He says he was at home when Joan was murdered and he claims to have a witness who saw him there, probably some woman who would lie for him."

"Do you still want him back?"

"No!" She blew her nose and sat quietly for a moment. "I'm so conflicted. I don't want him back now. I can't believe he started going out with Joan so quickly." She snapped her fingers. "He moved out and just like that he had someone else? That tells me a lot about how he really felt. He didn't care about me at all! If you love someone, you don't replace them in a matter of weeks or months. Sometimes not for years. You spend time pining and suffering and it takes a while before you can even think about loving someone else. Do you think he was seeing her before we separated?"

"I don't know." She was looking a little stronger. I preheated the oven, took some cookie dough out of the freezer, cut off chunks, and slid a tray of the chocolate chip cookie dough into the oven. They would be ready in minutes.

"Up until I found out about Joan, all I wanted was my family back. Jordan and my kids. That's all. I know I wasn't spending enough time with Jordan. Taking care of three kids keeps you busy. Plus, my business had been picking up and that was really important to me because Jordan was working sporadically. Someone had to keep money coming in, right?" She shook her head. "What a fool I was. I thought he was envious because things were going so well for me in my business. He wanted that kind of success, but has never managed to achieve it. Jordan always wants everyone else to do the work. He never worked his tail off like I did. I tried to overlook his jealousy, but now I realize what a jerk he was. I was getting four hours sleep a night! Even when I had a contract to provide charcuterie boards, Jordan couldn't be bothered to help out. He never had the time to take the kids to school or pick them up, or go to their after-school activities. I had to do everything."

Stella winced and rambled as if she were speaking her

thoughts aloud. "Of course he was seeing Joan before we separated. How could I not have realized that? I was too busy, that's how. That rat! And then when Dad died, he came around acting all sweet and sympathetic."

Stella sniffed the air. "Cookies? They smell delicious! Dad always disliked Jordan. You know what he did? On my wedding day, when Dad and I were outside the church, ready to walk in, he stopped. He came to a full, complete stop. The organ was already playing the processional music! Dad said, 'It's not too late to back out. I'll stand by you if you choose to do that.'"

Stella wasn't crying anymore. She pursed her lips, wiped her eyes, and looked determined. "I should have listened to him. I should have run off like Julia Roberts did in that movie. But you know, there's so much pomp and tradition and fuss leading up to the wedding that I couldn't imagine not going through with it at that moment. I was in love! Of course, I wouldn't have my wonderful babies if I had been a runaway bride. I suppose it's a trade-off. I wouldn't give them up for the world. But maybe they would have had a better father. Someone who really loved me and wouldn't have cheated on me at the first opportunity."

I took the chocolate chip cookies out of the oven and used a spatula to slide them onto a cooling rack.

"Sophie, I would die if I lost my children. I'm not joking. I couldn't take it. I won't be spiteful. I won't badmouth Jordan in front of them. That's not my style. No matter how angry I am, I won't make it their burden to carry. I'm okay with occasional weekends at Jordan's house, as long as he's with them. None of that nonsense about leaving them with a sitter while he goes out on dates. If he has them for the weekend, he should take care of them and focus on them. That's only reasonable, right?"

I moved some of the cooling cookies to a platter. "It seems reasonable to me. Milk, coffee, or tea?"

"Milk!" She managed a feeble smile. "I'm always taking care of everyone. You're being so kind. This is a treat for me. I feel just awful about what I said to you. Especially now that I'm here asking for your help. What a terrible person I am!"

I poured two glasses of cold milk and handed one to her along with the plate of cookies. "You're not terrible. You're in a big mess."

She moved to the banquette with her milk and bit into a cookie. "Mmm, all melty and soft!"

I sat down with my milk. "You had every right to be upset about your father's disposition of the store. I would have felt the same way in your shoes." I picked up a cookie and bit into it. She was right. They were so good fresh from the oven when the chocolate was soft. "Rumor has it that Jordan has a debt of some kind he needed to pay off. Do you know anything about that?"

Stella nodded. "I didn't sign on it, but he tried to get me to do it. He took out a loan to start a restaurant after he moved out. It's my guess that he spent most of it on renting an apartment. The kids say it's pretty incredible. It overlooks the Potomac! He went straight to the snazziest place in town."

"You'd think no one would have given him a loan. Didn't he have two failed restaurants before?"

Her eyes wide, Stella said, "I know! That's exactly what I said. What kind of person would have given him a loan at all when he didn't have a job and had a record of disastrous restaurants? It worries me."

"Why is that?"

"For starters, I think he spent it all and doesn't have a business to show for it. I haven't heard anything about him renting a building for a restaurant. And secondly, I can't see a bank lending him that money. That means it would have to be a private debt—a loan from someone. If they're pressing him for money like I've heard, then he's in serious trouble."

"Are you one hundred percent certain that your father didn't lend him the money?"

Stella choked on her milk. "Gah! There is no way he would have done that. None at all."

"I'm going to ask you a tough question. I'm sorry, but I need to be straightforward about this. Is there any chance that Jordan murdered your father in the belief that you would inherit the money to pay off his debt?"

Stella leaned toward me. "Oh, Sophie, I have wondered about that myself. The timing is certainly suspicious. And from the moment the ambulance left the engagement party until the reading of the will, Jordan was so nice to the kids and me. In a flash, he became the man I wished he had been. Reading to the children, playing with them. Saying all the right things to me. I'm not stupid, Sophie. He was a fool to imagine that I couldn't see through his act. Did he really think I would forget the way he treated me that quickly? Did he think I would erase it from my mind? Not a chance!" She sucked in a deep breath. "It's hard for me to imagine that he could be that devious and cruel. But I have seen his darker side. The one where Jordan is the only important person in the world. Yes, Sophie, I hate to think that I could have married a man who would murder my father, but it's entirely possible."

"Did he attend the engagement party?"

"He was there, but not with me. I can assure you of that."

Joan had been at the party, too. That was curious. They would have known Stella would be in attendance. Did they simply not care? Did they think no one knew and they could pull it off in spite of their relationship? Could Jordan and Joan have been in cahoots? I needed to move on to Stella's predicament before she remembered she had children to take care of.

"You parked in back of the art gallery on the day we helped you with the charcuterie boards. Did you see anyone back there? Anyone sitting in a car or hanging around?"

"Sophie, you know how heavy those boards are to carry once they're laden with food. Honestly, I don't look at anything else. Even if someone opens a door for me, I focus on the board and don't look up until the board is safely on the table."

"Did anyone open a door for you?"

"I don't think so. I learned early on that you can't rely on someone holding the door. They get called away, the phone rings, a customer comes in and then I'm standing there in the rain holding a heavy board with no free hand to open the door. Now I prop the door open, and I'm pretty sure that's what I did that day."

Chapter 21

Dear Natasha,
I love buying solid wood furniture at flea markets.
Sometimes, though, it's hard to tell if it's solid
wood or just a veneer. How can I tell the differ-
ence?
                    Flea Market Mama in Canton, Texas

Dear Flea Market Mama,
Follow the grain of the wood over the edge. Does it
continue? If not, it's likely veneer. Open a drawer.
If they went to the trouble of making dovetail cor-
ners in drawers, it's more likely to be solid wood.
But be careful, as some pieces are made of solid
wood and veneers.
                                              Sophie

"Was the back door open when you arrived or did someone have to open it from the inside?" I asked Stella.

"I rang the bell and Joan opened the door."

"Did she say anything?"

"She was very nice. She said how sorry she was about my dad and how grateful she was that I didn't cancel on them. That she had been afraid they would have to find someone else, and no one would be available at the last minute."

"How did Joan look?"

"Fine."

"Was she upset or flushed or fussing about something?"

"No. Not that I noticed."

"What happened next?"

"I carried the first board in. When I was arranging it, I remember Tripp saying he'd forgotten the flowers and had to go pick them up. Joan told him he'd better hurry."

"Did they sound angry?"

"No. I don't recall any animosity between them. I went out to the van and got the second board. When I positioned it, Joan admired it."

"So she was near the table with the boards?"

"Yes."

"Did you see Tripp?"

"I didn't notice him. I don't know if he had left or not. Then I retrieved the third board. When I came in, I remember feeling something squishy under my shoe. That was when I noticed the contents of a board all over the floor and I saw Joan sprawled in the middle of it."

"Any sign of Tripp?"

"Not that I noticed. It all happened so fast. I felt the squishy thing, saw the food on the floor, and then Joan. That's when I screamed. It only took seconds. Then you and Nina entered the store through the front door."

"Does Tripp have a reason to dislike you?"

"Gosh, I hope not."

"Have you ever had any arguments or discussions with him?"

She seemed surprised by my question. "No!"

"How about your dad or Jordan? Did they have any run-ins with Tripp?"

"If they did, I don't know about it."

I tried hard not to sigh. I wasn't getting anywhere. "What do you know about Joan?"

"Except for dating my husband, she was a nice person. At least I thought she was. Last year we were part of a group that was organizing a summer vacation art class for children, so I had a chance to get to know her a little bit better. She grew up in Old Town. It was just her and her mom, no siblings. She went to George Mason University, and majored in art. She was into making pottery and I think she said she also dabbled in painting with watercolors and was taking some classes in it."

"Did she know your dad?"

"Everybody knew Dad." She frowned and thought for a moment. "Yes! I think she bought a painting from him. I don't know much about it, but I recall how excited she was." Stella checked her watch. "Good grief, listen to me just rambling on. I need to get over to my mom's to feed my babies. We're staying over there for the time being. I feel safer there."

"Has someone threatened you?"

"Only the police. I never want to go through *that* again. We're moving anyway. It will be easier to move if we stay with Mom for a few days while I sort through Dad's house and bring all our stuff over."

Dad's house. The words rang in my ears. His desk or bedroom might contain something of interest. "His home must be very special."

"It's nice but it needs updating. I'd love to get rid of the wallpaper and paint some of the walls white to give it a more modern style. Sophie, what didn't fit in the store went into his house. My dad was a savvy businessman, but he kept all kinds of things. Is it okay if I bring some items down to you to sell?"

"That would be great." I would have to drop by when I thought she was working in the house. A little rude, I guessed, but it could be helpful to snoop around.

"Thank you for listening to me. Do you think you can figure out who murdered Joan? It's so important to me and my children."

"I can't make promises, but I'll do my best." I packed up the rest of the cookies for her kids. "If anything comes to mind, however unimportant it might seem, I want you to tell me about it."

"What if they try to arrest me?"

"Call Ronin right away to let him know. But I don't think they'll do that. Wolf seemed a little miffed about it. My guess is that they're going to be very careful." I didn't mention that they might bring her in for questioning in connection with the death of her father. She had enough to worry about.

"Thank you, Sophie." Stella walked away clutching the little box of cookies I had given her.

That night I whipped up some banana walnut bread to use up bananas before they went bad. While it baked, I made a list of people who might have wanted Orson dead. It wasn't long. His former business partner, Karl Roth, seemed a little off kilter to me. He was my top suspect, followed closely by Jordan St. James. I had to assume that Jordan would have thought Stella would inherit Orson's entire estate outright. That would fit with the sweet behavior she described when Orson was in the hospital and died. It changed abruptly when the will was read. Myra was miffed with Orson for not leaving the store to Stella, and rightly so. She was one of Orson's suspects, so I had to consider her.

As much as I loathed adding Stella's name to my list, I did it anyway. I couldn't count her out. She had provided the food for the engagement party, which was the perfect way to have poisoned him. It dawned on me that someone who knew Stella would be preparing the food might have seized the opportunity to poison Orson at the party because blame would fall on Stella.

And then there was Audrey, the nurse who had dated Orson. I needed to find out more about her. I added only one person who hadn't been on the list Orson made, Doreen Donahue. I folded the paper and left it on the kitchen table, in case I thought of anyone else. After the bread cooled, I covered it with a cake dome and headed upstairs to bed.

The next morning, Nina jogged across the street with Muppet and Rosebud.

I opened the kitchen door when I saw them coming. She carried two bags and a drink tray with three cups in it. "I brought lattes. Have you had breakfast?"

I took one of the steaming drinks and sipped it. "That was thoughtful of you." I drank a little more. "Caramel and mocha?"

"Exactly." She held up a bag. "Fried eggs and croissants. Shall we eat outside so the dogs can run around before it gets hot?"

"Sounds like a good plan. Are we expecting a third or are you terribly thirsty?"

"I figured we could invite Francie."

I nodded approvingly, gathered up a round tablecloth, napkins, and forks, and followed Nina outside. Daisy romped toward the backyard, followed by Rosebud and little Muppet, who was surprisingly fast for her size.

As I spread the purple-and-blue-flowered tablecloth

over my cast iron table, we could hear my neighbor Francie talking to her golden retriever, Duke.

"Now, Duke, you know you're never going to catch that squirrel. I'd think you would have given up on that quest by now."

Nina peeked over the fence between our houses. "Would Duke like to play with Daisy, Muppet, and Rosebud?"

Duke barked joyfully and ran to the gate.

Daisy responded and waited on the other side.

"Sure. Are you having breakfast? I'll come join you."

Nina opened the gate for them. Duke shot through at hyper speed and raced off with Daisy, followed by the other dogs. I carried Francie's mug over to the table under the tree where we would be sitting. The scent of coffee wafted to me.

Francie ambled over with a bowl of Cream of Wheat. About the same age as Wanda, or a little older, Francie had spent a lot of time in the sun gardening and bird-watching. Her face bore the wrinkles of a lifetime outdoors. Straw yellow hair stuck out from under her baby-blue sun hat. She had lived in Old Town most of her adult life and knew a lot of people.

Nina pulled three breakfast boxes out of the two bags. "I brought enough for everyone."

Francie opened hers eagerly. "The doctor said I'm not supposed to eat eggs because of my cholesterol," she grumbled, pushing her bowl of Cream of Wheat away. "I think eggs are the healthiest thing I can eat! I'm not giving them up, no matter what that bossy doctor says about it. Eggs got me this far. Mmm. Croissants. Is there chocolate in them?"

"They were all out of chocolate ones. These are plain," Nina apologized.

"Too bad, if they were dark chocolate, then they'd be good for us!" She tore a piece off one and munched on it.

"I like the way you think, Francie!" Nina laughed and handed her a latte.

"Francie, do you know Audrey Evans?" I asked.

"Oh, sure. She was a nurse for years. When she retired, she started volunteering at the library and the blood drive. I guess you're asking because of Orson?"

I nodded. "Someone said she was his girlfriend before Wanda?"

"Girlfriend? They were a *couple*. I was shocked when I heard about Orson's engagement to Wanda. Don't get me wrong. Wanda is a lovely person. Her earthiness is positively refreshing. She makes me feel like the world isn't so complicated, like it's still as easy and simple as when we were young. I don't know what happened between Audrey and Orson. Everyone has been talking about it."

"Think she could have killed him?"

"She's a nurse!"

"That doesn't mean she's an angel."

"I bet a lot of her patients would disagree with that."

"She would know how to poison someone," said Nina.

Francie gasped. "I heard Orson was poisoned, but I didn't believe it."

"Were you there?"

"At the engagement party? Wouldn't have missed that for the world. It's not often one of my more mature friends gets hitched. It's a miracle to meet a man at our age, much less love him enough to marry the guy. And Orson could be a little cranky, I think. He was quite opinionated. But then, after a certain age, I guess most of us are."

"I'd like to talk with Audrey."

Francie poured her latte into her mug and thought. "I could invite her to lunch. Would you be available today or tomorrow?"

Nina and I nodded.

Francie pulled out her telephone and made a call.

We only heard Francie's end of the conversation, but it seemed to be going well. She ended with, "I would love that! I'm supposed to meet with a couple of my friends. Would you mind if I brought them along?" Francie gave us a thumbs-up. She ended the call. "We're on. She has a new bird and wants us to stop by before lunch."

"Today? That would be perfect!" I said.

Francie beamed and laughed aloud. "I'm getting good at sleuthing. You two are a terrible influence on me."

I checked the time, but it was still early. "I thought I'd go have a look at Karl Roth's store this morning, but he threatened me at Natasha's house."

Chapter 22

Dear Natasha,
Why are these boards of food all the rage? What
happened to cooking and baking?
        Blue Ribbon Country Cook in Board Camp,
                                        Arkansas

Dear Blue Ribbon Country Cook,
The boards are easy to make and are very attrac-
tive to the eye.

                                        Natasha

Nina gasped. "He didn't!"

Francie shook her head and said, "You are not going alone, then."

"It wasn't an *I'll get you* kind of thing. He said I would end up like Orson. But when he said it, I felt as though it was something he threw out there to scare me. Like an old man trying to frighten kids so they wouldn't play in his yard."

Nina cocked her head. "You think he's hiding something?"

"I don't know. He's an unusual guy. He can flip back and forth from a saccharine sycophant to an ogre."

"Really?" Francie smiled. "That's good to know. I'll tag along."

We agreed to meet at Francie's house in an hour. I cleaned up our breakfast packaging and headed inside for a shower. I dressed in a sleeveless white dress with a cherry-red floral print. Simple and cool, but ladylike and appropriate for almost any daytime event.

Francie had donned a wide-brimmed hat with a loose linen pant outfit. Nina opted for a cool turquoise linen dress.

The heat was still bearable as we walked toward Karl's Fine Antiques. The exterior of the store would not have lured me inside unless I was in the market for a rusted frying pan. It had large show windows, but otherwise gave a rundown impression. It needed a good cleaning. I paused to look at the windows. They weren't even being put to good use. Instead of featuring lovely pieces that might encourage people to enter the store, they were piled with a hodgepodge of junk. Buckets, footstools, and chairs that were probably from the 1990s crowded together.

We stepped inside and I realized immediately why Karl and Orson split up. Paintings and mirrors leaned against furniture. Nothing hung on the walls except for a few spiderwebs. There were discolored rectangular blotches where it appeared paintings or mirrors might have once hung. Unlike Orson's store, which, crowded as it was, had a method to the madness, Karl's place looked like an indoor junkyard. Rusted lawn furniture mingled with coils of copper and a small collection of old tires.

"Not quite as elegant as Orson's shop," whispered Nina.

That was an understatement.

Francie had taken an interest in a side table that had

seen better days. She ran her hand over it. "I think I threw this out last year."

"Ladies!" Karl's voice boomed through the room. He hustled toward us, again looking quite dapper in a pale blue seersucker suit and a matching blue bow tie dotted with strawberries. "Welcome, welcome! What can I help you with today?" His gaze lingered on Francie as if he was sizing her up. "That's a very fine side table. You have excellent taste."

Francie's mouth twitched into a smile. "How much are you asking for it?"

"For you? I'll give you twenty-five percent off the asking price of two hundred dollars. It's a steal."

"I'll say," Francie said snarkily.

But then he turned in my direction. "You!" He sounded appalled and maybe a little bit worried. "Are you together?"

Nina quickly responded, "No."

I could see a wave of relief sweep over his face. In the sweetest tone imaginable, he said to me, "I'll be with you as soon as I can." He turned his attention to Francie. "This is genuine mahogany straight from Paris. You certainly know fine furniture!"

Straight from Paris? I doubted that.

I kept an eye on Karl and drifted toward the rear. I could hear Francie asking him to pick up the side table so she could see underneath it.

The door through which he had come hadn't closed completely. Hoping it wouldn't screech, I used the tip of my sandal to push it farther open.

To my surprise, it led to a kitchen. An old-fashioned one that had been pieced together. A skirt hung under a deep farmhouse sink. A tarnished copper kettle with a delft handle sat atop an aqua range that had to be from the 1960s. A newspaper and a remote control lay on a coffee table next to a Chinese food takeout container, and a plate of lo mein. Behind a plush brown sofa, a narrow stairway led to the second floor. A collection of framed photographs on the stairway wall were like a timeline of his life. I was fairly certain he was the adorable little boy jumping off a pier and riding a horse bareback. With a start, I realized that I was peering into his home. I'd bet anything that there were bedrooms upstairs.

I longed to peek at the second floor, but that would be wrong. I backed out of the doorway and moseyed toward the checkout desk. Pretending to be interested in a tall wire birdcage, I eyed the desk. There wasn't a cash register, a credit card machine, or a drawer with a lock. Of course, he could be using a tiny credit card swiper. But it was still curious. Didn't he take cash? When he made a sale, did he duck behind a magic curtain somewhere?

As I made my way back toward Francie and Nina, I spied a frosted glass Christmas tree topper for two dollars. It appeared brand new, as if never used, and was nestled on green velvet in what looked to be the original box. I had never seen one like it. It had been hand painted with a tasteful floral design. I picked it up and carried it over to Karl.

"I'll have to think about buying the table," said Francie firmly. If I hadn't known she didn't intend to buy it at all, I might have believed that she was wavering.

"I only have the one. These Parisian items go fast!" Karl warned.

I held out the Christmas tree topper. "Look what I found!" I pretended to be thrilled and pulled a twenty-dollar bill from my wallet so he would have to make change.

The edge of Karl's mouth pulled to the side as if he was aggravated.

He took his wallet out, handed me eighteen dollars, and pocketed my twenty. No bill of sale. No record of the sale.

And the money certainly didn't go into any sort of cash register.

I closed the box carefully. "Thank you." I couldn't be sure, of course, but I thought he was miffed that I interrupted his chat with Francie over the higher priced table.

He peered at me. "Is that why you came here? For an off-season ornament?"

"Of course. Did you expect something else?" I asked ever so innocently.

"Mmmfft. Excuse me." He turned toward Nina and Francie. "I hope you'll come back for the table. I don't hold anything, you understand. The next lady might snap this up."

Francie acted flustered and waved her hands around like a novice actor. "I can't make up my mind."

Nina checked her watch. "We have to go, or we'll miss that appointment."

I slipped out the door ahead of them and heard them thanking him as the door closed.

I hurried along the street, out of sight of the shop. Nina and Francie caught up to me.

"Honestly!" Francie exclaimed. "That is the very table I put out for the trash collector. I know it is because there's a ding on the corner where Duke knocked it over. He must be collecting things that people are getting rid of."

"Imagine his nerve trying to pass it off as Parisian. Although," Nina said, "we've become such a disposable society that we throw out a lot of perfectly good things. So maybe there's *some* good in collecting serviceable items and saving them from landfills."

She had a point. "I've seen the horrible side of him, but in spite of that, I feel sorry for him now. I think he lives in the back of the store and upstairs."

"In my day, a lot of people did that when they owned

stores. There's nothing wrong with that." Francie directed us toward Audrey's house.

"With prices the way they are in Old Town, I'm surprised he doesn't rent out the upstairs. It might look downtrodden, but I bet he could charge a lot of rent. Is this the house?" asked Nina.

Cream-colored, with seashore-blue shutters, the house was small but exceedingly well kept. Gauzy white curtains prevented people on the sidewalk from looking inside. A flower box hung underneath the window, overflowing with cascading petunias in shades of rose and lavender.

The front door, which matched the blue shutters, opened and Audrey stepped outside. "Hi! Come in out of the heat. I've prepared watermelon spritzers."

We filed inside. Audrey clearly loved blue. The cream-and-blue theme continued with loads of chinoiserie accents. A small dining nook was set up with a gorgeous Hepplewhite sideboard. I pegged it as an antique or a remarkable reproduction.

A little voice called out, "Come in. Come in." A vibrant blue parakeet squawked from his perch in a white cage.

"You shouldn't have gone to any trouble for us," I said.

"And why not? I love entertaining guests. People got away from that for a while, but I think we're moving back in that direction now."

"Show them your garden!" said Francie.

Audrey led us past the dining nook into a combination kitchen and family room. She had abandoned the formal white-and-blue motif in favor of flowers. It was reminiscent of an English country cottage with vibrant floral patterns on the sofa, chairs, and pillows. Beyond the family room, real flowers bloomed in a riot of colors. Except for a table and two chairs, Audrey had filled every inch of her garden with tomato plants, cucumbers, herbs, foxglove, geraniums, roses, hosta, and daisies. There were so many plants, and they were all mixed together.

"This is beautiful," I said. "Is that a set of cast aluminum garden tools?" The pretty stand meant to hold them only contained two. She must have left the trowel where she was last using it. I did that all the time and then had to search for it.

"It is. I'm never going back to wood handles. Even when I leave them outside, they look like new. They were a gift from Orson."

"How do you have time for this? You must garden all day long. I don't see a single weed," said Nina.

"It's only a weed in the eye of the beholder. I love a lot of invasive plants like thistle and . . . see that yellow one over there? The tall stalk? That's a yellow mullein. In the old days, people made tea out of them for colds and coughs because they're an expectorant. Today, though, they're considered a noxious weed because they spread their seeds like crazy. But I think they're lovely."

Nina and I agreed with her, but Francie laughed. "You're the only person I know who intentionally plants those things. I'm not coming over here to help you pull them all out of the garden next year!"

Audrey laughed along with her and led us back to her living room. She gestured toward a cream-colored sofa.

A tray of frosty glasses and a pitcher of watermelon-red liquid were on the coffee table next to a platter of pastries.

Francie asked, "What is the bird's name?"

"You have to see this." Audrey opened the cage door and the bird readily stepped onto her finger. "What's your name?"

"Bond. James Bond," said the bird.

We all cracked up.

"His previous owner taught him that. Isn't it adorable?"

"Are you a pretty boy?"

"Dishy hunk!" James Bond said as if he understood.

She fed him a morsel and brought him over to show us. "Hello! Hello!" he called.

We chorused, "Hello."

"He's so entertaining. My nephew lived with me for a while when he moved to Old Town. He has his own place now and I hated the silence in the house. You know how that is? Kind of like being an empty nester, I guess. But with James Bond in the house, I can't help being happy. He was just the ticket for, well, everything that ails me."

"You mean Orson's demise, I suppose?" Francie picked up her watermelon spritzer and pressed the cool glass against her face.

"Orson!" James Bond looked around and up at the ceiling.

Audrey took a deep breath. "It came as such a shock to me. I feel his loss so deeply."

"The death of a close friend is hard to deal with." Nina eyed the pastries and selected a mini cream puff.

"I can't believe he's gone. I catch myself picking up the phone to call and tell him something, and then there's the sudden blow again when I realize that he's not here anymore. I think the hardest part for me is that he never told me about Wanda. And now, I'll never know what happened there."

"Orson never told you?" I asked. "How could that be?"

"How could he? Howwww could he?" sang James Bond.

"You went out with him for a long time, didn't you?" asked Francie.

"For years! If anyone was going to marry Orson, I thought it would be me. Imagine my shock at learning that he was engaged to another woman. For the life of me, I still cannot understand why he wouldn't have had the decency to tell me. And really, Wanda? Of all the women in the world, I never would have thought he would choose her. She's not his type at all. She's, she's, well, I can't find a nice word for what she is. I hope she's not a close friend of yours, but the woman is what we used to call a country cousin. You know, unsophisticated and dowdy. I can't imagine what he saw in her."

I resisted the urge to defend Wanda because I wanted Audrey to keep talking.

"And that worries me." Audrey shook her forefinger in the air. "I have to wonder if that's why he never mentioned her. Was he ashamed? Embarrassed?"

"He probably didn't want you to know he was two-timing you," said Nina.

"I certainly thought that in the beginning, but the more I consider everything that happened, I have to wonder if there was something else."

Francie appeared doubtful. "Like what?"

"You see, that's what I don't know. I wonder if she had some hold over him. Maybe she forced him to change his will in her favor."

"You mean like a spell or something?" It was far-fetched, but Wanda did believe in potions and the like. I couldn't help thinking of the daffodil-based products she sold.

Audrey flapped her hand in the air. "I don't give any credence to that kind of thing. I hear Wanda does, but Orson wasn't the type to fall for incantations or curses. He would have laughed at that as nonsense. Do you see what I'm saying? He didn't buy into that backcountry mysticism. Orson was a curious man and by that I don't mean peculiar. He was well read and interested in many things. People associate him with antiques, and he knew more than anyone I've ever met in that arena. But he was also into genealogy and human behavior. Oh! And woe be the person who got him started on Jordan, his son-in-law."

Francie smiled. "No love lost there, eh?"

"I should say not. Orson treated Stella like a princess. That girl could do no wrong in her father's eyes. But he ranted about Jordan. Did you know that Orson anteed up the funds for Jordan to open a restaurant not once but twice? He wanted so much for Stella to be happy and financially stable." Audrey shook her head. "It never happened for her. But not for lack of trying on Orson's part."

For a moment, she sat quietly and nibbled on a miniature chocolate eclair. "No. Something happened for sure. I wonder if I'll ever know what. I don't trust Wanda. And then he went and left his store to some other woman. Why in the world he didn't leave it to Stella is a mystery. Who knows what kind of influence that woman and Wanda had over him!"

Chapter 23

Dear Sophie,
I love butter boards! How can I dress them up for
the holidays?
    Crazy for Christmas in Christmas Cove, Maine

Dear Crazy for Christmas,
Instead of smearing the butter on the board, how
about piping it on in the shape of a Christmas tree
or a reindeer? Or you could compound the butter
with cranberries! Or how about piping three small
stars on each individual butter plate?
    Sophie

I waved at Audrey. "I'm afraid that woman would be me."
Audrey froze and studied me for a long moment. "Would
it now?" She forced a smile. "How nice to make your ac-
quaintance." Her eyebrows rose. "You were there when
Orson fell to the floor. I remember you. I knew you looked
familiar."

She stopped short of saying it, but I would have bet anything that she was thinking I might be the person who killed Orson.

"Perhaps you can enlighten us. Why *did* Orson leave the store to you?"

I fabricated something I thought she might accept. "Honestly, I think it was to keep it out of Jordan's hands." I didn't even feel a twinge of guilt. After all, it wasn't a complete lie. Orson had been worried about Jordan, just as Audrey suggested.

"Do you know that for a fact? He could have easily accomplished the same thing by leaving it to Wanda or me."

Audrey was pretty swift. Probably a good thing for a nurse. One wouldn't want a nurse who didn't pay attention to details. "Perhaps he didn't want to trouble you with the minutia of running the store."

Nina nodded. "Sophie has already spent a lot of time over there. There's so much to be done."

"Really? I walked by the other day and noticed that it was closed," said Audrey.

"She's putting in an updated alarm system," Nina explained.

"Have there been problems?" Audrey studied me.

I tried to sound casual. "The employees think it's overdue and I tend to agree."

"I used to bring Orson lunch. We would eat in the office and dream of going on antique-buying trips in exotic places. I thought we would really go on one someday, but all that is over and done now." Audrey dabbed at her eyes.

"Orson is a beast!" squawked James Bond.

Audrey laughed at him and recovered. "Well! I guess Wanda got what she wanted from him. Do you know how much money he left to her? I've heard it's a substantial amount and that she's set for life."

"I don't know any figures." I sipped my cold drink.

"I gather it was based on need. Like if she should get sick and need care," said Nina.

"He didn't leave *anything* to me. Not a single thing. Wouldn't you think that a man who claimed to love me and had no qualms at all with me spending my meager retirement funds to feed him on a regular basis would have left me something? Did all those times we spent together mean nothing to him?"

I felt terrible for her in spite of the fact that she seemed fixated on his money. I suspected that if he had left her a trinket of some sort, she would still be complaining, but anyone could understand her disappointment, especially since Wanda had stepped into the shoes Audrey thought she would be wearing.

Francie patted Audrey's arm. "One would think so, dear. It just shows that he wasn't the right man for you."

"He most certainly wasn't."

"You can't dwell on it, Audrey." Francie held her finger out for James Bond, who readily walked onto it. "You will only make yourself miserable. That chapter is closed. There's absolutely no point in 'what ifs' or asking why. He did you wrong, my dear, but you are still alive and vibrant. You need to live your life to the fullest. It's the best revenge, you know."

"He did you wrong," chirped James Bond. "He did you wrong!"

Audrey chuckled wryly. "Some revenge. I heard he left his former wife one dollar in pennies. Is that true?"

Nina nodded. "I'm afraid so."

"I suppose I shouldn't be surprised. Their divorce was quite contentious. The woman was relentless. Why, I saw her knocking on the door of Orson's house the night before the engagement party!"

"Are you certain about that?" I asked.

"Absolutely. She's hard to miss in those caftans she wears."

"You just happened to be passing by?" asked Nina.

Audrey turned blazing eyes on her. "Unfortunately, I walk by Orson's house quite often. It's on a rather prominent street. I would wager that you two have walked by it as well."

She had a point. But somehow, I didn't think it was a coincidence that she saw his ex-wife at his door. "When did you last see Orson before the engagement party?"

"That night, I suppose. I saw him open the door to let her in. You know, Orson put forth a persona of the successful businessman, which he was. But I always had the impression that there was something he wasn't telling me. A secret of some sort from his past that left him melancholy. Now I'll never know. He took all his secrets with him when he died."

"You need to focus on yourself now." Francie made kissing noises at the parakeet. "Have you thought about a girlfriend for James Bond?"

"It's funny you should mention that. My nephew was just telling me about a friend of his who has a lonely female parakeet. He was going to check into it. I think James Bond would love to have a friend."

"That cage is plenty big for two." Francie placed her glass on a tray, signaling her intention to wrap up our visit. "Audrey, if you feel lonely or want company when you feel like going out for dinner, you just call me."

Nina and I thanked Audrey for her hospitality and headed for the door. When it closed behind us, and we were out of earshot, I asked Francie, "Do you think Orson had some kind of secret? Or is that just the kind of nonsense Audrey would say?"

"Sophie, everyone has a past. And that means the good

and the bad. No one is perfect. Perhaps there were things he came to rue as he got older. I'm no expert, but I suspect we all have moments in our past that we regret. It doesn't mean he robbed a bank. Not to mention that as we age, some of our loved ones have passed and we have melancholy moments because we miss them or wish they were still around."

Francie was right. It didn't mean Orson had a deep dark secret. I suspected that I overreacted because I knew about the bulletin board in his hidden room. And the mere fact that he'd found it necessary to have a private room hinted strongly at secrets.

It was a beautiful day. The three of us stopped for lunch at an outdoor café overlooking the Potomac River. The umbrella over the table and the breeze from the river cooled us off. But while Francie and Nina chatted about neighborhood gossip, I was thinking of Orson and remembered that Stella was getting his house ready to move into.

After a shared lunch of delicious spiced shrimp and a large white pizza with spinach, roasted red peppers, and zesty sausage, Nina and I put Francie in a cab so she wouldn't have to walk home in the heat and the two of us strolled over to Orson's house.

Unlike most of the homes in Old Town, Orson's place was set back off the sidewalk. A black wrought iron fence with a charming gate led into a lushly planted front yard with two benches.

The gate was open, and so was the door to the house. Three muscular men were carrying furniture inside and Stella stood in the foyer, telling them where to take things.

"Moving day!" I said.

"Ugh." Stella looked beat. "It's awful! I thought it would be best to leave everything of Dad's in the house for right now. That I could take my time later on to sort it all. But now I'm not so sure. I can barely get through some of the rooms because of all the furniture. And that's saying a lot because Jordan took some of our furniture when he moved out."

"Do you mind if we look around? Try to get a feel for your dad?"

"Of course not. Have at it!"

"Have you found any papers or anything of interest?"

Stella shot me a look of incredulity. "I haven't done a thing in that regard yet. Juggling the kids and making sure everything is out of our rental has been overwhelming."

Just then two of the men carried a sofa into the house. Nina and I hurried to get out of the way.

We passed through a formal dining room with a large chandelier and a gleaming walnut Victorian table with matching chairs. A large rug sat underneath it and paintings adorned pale red walls. While Nina roamed downstairs, I went in search of Orson's bedroom.

I found it on the second floor. It was furnished with a four-poster bed and a large desk with a comfortable chair. But my favorite part was the round-top windows with shutters to fit that opened inward.

For an hour I poked around. What must have once been a small bedroom had been made into a modern bathroom and a walk-in closet. I looked though desk drawers and old shoe boxes, but found nothing of interest until I accidentally knocked over a framed picture of Stella. It clanked to the floor. I was relieved that the glass hadn't shattered. But when I picked it up, the stiff velvet backing that covered the rear had been knocked out of position. When I tried to wedge it back into the frame, it wouldn't cooperate. I slid it out a bit to readjust it and discovered the problem. Two other pictures were in back of the photo of Stella.

One was of a pretty young woman holding a baby whom I guessed to be six months old or so. A little girl around age two sat beside them, clearly fascinated by the baby. The other photograph was of the baby. She wore a pink dress and held a stuffed kitten. It looked like a professional photo. The kind that people often paid a photographer to take of their young children. I flipped it over. It was stamped with the name of a photography business, Ludlow Family Portraits.

I studied the baby in the photograph. She was blond with an oversize pink ribbon on her head. Someone had dressed her in a fussy gown. Maybe for a baptism?

"Sophie? Where are you?" Nina called.

"In here."

"There's so much stuff to go through. How are you doing?"

I showed her the pictures. "Did Orson have a sister?"

"Not that I ever knew about. Stella probably knows."

I was torn about showing the photos to her. "They were hidden behind a picture of Stella."

"That's odd." Nina used her thumbs to shield the woman's hair.

"Oh wow!" My breath caught in my throat. The resemblance to Stella was unmistakable.

"Their outfits are coordinated," said Nina.

I nodded, beginning to feel a little queasy. "That woman must have gone to lengths to find a mommy and daughter match for Stella and the infant."

"Do you think Orson stole Stella?" Nina looked at me with fear in her eyes.

Chapter 24

Dear Sophie,
Friends are coming for breakfast with their lively
kids who have trouble sitting still. I'd like to make
a breakfast board. Any ideas about what I could
put on it?
Coming Up Blank in Childs, Maryland

Dear Coming Up Blank,
How about a pancake and waffle board? Line up
the pancakes and waffles along the edges and fill
the middle with all sorts of wonderful toppings like
berries, nuts, fruit, and chocolate. Be sure to get
some savory items in, too, like bacon and sausages.
Sophie

My heart pounded. "Let's not jump to conclusions just yet. Besides, if he stole Stella, why would he have the picture?"

"Then why did he hide the photo?" asked Nina.

"It could be Stella's aunt with her child and Stella. Maybe the photographer can identify them." There was someone else who might know—Myra Chatsworth. However, since Orson had gone to the trouble of hiding them, it was worth looking into the identities of the three people in the photograph before I started questioning Myra.

There wasn't anything disturbing about the picture. Just a little girl looking adoringly at a baby and the woman who likely was the mother. Anyone looking at it would assume that the woman was the mother of the two children. But there was no way that the woman was a young Myra.

I could hear Stella guiding the movers upstairs and quickly hid the photos in my purse before reassembling the frame that held Stella's photo and propping it on the desk.

Nina and I got out of the way as the movers shoved furniture aside to make room for more.

"Is the store open yet?" asked Stella.

"Actually, I was thinking of opening it this week. I believe the employees are ready to get back to work."

"Great. I'm going to have quite a few things to sell."

"Call me when you're ready. I'll be sure it's open when you need it. There's extra room in the storage in back, so anytime is fine."

Nina and I headed home. She stopped at her house to collect the dogs, who were happy to romp in my yard with Daisy. Mochie yawned and stretched. After a bite to eat, he watched the three dogs from the sunroom in the back of the house, unconcerned about them.

I brought my laptop to the kitchen table while Nina sliced banana walnut bread and made decaf coffee.

The backs of the photos were stamped *Ludlow Family Portraits, Alfonso Ludlow*. A quick search for Ludlow Family Portraits yielded loads of results. The studio had been in business about thirty to forty years earlier in Baltimore, Maryland. The Web site showed photos of babies, young children, and doting parents with their offspring. On the remote chance that someone might answer the phone, I called the number.

Nina set coffee in front of me along with a slice of the banana walnut bread. As I expected, my call ended abruptly with a recording that told me the number was not in use. I looked up Alfonso Ludlow. That search yielded a different phone number. I tried calling it.

"Hello?" The male voice sounded elderly and soft.

I put the phone on speaker so Nina could hear. "Hi. This is Sophie Winston calling. I'm looking for an Alfonso Ludlow who was a photographer in Baltimore."

"Is this one of those weird calls? What do they call them? Spam?"

"No, sir. It's not. I live in Old Town, Alexandria, Virginia, and I found a couple of your photographs."

"Well, that's nice. How can I help you?"

"I'm trying to identify the woman in one of the pictures. She's holding a baby, maybe about six months old, and a little girl in a pink dress is fascinated by her new sibling or perhaps cousin?"

"That describes an awful lot of the photos I took. I wouldn't be able to say who they were unless I saw it."

"I see. Could I text a picture of it to you?"

"Text?"

"Through a mobile phone?"

"Martha," he called. "Can you get a text on your phone?"

Someone replied, but I couldn't make out what she said.

"Okay. She gave me this number." He rattled it off.

I took pictures of the two photographs with my phone and texted them to him.

"Where? Oh, there." I heard the intake of a raspy breath. "Oh. That was a terrible matter. Saddest thing I ever heard of. I never expected it. You know, a photographer often sees things through his lens that make him wonder. But I had Mr. Harris pegged as a gentleman. Probably because he worked for a bank. You expect bankers to be honest, solid people."

"Who is Mr. Harris?" I asked.

"Oh! Well, he's the one who murdered his wife and stole the children in this picture."

Chapter 25

Dear Natasha,
We're supposed to be eating more salmon. I was
planning to serve it at a big family dinner, but my
brother-in-law has announced that he won't eat At-
lantic Salmon. We live on the East Coast and it's a
lot cheaper! I think he's being snooty, but my hus-
band says we should indulge him. What do you
think?
            Love the Atlantic in Ocean City, Maryland

Dear Love the Atlantic,
Your brother-in-law isn't being snooty. While there
are species of salmon that are native to the Atlantic,
most salmon labeled Atlantic Salmon is farm raised.
You'll have to read the label carefully to know. Wild
caught salmon is said to be healthier.

                                            Natasha

"Murdered?" Nina spilled her coffee.
"Who's that?" asked Mr. Ludlow. "I heard someone else."

"It's Nina Reid Norwood, Mr. Ludlow. I'm working with Sophie. I never expected to hear this lovely woman was murdered."

"Neither did I. Mind you, I only know what I read in the papers. As I recall, they never did find Mr. Harris. I believe he came home from work and found his wife with another man. He shot her dead and disappeared with his children."

"How old would they be now?" I asked.

"Sakes alive! I'm sure I don't know that."

I thanked him for his help and gave him my number in case anything else occurred to him.

Breaking off a piece of the banana walnut bread, I looked over at Nina. "Are you thinking what I'm thinking?"

"That Mr. Harris is, or was, Orson Chatsworth?"

Nina turned the laptop in her direction and typed something in while I ate. "Here it is. Pretty much what Mr. Ludlow said. *Mr. Harris, manager of the First Trust Bank, went home after work and in a fit of jealousy on finding his wife with another man, shot her and stole their two daughters, Sandra and Callie.* According to this, they would be right around Stella's age."

"Maybe they're Orson's nieces." I didn't think so, but I desperately hoped Orson wasn't the terrible Mr. Harris. "I know women who look like their aunts." It was a weak rationalization, but I did know a few women for whom that was the case.

"That would make more sense," she agreed. "As far as I know, Stella never had a sister."

A chill ran over my shoulders. What if that was what Orson wanted to tell me? What if he wanted Stella to know that she had a sister? Or worse—that Myra wasn't her mother? I blurted what I was thinking. "Myra Chatsworth would know the truth. Either she gave birth to Stella, or she didn't."

"It's not the sort of thing a woman would forget. Maybe we should pay her another visit."

I nodded, feeling sad for Myra and Stella.

While Nina tidied the kitchen, I made copies of the two photographs. We left Rosebud and Muppet with Daisy and Mochie. They would all probably nap while we were gone anyway.

We walked over to Myra's house and Nina banged the door knocker.

Myra opened the door wearing a red caftan and large opalescent, dangle earrings that matched the white trim on her dress. "Good grief. Not you two again."

"Could we have a minute of your time?" I asked.

Nina was already walking into the house.

Myra showed us to the same living room. Her cats followed along, curious about us.

"Are your grandchildren here?" I didn't hear them.

"The sitter took them to the pool."

I sat down and sucked in a deep breath. How could I approach a sensitive topic like this? "Some information has turned up and we thought you might know something about it."

Myra pursed her lips and looked away, more annoyed than anything else. "I did not kill Orson. That's it. I have nothing else to say." She rose, as if signaling that we were done and should depart.

I didn't budge. "Is Stella your biological daughter?" I knew it was a brusque way to go about asking such a sensitive question, but she was intent on getting rid of us.

Myra's shocked expression told me the answer. Her face sagged. She parted her lips and took several deep breaths. She looked at each of us and then away before sitting down again. "I don't believe that my maternal history is any of your business."

I nodded. "Ordinarily, I would agree with you. But

something has come to light. Otherwise, we would not be here asking you anything so personal."

"I cannot imagine what that might have to do with finding Orson's killer. Not even that"—she fluttered her hand—"policeman, Wolfie whatever, had the audacity to approach me with something so ridiculous. Will my answer help you find the murderer?"

I had to be honest. "I don't know. But it might. There could be people who held a grudge against Orson for something he did in his past."

"Stella is my daughter in every sense of the word."

"You and Stella are very close," said Nina. "You're lucky that way."

Myra's bottom lip quivered ever so slightly, and she toyed nervously with one of her earrings. "Have you made mention of this to Stella?"

I met her gaze. "No."

"Well, thank heaven for that small comfort. What is it that you have uncovered?"

"Photographs," I said.

Myra scowled at me. "I have plenty of photographs of Stella as a baby."

"Do you have these?" I handed her the copies.

Myra caught her breath when she saw them. "Where did you find these?"

"Among Orson's things." I figured I didn't need to be too specific.

Her brow furrowed. "I never saw Stella's birth mother before. The likeness is remarkable." She studied them. "Orson, you old goat, what have you done?" She looked up at me. "Please, all I ask is that you let me tell Stella myself."

"We have no need to break this news to her. Not right now, anyway."

Myra nodded. "Thank you for that courtesy. Honestly, I

hoped this day would never come. I love Stella more than life itself and I can't bear to imagine how painful this will be for her. I wasn't able to have children of my own. When I met Orson and he had this precious little girl, it was like a gift from heaven for me. I yearned to be her mama. Orson and I debated telling her the truth. At this moment, I wish we had. But there were other factors, and in the end, we decided against it, at least while she was a child. Now I have no choice."

"What other factors?" Nina picked up a Siamese cat.

"Orson was a banker. One of his depositors was a rather unsavory man who had a bad reputation. When he applied for a loan, Orson had to turn him down. The man was livid. He threatened to kill Orson. A few weeks later, when Orson came home from work, he could hear Stella crying when he parked his car. Orson found his wife inside. She had been shot and was dead. From the way she lay, he thought she died trying to protect Stella. He never mentioned a baby. The man had violent brothers." Myra shook her head. "A despicable family, from what Orson told me. He had no choice. If they returned, he and Stella would be next. He had to protect her. So he drove through the night to Florida where he was able to procure identification under the name Orson Chatsworth. He worked a few odd jobs and was offered a position at an auction house in northern Virginia. That was where he picked up the antiques business. He settled here in Old Town, where I met him."

"So you knew all along that he was really Mr. Harris," said Nina.

"Yes. In the beginning, I admit that I was concerned. We're not that far from Baltimore. But our lives seemed so tranquil that I didn't even think about it anymore as the years passed."

Her story rang true in a way, but why would the police

have thought that it was Mr. Harris aka Orson who killed his wife? And what about the other child?

In that moment, I realized why Orson had posted the pictures of the five girls in his secret office. He wasn't some kind of pervert. He was a father, searching for his missing daughter. "Do you know anything about the other child in the photo?"

Myra glanced at the picture again. She shook her head. "I haven't a clue. Orson never mentioned another child."

"Can anyone else confirm this?" I asked.

"Not that I know of. Orson was very private about it. We really never mentioned it after we were married. I think he told me because he wanted me to know what I was getting into. Lay his cards on the table, so to speak. I have to admit that the thought of being his second dead wife scared me. But I loved him and believed what he told me, and I loved little Stella, so I took a chance that the terrible man who murdered Orson's wife had gone on with his life."

Nina's mouth skewed to the side. "Really? Didn't people think it odd when you turned up with a little girl, but you hadn't been pregnant?"

"Not at all. People weren't as intrusive back then." She shot each of us a look that let us know she thought we had stepped over the line of polite society. "We lived in Manassas when we first married and then we moved to Old Town."

"But your family must have known," Nina persisted.

"They knew she was Orson's little girl. They adored her just like I did."

"Did you know that the police think he murdered his wife?" asked Nina.

Myra looked appalled. "No," she said softly. "I wouldn't have married him if I had known that."

"What was the name of the man who allegedly killed Orson's wife?" I asked.

"Oh! Well, now you're asking ancient history." She thought for a moment. "Mickey Finn?" she mused.

"That's a drink that knocks a person out," said Nina.

"Maybe it was Mike Hammer?" said Myra uncertainly.

"Mike Hammer is a character. A private detective," I said.

"Well, it's something like that. I think. It's been a very long time. Why would he kill Orson now, after all these years?"

There were too many possibilities. "Because Orson could finger him? Myra, you should expect another visit from Wolf. I'm going to have to tell him about this."

"No, no. Why would you do that?"

"Because the police are looking for the person who murdered Orson, and Mickey Finn Hammer could be the one."

"Nana?" A child called.

"The children are back. Not a word about this. In fact, it would be better if you left. Hurry!"

It was unnecessary, of course, but in the heat of the moment, we went along with Myra as she ushered us through a butler's pantry to the kitchen and out the back door.

Nina came to a halt and gazed around. "This is a lovely backyard. Look at those roses! And the cardinal flowers. I love the bright red of the blooms."

I hurried her toward the gate. "Come on before the children see us and ask Myra questions."

We slipped out the gate as quietly as we could and walked along the cobblestone alley.

"I'll make dinner tonight and invite Mars, Bernie, Francie, and Wolf. Something simple, like salmon and roasted veggies. Does that suit you?"

"Of course. I'll bring drinks. Will we eat outside?"

"It would be nice. But this is sort of sensitive. I'd hate for anyone else to hear. Maybe we'll eat in the dining room for a change."

"Fancy!"

I laughed at her. "Hardly. But it's an excuse to get out the nice china."

Nina peeled off at the grocery store and went her own way. I entered the store and bought an iced coffee to sip while I phoned Mars, Bernie, and Wolf to see if they were available for dinner. Happily, they were, and Bernie insisted on bringing dessert from his restaurant, The Laughing Hound.

I picked up corn on the cob, bacon, red peppers, and a bag of lima beans. I was choosing salmon when Colin Warren, who was opening the new event venue in Old Town, approached me. "Looks like you'll be eating well."

"I'm having a few friends over for dinner. Nothing fancy."

"I was so sorry to hear about Orson. I didn't know him personally, but what a blow. To meet a wonderful woman at his age is like a miracle. I wish my uncle could find someone."

I thought back to the unfriendly man I had encountered at Colin's new place. It wasn't much of a surprise that *he* would have trouble finding a girlfriend!

"Natasha has been wonderful. Even though they won't be needing my space, she's coming over to film her TV show there. The publicity is more than I could ever have hoped for."

"I'm glad it worked out for you after all."

"Has she told you about her new project?"

"Noooo," I said slowly.

"I don't dare ruin the surprise. Hmm. Funny, I thought she said you would be one of her first customers."

"Really? I'll have to find out more about it."

"Enjoy your dinner. I just wanted to thank you again for putting Natasha in touch with me. You did me a huge favor." Colin walked away.

I couldn't help noticing that his shopping cart contained ribs and barbecue sauce. Enough to feed a lot of people. I checked out of the store and walked home, wondering what kind of business Natasha had in mind this time.

Chapter 26

Dear Sophie,
I went to a party where they had gone to a lot of
trouble to make food boards. They were so unap-
petizing that I didn't want to eat anything. How
does one avoid that?
                    What a Mess in Clearwater Florida

Dear What a Mess,
I have seen those boards, too. Place anything
shredded, diced, or grated in a bowl with a serving
spoon. Don't use foods that can wander or melt. If
you can't pick up a piece of something with a fork
or your fingers, don't use it on the board. Lastly,
use multiple pieces in interesting rows, circles, and
patterns. This also helps the board remain attrac-
tive as the food is consumed.

                                        Sophie

I had never been quite so heralded as I was when I arrived at home. Three dogs wanted my attention. All of them certain that Nina and I might not return. Mochie yawned as if he thought they were all being silly.

I popped the salmon in the fridge before I let the dogs out. They chased one another and sniffed the yard while I plucked fresh, ripe tomatoes from my garden. I tweaked off some fragrant basil leaves and sprigs of savory rosemary as well.

Thanks to the heat, it didn't take long for the dogs to be waiting in line at the door to return to air-conditioning. They settled down immediately in the air-conditioned house. I donned an apron, washed my hands, and set to work on our dinner.

I preheated the oven for the salmon, then microwaved the bacon. I thought the dogs would beg for bacon because it smelled so wonderful that I wanted to eat it, but they sprawled on the cold floor and behaved very well.

I diced a red onion and sauteed it, then added fresh corn kernels, diced red and yellow peppers, diced zucchini, and lima beans. While they cooked, I covered a baking sheet with aluminum foil, then cut potatoes into cubes and tossed them with olive oil, paprika, and salt before spreading them onto the baking sheet and popping it into the oven.

Nina arrived first, pulling a cooler on wheels. After greeting the dogs, two of whom were clearly relieved that she was back and hadn't abandoned them at my place, she opened the cooler to reveal three large pitchers on ice. They contained a beautiful peachy pink liquid. She removed one and closed the top.

"That's a lot of drinks."

"Not really. It's peach bourbon iced tea. Rather mild on the bourbon."

She accompanied me to the dining room where I set the table with a white tablecloth and Lenox Tuscany china.

The intricate design around the edge in gold was stunning and way too formal for our gathering, but I was pleased to have an excuse to use it. While Nina filled water glasses and iced tea glasses, I hurried outside with the dogs and snipped pink and peach zinnias and roses. Back inside, I mixed them in two vases. They looked perfect with the pinkish tea.

I checked the time and set out a cheese board. It only took minutes to place a wedge of Brie, slices of Gouda, crackers, black olives, and some sliced salami on it. The quickest and easiest hors d'oeuvres ever.

I finished just as Mars knocked on the kitchen door and walked in with Bernie right behind him carrying a cake box.

"Is everything all right?" asked Mars.

"Of course. Why wouldn't it be?" I asked.

Nina held out a glass of iced tea to him.

Mars peered in the dining room. "Thanks, Nina. Okay, now I'm really concerned."

I thought about it and realized that I hadn't used the dining room since the holidays. "Nothing's wrong. I just thought we'd be more comfortable in the dining room. Okay, that's not really true. I have information that needs to be kept confidential."

He turned and looked at me with raised eyebrows. "Sounds intriguing."

Wolf knocked on the door and held it open for Francie. Everyone chatted amicably as they nibbled goodies from the cheese board. I slid the salmon trays into the ovens. Minutes later, my friends migrated to the dining room and sat down.

I transferred the salmon and veggies to dishes, garnished them with slices of roasted red and yellow peppers, and added a helping of the potatoes. Nina and Bernie carried the plates into the dining room. I filled serving dishes with the rest of the food and brought them to the table in case anyone wanted seconds.

When we were all seated and everyone had started to eat, Wolf asked, "Why do I think we were invited here because of Orson's death?"

Bernie chuckled. "It does feel a bit as if Hercule Poirot might walk in and point the finger of guilt at one of us."

The laughter subsided and I told them the story of the untimely and horrible death of a woman we believed to be Orson's wife. "Sadly, Stella's birth mother was murdered. The newspaper report indicates that her husband killed her, but Orson told Myra that the murderer was a ruthless man whom he feared. That was why he took Stella and left."

I retrieved the photographs I had printed out, and stopped talking while they made the rounds through my guests.

"So Orson may or may not have been a murderer," said Bernie. "How would we ever find out? That happened decades ago."

Everyone looked at Wolf. He examined the photographs. "I can make some calls. This case probably went cold a long time ago when they couldn't locate Orson. Still, sometimes something turns up. DNA tests have gotten more sophisticated over the years, too. You don't need as big a sample anymore. If they saved something from the crime scene, it's possible that it could be tested."

"But would that really prove anything?" asked Mars. "After all, if Orson lived in that house, wouldn't his DNA be all over the place?"

Wolf smiled at him. "That's certainly what the lawyers would argue."

"Who is this other child?" asked Francie.

"The article says he took his *two* daughters. So, presuming that Orson was this Mr. Harris, she must be Stella's sister." I bit into a piece of salmon.

"Does she have a sister?" asked Mars.

"Not according to Myra," said Nina. "The question is, what happened to her?"

I had forgotten that Francie didn't know about Orson's corkboard with pictures of young women. I quickly explained that I had thought it was sort of creepy. "But I now think I was wrong. My theory is that Orson was looking for his other daughter."

"That doesn't make any sense." Mars shot me a skeptical look. "If he took her when he killed his wife, then why wouldn't he know where she was?"

"Mars has a good point." Nina poured more of her spiked tea for everyone. "More likely something happened to her, and she died before he met Myra."

I hated to imagine that because it sent me back to thinking the pictures on the corkboard were something unpleasant. "That could be. If she was still living, I'm hoping it wasn't Joan," I said. "To gain a sister and lose her at the same time would be too much to take."

"Let me get this straight," said Mars. "Orson may or may not be a killer."

"At least we don't have to be afraid of him now," said Francie.

Bernie winced. "I admit that I have trouble believing that he didn't stay by his dead wife and call the authorities. Who would run off and leave a loved one like that?"

"Someone who feared for his own life or the lives of his children. There's no time to be sentimental. Good or bad, you have to make a decision. And sometimes that might mean leaving the dead to save the living." Mars helped himself to another piece of salmon.

Wolf nodded. "I've learned that it's easy to guess what

we might do in a given situation, but when it actually happens, there can be circumstances that change the way we react. If he thought the killer was still in the house, for example."

"Or if the killer was there and threatened the children," Nina added.

"In any event," I summed up, "killer or not, Orson fled the scene of the crime and eventually arrived in Old Town, at which time he only had one child instead of two."

"Maybe the killer harmed the little girl in some way, and she died," said Francie. "Or Orson could have left her with someone he trusted, like a sister or an aunt. Maybe that was the real reason that he fled to Florida."

"And he never went back for her?" That was something I couldn't understand. "Why would he do that?"

Francie cocked her head. "Things happen. Historically, there were people who couldn't afford all their children. If relatives didn't take them in, they landed in orphanages. Maybe the sister didn't have children of her own and had grown close to this child and they felt it was better for her to stay in Florida."

"Possible, I suppose," I grumbled. It blew a big hole in my theory that Orson had been looking for her, unless he had reason to know she had moved to Old Town.

Nina smiled at me. "I don't want to think Orson killed his wife, somehow ditched one daughter, and was a creepy old man spying on women."

She had summed it up perfectly. That was exactly what I had been thinking. "Honestly, if that was the truth, then Wanda was lucky he died before he hurt her, too."

Mars and Wolf helped carry our dinner dishes into the kitchen.

Bernie insisted I stay put and returned with a beautiful chocolate cake. It was only one layer, with a creamy ganache running down the sides. To make it even more sinful, it had been topped with whipped cream and sliced straw-berries.

"It's currently the best-selling summer dessert at the Laughing Hound. Even the people who turn down dessert end up ordering it when they see it."

Bernie sliced it, and placed the slices on my formal dessert plates, taking care to be sure that everyone received some cream and strawberries.

Mars and Wolf surprised us by bringing in pots of tea and coffee. I didn't say anything, except thank you, but I thought that Nina and I had trained them well over the years.

We lingered at the table, laughing and enjoying the warmth of dear friends.

They offered to do the dishes before they departed, but I insisted on doing them myself and shooed them out the door.

Wolf gave me a big hug and whispered, "I promise I'll make some calls about the cold case."

"Harris," I reminded him. "That was the name of the man married to the woman in the photos."

"I'll keep you posted."

It was unsettlingly quiet after they left. Even Mochie and Daisy seemed at a loss when Muppet and Rosebud went home with Nina.

I took my time hand washing and drying the dishes and the stemware, thinking all the while about Orson.

Myra might have loved him once, but something must have spurred their divorce. She had seemed legitimately shocked when Nina and I turned up Orson's real identity. She didn't deny it. But he may well have lied to her. That would certainly fit the profile of a man who had killed his first wife. My heart sank at the thought. Why had they divorced? Was it something worth killing him for? Had it been so combative and hostile that she still wanted him dead?

Karl definitely had a dark side and was two-faced. I couldn't forget him telling me that I would end up like Orson. He was an ugly man, not in appearance but in spirit. Loads of people had committed murder out of jealousy. And if there was one thing I was certain of, it was that Karl had plenty to be jealous about when it came to Orson.

I liked Stella, which made it more difficult to consider her as a suspect in her father's death. But as far as I could tell, she didn't have much of a motive. He'd left her children well cared for and given her two houses. I suspected that Orson's reason for all the trusts was to keep his money out of Jordan's hands.

Ah, I had forgotten about Jordan. I would make a point of talking to him tomorrow. It would be interesting to hear what he had to say.

Chapter 27

Dear Sophie,
Can you settle an argument? I bought an antique chair that was made in 1911, over one hundred years ago. My mom says it's not an authentic antique unless it was made before 1830. Who is right?

                    Proud of My Antique Chair in Old Town,
                                        Alexandria, Virginia

Dear Proud of My Antique Chair,
To be called an antique, an item must be over one hundred years old. However, some collectors claim only items made before 1830 are true antiques because machines came into use in manufacturing after that date. You and Mom will have to agree to disagree. Be proud of your chair and enjoy it!

                                                    Sophie

I was up early on Wednesday morning. After a walk with Daisy and a shower, I fed Daisy and Mochie. I skipped oatmeal in favor of shimmering blackberry jam that I had bought at the farmers' market. It was all I needed on whole wheat toast with a mug of tea. Then I baked a peach coffee cake to bring to the employees of Chatsworth Antiques.

It had been a week since Orson's death, and it was time to open the store. All the employees were scheduled to be there. If not to work, at least to meet me. The store would be back to earning its keep.

On my way there, I stopped to buy six lattes. Not everyone liked them, but I hoped it was a safe bet that most of the employees would appreciate them. Besides, I had seen a coffeemaker and a teapot, so they would have those options if they preferred. Juggling the lattes and the coffee cake, I unlocked the door and turned off the alarm. I set them down on the table where we had had dinner, added elegant paper napkins and a knife for cutting the cake, and then walked around turning on lights. The air was cool, and it was comfortingly silent. I wondered if Orson had enjoyed the quiet before everyone arrived as I was doing now. It didn't last long. Ian was the first to come in, all bubbly, his nose peeling slightly from a sunburn.

The others filed in somberly. An older woman, with gray streaks running through her black hair, introduced herself as Margie.

A tall, slender gentleman stiffly shook my hand and said, "Robert." He eyed me curiously. Not that I could blame him. Not only was I his new boss, but I had come by the store in a truly unexpected manner.

A redhead named Reba who was about Ian's age smiled at me shyly. And finally, a portly middle-aged man, who seemed displeased about my presence, briskly blurted, "Gene."

They gathered around me. "Thank you all for coming in today. I'm truly sorry to meet you under such sad circumstances. Please help yourself to lattes and the coffee cake."

"Is it true that Orson was murdered?" asked Margie.

"I'm afraid so."

"I heard you investigate murders. Is that why you're here? To spy on us?" Robert seemed highly suspicious of me.

"No!" I blurted. "Not at all. You're here because the store needs to be open and running again. I know they haven't had a service for Orson yet, so we'll close again on that day out of respect and so that all of you can attend. I have on occasion uncovered a murderer and I can use help from all of you in that regard. You spent a lot of time with Orson. You may have seen or heard something that now seems curious or out of place. Please don't be shy. If you know of anyone who held a grudge against Orson or disliked him for some reason, I hope you will share that information with me." I was relieved to see some of them nodding their heads.

"Anything we can do to help," Gene growled in his deep voice. "Orson was very good to me. I'd like to catch the person who did him in."

No one wrapped an arm around him or comforted him. I had a feeling he wasn't that kind of guy.

"In addition, someone broke into the store after Orson's death. As you can see, all the broken glass has been cleaned up. I have changed the locks and updated the security system. While you're here today, I would like to set up the work schedule and give each of you a new key and the code to the alarm, so you can open and close the store when it's your day to do so."

I could have been wrong, but I thought I saw some of them eyeing one another. That was curious. I would have to try to talk to them one at a time so they could speak privately.

"Lastly, I have no idea what the intruder might have taken. To a newcomer like me, there's a lot of inventory. But you are familiar with the items and where they were, so perhaps you can shed some light on what might have been taken. And that, in turn, might give us a lead on Orson's killer. Any questions?"

"Are you going to sell the store?" asked Robert.

"I really haven't given that much thought yet, but I promise that I'll keep you posted."

"Why did Orson leave you the store?" asked Margie. "I always thought he would leave it to Stella."

"I'm not sure. I think he had a purpose, but I haven't figured it out yet." It was a half lie. But I couldn't exactly tell them he thought someone was going to kill him!

They began to drift around the store, lattes in hand. I watched as they searched. I hadn't moved very much. Only a couple of items the night we had dinner, but I had taken care to put them back where they belonged.

"Should I turn on the music?" asked Margie.

"Music? Yes, please." I followed her to see where and how she would do it. It was actually very simple. Classical music filled the store, creating a warm and comforting atmosphere.

Ian tapped the glass cases. "Should we put out the jewelry?"

"Yes! Of course." I went into the office with him.

"Not everyone has the combination to the safe. Only Margie and me." He sucked in air. "Looks like the burglar wanted to get into the safe. These scratches weren't here before." He dialed the combination and swung the door open. "Whew! I don't think he got in."

Ian removed trays of jewelry and carried them out to the locked cases. I took more out and looked through them. To my untrained eyes they looked like antiques, in style anyway. Emeralds, diamonds, rubies, amethysts, and more. I set them aside and examined the door. Ian was right. The scratches certainly looked as if someone had struggled to break the lock. I had a feeling that was futile. I didn't know anything about getting into a safe, but if movies had even a little realism, and I thought they did, you couldn't get into a safe that way, which suggested to me that our burglar was not a professional. Whoever broke in didn't know what he was doing. Maybe he hadn't taken anything when he couldn't get access to the safe!

Robert entered the office. "I locked the front door."

"Oh?"

"It's a precaution. We always lock the door when we're putting out the jewelry or putting it back in the safe at night. It's when we're most vulnerable."

"I didn't know that. Thank you. Should I set up the work schedule in a particular order? Does someone have seniority?"

"I think we're in agreement that the previous schedule was working fine."

"Great. It sounds like you're a fairly amicable group."

"You could say that."

Ian returned for the rest of the jewelry. When he left, I asked, "Robert, would you like to be first?"

"For what?"

I closed the door and asked him to have a seat. "You've already indicated that the previous work schedule is fine with you. Is there anything you would like me to know?"

"In what regard?"

"About you or the store or Orson?"

"Nope."

I studied his face and wondered if he was the kind of guy who held everything inside. Maybe he just didn't warm up to strangers fast. And I was certainly a stranger. I took out one of the store business cards and wrote my personal number on the back. "Call me if you ever need anything."

"Like what?"

"If you have an emergency or there's something you think I should know."

"Can I go now?"

I nodded. "Please send in someone else."

Margie was much warmer than Robert. Ian was most helpful, and Gene was like talking to a brick wall. I wondered how a guy like that could sell anything.

Reba entered the office timidly.

I smiled at her. "Please have a seat."

She murmured something that I could barely understand. I asked her to say it again.

In a soft, little voice, she said, "Thank you for bringing the lattes and cake. They were a wonderful treat."

"You're very welcome. Are you satisfied with the schedule as it was before?"

"Yes." I could barely hear her. She went on, looking me straight in the eyes. "The piece that is missing is the face carved in stone and mounted on a post, except it's not actually stone."

Chapter 28

Dear Sophie,
I've heard that manufacturers use various methods
to make furniture look like antiques. I'm consider-
ing buying a chair that I love. How do I know if it's
a reproduction?
        Best Seat in Town in Seat Pleasant, Maryland

Dear Best Seat in Town,
There are entire books written on this subject. But
a quick method with chairs is to look for a wear
pattern. If the chair is worn all over, then it might
be a reproduction. But if it's worn only in places
that would have received a lot of use, like the arms,
then you might have the real thing.

                                                    Sophie

Her revelation took me by surprise. "Are you certain?"
Reba nodded.

"Can you describe it to me?" She nodded again and

studied the top of the desk where I sat. "May I?" She held
up a piece of paper.

"Yes, of course."

With a practiced hand, she drew a somewhat triangular
shape with crude eyes, nose, and a mouth.

"How big is this?"

She held her hands up to show me. "About eight inches
high."

"Is it valuable?"

She shook her head.

I waited for her to say something more.

Speaking softly, she said, "The edges are intentionally
rough to make it appear to be cut from a wall of some
kind."

"But it's worthless?"

"Yes."

"How do you know all this?"

"Orson told me." She pointed at the items in the office
that I had wondered about because they looked like valuable remnants. "He liked it because it reminded him to be
careful. People go to lengths to make fake antiques. And
right now, there's a decorating trend to use fakes like that.
Most people won't know if you have the real thing."

"Why would someone break into the store to steal it?"

She shrugged. "Maybe the thief thought it was real. We
have genuine antiques, but we only carry mock antiquities. Orson was very firm that we had to be clear about the
difference. Things like that appeal to our buyers, but he
didn't want them to think they were getting a valuable antiquity. Some of them can be quite expensive, but they're
still fakes."

"Thank you, Reba. That is very helpful."

She smiled bashfully and ducked her head.

"Is there anything else you would like me to know?"

"I'm glad to be back at work."

"I'm happy that you're back, too."

Reba and I left the office together.

Ian was at the checkout desk. He handed me a work schedule. "Reba and I are a team. Right, Reba?"

She giggled and blushed.

The other three employees went on their separate ways.

I hung back and asked, "Is there anything you need? Supplies or anything?"

Ian shook his head. "We're good."

"Customers!" said Reba in her tiny voice.

Ian grinned. "Feels good to be back." He strode toward two men and greeted them.

I squinted a little, but was fairly certain the customers were Colin and his uncle.

"He's so good at this," said Reba.

I hoped she was, too, and that people could hear her. "Excuse me, Reba." I walked toward Colin, shook his hand and said "Welcome" to his uncle.

"We're looking for some majestic pieces for our building."

"Majestic! That's a tall order. I'm sure Ian can help you with that."

Ian wasted no time in directing them to oversize mirrors and consoles. I couldn't help noticing that Ian and his uncle looked up at the chandeliers. I thought it best to leave Ian to do his job. I didn't need to butt in and there wasn't any point in hanging around.

I waved at Reba and left the store. When I arrived at my house, it turned out my mail had arrived early that day. It was mostly junk, but one envelope drew my attention. It was definitely the high-quality type of heavyweight, cream paper that I recommended for formal invitations. I slit it open and pulled out the enclosed invitation.

You are cordially invited to the launch of
Natasha Style
on Friday, August second, six p.m.,
on board the glamorous Carpe Diem.
T Pier, B Dock.
RSVP CarpeDiem@NatashaStyle.com
Semiformal Nautical

The last line cracked me up. I supposed it was semihelp-ful since I had never seen it worded quite that way. In any event, it should be interesting. A boat! That seemed way out of Natasha's wheelhouse.

I was holding the invitation when Nina opened my kitchen door. I held it out in her direction. "Did you get one of these?"

Nina read it. "Natasha Style? What is that supposed to mean? And no, I did not receive one."

"It will probably arrive tomorrow. Not much lead time, though. Most people probably have plans for this Friday."

"What is semiformal nautical?"

"I wondered about that, too. Navy blue and white, but no T-shirts or shorts?"

"Makes sense."

"I was planning to track down Jordan today and see what he has to say for himself," I said.

"I'm game. Lunch after? I'm starved."

"Sounds good. Now, how to find him?"

"Let's go by Orson's old house. If Stella is there, she might know where he is."

I nodded in agreement. Daisy and Mochie were already napping, so we left the house quietly, and I locked the door behind us.

Outside, the sun beat down on us unmercifully and the

humidity only made it worse. We hustled over to Stella's new house.

She was there, looking exhausted. Her beautiful long hair had been clipped up without a care and was falling over the clip in a lopsided manner. She wore no makeup at all, and her clothes bore the marks of moving dusty items.

"Stella! How's it coming?" asked Nina.

Stella gave her a dirty look. "Everything is out of the rental, and I have cleaned it from top to bottom. I started at five this morning. Now to tackle this house and try to get beds set up for the children. And look what I found when I got here."

She beckoned us into the kitchen. The glass in the top portion of the door was missing. Sharp, evil remnants jutted from the frame. "It was unlocked. Someone broke in."

"Where's the glass?" asked Nina.

"I swept it up. Someone is coming this afternoon to replace the glass."

"Is anything missing?" I asked.

Stella gestured at the boxes that needed to be unpacked. Several had been opened. Pictures, outdoor cushions, and various gadgets leaned against the walls. "It's impossible to tell!"

"Did you call the police?" asked Nina.

Stella bit her lip. "No. I thought about it, but decided it was ill-advised after what I went through with them. They might make something out of it that I wouldn't have anticipated. I'm still a suspect in Joan's murder, and with the custody of my kids on the line, I can't take any chances."

"I'm so sorry, Stella. It was probably someone who read Orson's obituary and thought he'd take advantage of an empty house. We could give you a hand with the beds," I offered. After all, it was only three beds, right? How hard could that be?

"Really? That would be great!"

We followed her into the house and upstairs to a bedroom that would clearly be for one of the girls. Unicorns and pink fabrics dominated the room. I saw why Stella needed help. The movers had brought the components of the bed into the bedroom, but it needed to be assembled. Definitely a job that would be easier and faster for two people. While Stella hung clothes in the closet, Nina and I quickly assembled the bed and dressed it in adorable ballerina sheets.

"If you notice a baby-blue blankie anywhere, please tell me. For the life of me, I don't know what I did with Olly's blankie. He carries it around with him everywhere and the little stinker won't accept anything else as a substitute. I must have packed it, but I don't know which box it's in!"

"Where are the children now?" I asked.

Stella grinned. "At my mom's house. She has hired a sitter to help out for a few days."

Stella directed us to another room that looked a little more mature but was still dominated by pink. After assembling the bed, we put on pink gingham bedding. From there we moved on to a room for Olly. His mock firetruck bed was easier because it had not been disassembled. Yet it was also a little more complicated because the bright yellow sheets had to be tucked inside the side rails of the firetruck. Still, the two of us managed it quickly. Unfortunately, there was no sign of Olly's favorite baby blanket.

"Jordan insisted on that bed for Olly." Stella rolled her eyes. "I'm not crazy about it, but Olly loves it. I figure he'll outgrow it pretty soon and I can buy what I want then."

"Too bad Jordan isn't helping you," said Nina. "Where is he?"

"Wouldn't you think he could give me a hand? He was being so sweet and accommodating but—"

"But what?" I asked.

"He stops by every single day to see them, which he never did before. It's like he's spying on us."

"Is he working?" Nina asked.

"I have made a point of not asking about that. But he comes by in the middle of the day, so I doubt that he has a job unless he works nights, which wouldn't be like him."

"He must be doing something. He has expenses just like the rest of us," I persisted.

"Stella?" a man's voice called from downstairs.

"That's him, now," she whispered.

The three of us walked down to the foyer, but there was no sign of him.

Nina and I followed Stella to the kitchen.

Jordan was examining the damage to the door. "What happened here?"

"Just an accident. One of the movers busted the glass. I have a repair person coming. What are you doing here?"

Jordan stared at his wife. "Are you sure? What did he hit it with?"

"Jordan, what do you want?" Weariness tinged Stella's words with impatience.

He smiled and held up a sack. "I brought you lunch. Thought you might need a break."

There was no surprise or pleasure in Stella's eyes, only dubiousness. "Thank you."

"What luck that you happened by," I said. "Nina and I wanted to talk with you."

"I'm starved. We could buy you lunch," offered Nina.

Jordan regarded us with suspicion. "Yeah, I don't think so."

Nina smiled at him. "I bet you know where to get the best pulled pork in town."

Jordan's expression changed and the hint of a grin floated across his lips. "I do. It's a little place, probably not the kind of joint you ladies visit."

"Oh! A new place?" asked Nina. "Now I have to go there!"

She was handling him beautifully. I kept my mouth shut and let Nina sweet-talk him.

"C'mon," he said. "See you later, Stella." Jordan walked toward the front door.

"Thank you," mouthed Stella.

I found it interesting that he didn't ask where the children were.

When we reached the sidewalk, Jordan turned to us. "It's on the outskirts of Old Town, so it would be better to drive in this heat. Shall we meet there in twenty minutes?"

We agreed, and he gave us directions. But when we turned to walk home to get a car, Nina stopped me. "I'm going to follow him," she whispered.

"What?"

"I want to see where he lives. It'll be fine. I'll have my phone with me. I can message you and tell you where to pick me up."

"No way. In the first place, he might see you and that would blow any chances of him talking to us at all. Not to mention that you seem to have forgotten that he might be a murderer. Of two people! What's to stop him from adding one more? He's gotten away with it so far."

Nina stuck her tongue out at me. "You're no fun at all."

"I am so fun," I protested. "It's just that I'm trying to be sensible. How about this? After we talk with him, we'll follow him back!"

"That's not bad. I think you have potential as a sleuth."

We hurried along the street and turned down the alley to my garage. Minutes later we were in the car and on our way.

"I'm glad he suggested taking cars. 'On the outskirts of Old Town' is a little bit of an exaggeration," said Nina.

I had to admit that we were entering an area that wasn't Old Town chic.

Chapter 29

Dear Sophie,
I bought some things at an antiques store today
and overheard the saleswoman tell someone that
she loves grandmillenials like me! Should I be of-
fended? Does that mean I look old?
            Uncertain in Charleston, South Carolina

Dear Uncertain,
Were you buying chintz? Items for a blue and
white room? Crystal? Some millennials have tired
of midcentury modern and are styling their homes
with items their grandmothers enjoyed. They grav-
itate to wallpaper, flowers, gallery walls, and vin-
tage decor!

                                    Sophie

I wouldn't have called it seedy. Not at all. But it was more industrial with car repair shops and the like.

"There it is!" Nina pointed ahead and to the left. A tiny hole-in-the-wall place called Sweet Jimmy's.

I pulled into a parking spot, and we got out of the car. Both of us sniffed the delicious air.

"I don't think he was jerking us around. It's gotta be good if it smells like this."

I had to agree. "Why didn't we know about this place?"

Nina pulled open the door and cold air wafted out. The interior could have used better lighting. The chairs were cheap molded plastic and the tables looked like faux wood with tops that were easy to wipe clean.

A pleasant-looking redheaded man in an apron that needed washing called out, "What can I get cha?"

"Are you Sweet Jimmy?" I asked.

"That's me. Couldn't decide whether to call it Jimmy's Revenge or Sweet Jimmy's."

"What was the revenge for?" asked Nina.

"For firing me from my boring old desk job." He held out his arms. "She ain't much, but I love her."

The door swung open, the bright sun hurting our eyes.

"Hey, Jimmy!" Jordan ambled in. "I see you found the place."

"I can't recall you ladies eating here before," said Sweet Jimmy. "I'll bring you over a Jimmy's sampler. Pick a table."

As we selected a table, I recognized Colin's Uncle Terry seated at a table in the back. His eyes met mine and I gave him a nod and a smile. He stared at me. I wondered if he remembered me or was trying to place me.

We sat down and Sweet Jimmy immediately brought us a huge board of meat. Bowls of barbecue sauce were surrounded by sausages, ribs, sliced brisket, and mounds of pulled pork. I had never seen anything like it. But he wasn't finished. He added a basket of fresh-from-the-fryer hush puppies, butter, and individual bowls of red cabbage coleslaw along with forks and knives for three. Wiping his hands on a towel, he asked, "Iced tea or bottled water?"

We didn't wait for our beverages to be delivered. The aroma was too tempting. We wiped our hands on the sanitary towelettes that came with our meal. Jordan, who was wearing a long-sleeve shirt, rolled back the sleeves and dug in. It definitely wasn't the right place for anyone prim and proper who was afraid to pick up their food. But that simple act revealed a pale spot on his arm in the shape of a watch. Had he sold his Rolex to pay off the big debt he supposedly owed someone?

"How did you find this place?" I bit into a rib and savored the smoky flavor.

"Amazing, isn't it? A chef I know told me about Jimmy. I always wanted to have a restaurant." He looked around and said in a softer voice, "Not like this. A big one with brass fixtures and a long shiny bar. Jimmy says he can manage by keeping his menu basic. Only two drink selections, no deviations from the menu. No desserts. No employees. That's how he keeps his costs down. He's considering beer, though. Alcohol is a moneymaker."

"Someone told me that you tried twice." I sipped my tea, which was brewed, not from powder. Jimmy might be smart about keeping his costs down, but he didn't skimp on ingredients. The place was rustic at best, but I didn't think anyone in Old Town could beat Sweet Jimmy for flavor.

"Yeah, old Orson took a chance on me twice. But restaurants are a tough business. And very expensive if you want to do it right. I'm not like Jimmy. I have no interest in starting a smoker at four in the morning every day."

"What are you doing now?"

I marveled at how innocently Nina managed to ask that question.

Jordan helped himself to another rib. Holding it in his fingers, he said, "I was not lucky enough to inherit a valuable business from someone." He looked at me over the rib.

Why hadn't I figured out some clever way to explain the situation? Or at least a good comeback. It was odd that Orson had left the store to me, there was no way around that. "No one was more surprised than I."

"What did you do in between restaurants?" Nina slathered butter on a hush puppy.

"I've worked in gyms and driven an Uber. Did some construction when I was younger. I've been a softball coach, too, which I hope will come in handy when my kids are a little older. Julie doesn't have any interest in it. She's all about ballet, which is new to me. I now know how to plié."

Jordan surprised me. He had a certain charm. I could see why Stella would have fallen for him. "Were you at Orson and Wanda's engagement party?" I watched him carefully.

He didn't seem perturbed by my question. "That was an awful thing. You know, I've seen some people at the gym who are not in shape to do certain things, like bench press. And you watch them, thinking *this is not going to end well*. But Orson just collapsed. It should have been a happy day for him, and he just fell over in front of everybody. I sure did not see that coming."

He sounded so innocent, but I noticed that he didn't mention the fact that Orson was murdered. "You say that as though you liked Orson."

Jordan wiped off his fingers. "Orson and I had a weird relationship. I think he wanted Stella to be happy and he knew that she loved me. So he tried to help us financially. He didn't like that I wasn't *somebody*. You know what I mean? I wasn't a guy with a great future. I wasn't a doctor or on track to be the mayor. He wanted to do what he could to make our future bright. And I respect him for that. I don't, however, understand why he didn't leave his entire estate to Stella. She deserved it."

I finished my pulled pork. "Does Jimmy deliver?"

Jordan laughed. "I wish. I've been trying to talk him into getting a barbecue mobile. Wouldn't that be great? He could drive into Old Town, park, and be sold out in an hour."

"Did Orson know about you and Joan?" Nina didn't look at him when she asked.

But Jordan took note and paused before he answered, as if he was trying to think of the right thing to say. "What do you mean?"

"I mean you were having an affair with another woman."

"Come on. That's just rumor. Silliness. You know how it is around here. Something like that gets started and then it grows."

I couldn't help noticing that he was watching our reaction to his blatant lies. "You did a good job of hiding it from Stella."

He leaned toward me and said defensively, "You can't prove it."

I gave him my best are-you-kidding look. "People saw you. Joan talked about it. So did Tripp Fogarty."

Jordan paled. A sad sigh escaped him, and he rubbed his forehead. "I never imagined that getting involved with Joan would lead to so many problems. I'm trying to convince Stella that it was meaningless. It was! But I don't think she'll ever forgive me. She claims if I hadn't been seeing Joan, she never would have become a suspect in Joan's death." He leaned his head down, as if inspecting his plate. "She's right, you know. She would have just been a bystander. Another person in the wrong place at the wrong time." He brightened up. "Like you guys. No one hauled you down to the police station and treated you like a criminal, but you were there."

"Who would have wanted to kill Joan?" I picked at a piece of pulled pork on the board.

"I don't know. Maybe she was seeing another guy that I didn't know about? Maybe she had dumped some guy and he was mad at her?"

"Do you know of another man in her life?" I asked.

"No. But that doesn't mean there wasn't one."

"Nor does it mean there was one. Joan was at the engagement party, too." I left it at that to see where he would go with it.

"Oh man!" Jordan rubbed his forehead again. "That was a nightmare. Can you even imagine it? What were the odds of that? I was doing my level best to keep away from Joan, but she kept coming up to me to talk."

"Were you angry with Joan?" asked Nina. "She must have realized that Orson was your father-in-law."

"Of course I was ticked off with her. She knew exactly what kind of position she was putting me in by coming to that party. She didn't have to be there, you know? I think she did it on purpose to put me on the spot."

He had the most to gain from Joan's death. I was surprised that he admitted as much as he had.

At that moment, Colin's uncle Terry finished his meal and stood up to leave. As he walked by our table, he gave me a nod. I smiled back at him.

"You know Terry Warren?" Jordan squinted at me and sounded surprised.

"I know his nephew, Colin. Terry has been doing some work for Colin, so I've seen him around. Is there something wrong with that?"

"No. Not at all. The Warrens aren't what you'd call high society." He shrugged it off.

"What is that supposed to mean?" Nina wiped her hands.

"They're a little rough around the edges is all. It's not a slight. I don't come from society people either. The Warrens think they're tough guys and can be a little coarse is all."

I shifted the topic to get to what I wanted to know. Leaning toward him, I hoped to give the impression that I was on his side. "Jordan, there have been two murders. You must realize that you're a suspect in both of them. Who would have wanted to murder Orson or Joan?"

Jordan shifted uncomfortably and rolled down his shirt-sleeves, but not before I saw what appeared to be a cut on his arm about two inches down from his elbow. "Stella's mom was pretty miffed with him. Some people never get over divorce issues. And that woman he dated before Wanda, Audrey somebody, I could tell she was crushed."

"What about the business? Someone broke in there. What did Orson have that someone might want?"

He shrugged. "Expensive stuff. The inventory in that place is worth a lot of money."

"Did Orson blackmail people?" asked Nina.

Her question caught me by surprise, and from the look on his face, Jordan, too.

He shook his head. "I don't think so. No. I'm sure of it. If he'd been that kind of guy, he would have tried to bribe me into doing what he wanted. No. I can't see that. He had that weird partner, though. Maybe he thought Orson owed him something."

"Karl?" asked Nina.

"Yeah, that's him." Jordan sat up straight. "I did my share of complaining about Orson. I'll admit that. He had a lot of money, and he could have made our lives easier if he'd helped us out. There were times when Stella and I were scraping by. But the truth is that he was a decent man. A lot of people would be surprised to hear me say that considering the way I complained about him, but he was good to my children, and as angry as I was about the store, I am grateful for that."

"Did you want the store?" I asked.

Jordan's eyes opened wide. "Would have been nice. I'm sure we would have been able to sell it for a lot of money."

He checked his watch. "Ladies, I'm afraid I have to go."

"Thanks for introducing us to Sweet Jimmy's. We'll pick up the tab. You go ahead."

Nina echoed my thanks while I paid the check.

I met her at the car.

"Hurry! He sat in the car for a few minutes looking at his phone and then he pulled out and turned left like he was going back to Old Town."

I unlocked the car, and we hopped in.

"He's driving a white Toyota Prius."

I groaned. "Great. Not many of those around here."

She ignored my sarcasm. "Maybe we can catch up to him at the light."

I drove a little faster than I should have and nearly hit the brakes when Nina screeched, "That's him! That's him!"

I tried to hang back a little bit so he wouldn't notice us. We lived in Old Town, though, so it was only natural that we would be driving in the same direction. Once we were back in Old Town proper, it was more difficult to tail him in the slower traffic.

"He's turning left," said Nina. "And his license plate says *SAINT*. That's a misnomer if ever there was one!"

I slowed as much as I could. He cruised onto our street and pulled into a parking spot in front of Francie's house.

"What's he doing? Is he planning to spy on us?" asked Nina.

There was no alternative but to drive by his car.

"Park already!"

I found an open space and parallel parked into it.

Nina twisted around in her seat. She unfastened her seat belt. "He's getting out of the car!"

I shifted to see for myself.

"He's opening the back door. Good heavens! Sophie, Francie is getting in his car. He's closing the door. Duck so he won't see us." Nina slid down in her seat as far as she could.

"Nina, he's an Uber driver. I bet Francie called an Uber to take her somewhere."

She turned her head to look at me. "Ohhh. You're probably right." Nina returned to a normal sitting position. "What did you think of him?"

"He had some appeal. But he's a practiced liar."

"I agree. Not as scummy as I thought he'd be."

Someone rapped on the back window and we both screamed.

Chapter 30

Dear Sophie,
How can I make my board appropriate for an event like a birthday or a holiday?
Christmas Is Coming in Santa Clara, Oregon

Dear Christmas Is Coming,
Cheese is your friend. Slice semisoft cheese like havarti, then cut out figures or numbers by hand or with cookie cutters. For a birthday theme you might use numbers for the person's age and items the person is fond of, like a cat, baseball, football, ballerina, etc. For Christmas you could cut out stars or bells and arrange them on a board with other favorite foods.

Sophie

Wanda walked up to the driver's door and peeked in at us. She carried a small folder.

I rolled down the window, but she opened the back door and got into the car. "I didn't mean to scare you. What are you doing sitting out here?"

"We had lunch with Stella's soon to be ex-husband. I'll park the car in the garage and make us something to drink."

"No alcohol for me this early in the day. Gotta keep my wits about me," said Wanda.

Minutes later, the car had been parked in my garage. Nina, Wanda, and I walked into my house.

Daisy spun in circles with excitement and Mochie mewed at us.

We all patted Daisy and Mochie before moseying into the kitchen where I whipped up iced coffee and milk in the blender. I poured it into glasses and added a scoop of vanilla ice cream and a spoon to each glass.

We sat around the banquette and Wanda opened her folder. "I wanted you two to see this and to talk to you about the notes I've made." She took a deep breath and shoved black and white photographs in front of us. "These are still pictures of our burglar."

The person wore dark clothes, probably black, and carried what appeared to be a giant trash bag. The clothes looked like a sweatshirt with a hood and skin-hugging sports tights. I sipped my rich coffee.

"It's a woman," said Nina, sounding surprised.

"Griselda and I think so, too." Wanda tapped her finger on another picture. "Lookie here."

The burglar reached up for items on a high shelf, but she didn't have to reach far. She was tall, and from the looks of the sports tights, she was very thin. I thought I knew who it was, but didn't want to say so. I wasn't sure whether Natasha's mother realized that her own daughter had broken into her store.

I gazed at Wanda.

"I can see it in your eyes, Sophie."

"See what?" asked Nina before slurping some melting ice cream.

"It's Natasha," I said.

Wanda slapped her hand on the table. "I think so, too. I know my daughter and that is her. You can tell by the way she's standing and carrying herself. A cop might not be able to see that, thank goodness, but I know my baby. We thought the person who broke into our store picked the lock, but I bet you anything that she took my key and let herself in. But why? She could have had anything she wanted. She knew we would give it to her. She didn't have to sneak around and steal it in the middle of the night."

Nina looked at the photos again. "Now that you mention it, I can see it, too."

Wanda drummed her fingers on the table. "I just don't know what to think. I thought maybe you would know what she was doing."

I went with the only logical thing. "Do you suppose she's sick but doesn't want to tell you?"

"That does sound like something she would do. But she could swipe a box or two when the store is open. It's not like she would have to take our entire inventory of certain items."

"She's a kleptomaniac!" Nina's eyes were wide. "Do you think she's the one who burgled Orson's store, too?"

"I know of one way to find out," I said.

"Now, I don't want to get the police involved. I'm sorry we called them when we discovered the burglary. Even if she is a thief, she's still my baby girl."

"Is Natasha home right now?" I asked.

Wanda nodded. "That's why I hopped into your car. I didn't want her to see me."

"Does she have plans to go somewhere?" I asked. "We need to snoop and see if we can find what she stole."

"Okay. I'm with you on that. Then we'll know for sure." Wanda pulled her phone out of a pocket and appeared to text someone.

We heard a little *ding* when someone responded.

"We're all set. We can sit here and enjoy these delicious coffees. Griselda will text me as soon as Natasha leaves the house."

"Sounds good to me. There's something I've been wanting to ask you. Did Orson say anything about his ex-wife paying him a visit on the night before your engagement party?"

Wanda drew back and gazed at me. "Sophie, I have long suspected that you have the gift. How could you know about that?"

I laughed at the thought that I might possess some kind of magical abilities. "Wanda, I ask people questions. That's how I know."

"Well, darlin', you are absolutely right. They had an argument. Myra wanted Orson to give Jordan a *lot* of money so he could repay a loan. Orson told her 'no way.' After all, Jordan had left Stella. They were in the process of getting a divorce, so he didn't see how it would benefit Stella. And he thought it was time Jordan was responsible for himself and his own decisions. You know, he helped out Stella and Jordan for years. Orson told Myra that she could give Jordan all the money she wanted, but he was through funding Jordan's lifestyle. If he made a poor decision, then he needed to be responsible and work for the money to pay back the loan. I told Orson that he did the right thing. Jordan wasn't his responsibility."

I wondered if Stella had asked her mother to speak to Orson on Jordan's behalf. She didn't mention it when she was in my kitchen, but at the time, she was very upset with Jordan for having an affair with Joan. If Orson hadn't been murdered the very next day, Myra's visit to him probably wouldn't have mattered. But now I wondered why Myra hadn't told us she visited Orson that night.

For the next forty-five minutes, we speculated about

Orson's killer and finished our drinks. When Wanda's phone *dinged*, we left the house and hurried across the street to the other corner of the block. Griselda waited for us at the stairs to Natasha's house.

I volunteered to check Natasha's workshop that was attached to the garage. I had found a body once in one of the storage closets. I hoped that wouldn't be the case again, but Natasha was very possessive of that space, and I had a hunch that was where she might have hidden the stolen goods. While I was outside, Nina, Griselda, and Wanda would search the house.

Natasha had been correct about one thing. Her backyard was in no shape for a wedding. The gazebo was still there, but the grass was gone and almost the entire backyard had been turned into a vegetable garden. An occasional patch of daisies or colorful zinnias interrupted the tomatoes, peppers, and beans. The scent of various herbs wafted to me as I walked by.

Wanda had given me a key to Natasha's work space. I slid it into the lock and opened the door. The first thing I did was look around for cameras. If Natasha had any, I didn't see them. But I knew how easy it was to hide a camera, having done so myself.

I opened drawers chock-full of ribbons, bows, and assorted floral arranging items. Impatient, I didn't finish in that room and headed toward the larger locker style closets in the garage. Her car was gone, giving me loads of space to open them and look inside. In the fourth one, I found a black plastic bag, the kind used for lawn garbage and big items. I took a photograph of it, then untied the top, which was harder than I expected. I managed, though. I turned on the light in my cell phone and looked inside the bag. It contained dozens of boxes of homeopathic medicines.

"Oh, Natasha," I murmured. "What have you done?"

I texted Nina to let her know I had found the goods. I carried the bag into Natasha's workshop and poured the contents on a table. They all seemed to be in good condition. None of them appeared to have been opened.

Behind me, the door swung open. I whirled around, fearing it could be Natasha, but it was Nina, Wanda, and Griselda.

Wanda gasped when she saw the pile of boxes. "They're all here. Where were they?"

"In a storage locker in the garage."

Griselda examined them. "They're in perfect condition. What does she want with these? She didn't have to steal them. Natasha can have anything she wants. All she had to do was ask."

"What are these for?" asked Nina.

"Most of them are for coughs and colds." Wanda picked one up and frowned at it. "Do you think she has developed some kind of respiratory problem and doesn't want to tell us about it?"

"Let's say that's true." Griselda counted some of the boxes. "Why would she need so many? This looks more like she's hoarding them."

"Ah." Wanda nodded her head. "She's afraid she won't be able to get them and will run out. I've heard of people doing that with things they love and don't want to be without. Like soda when they change the flavor or cosmetics that they stop making."

I met Nina's eyes and had a feeling she was thinking the same thing as me. Wanda and Griselda were looking for excuses. There wasn't a good reason at all for having stolen all these boxes of homeopathic medicine. The only good news, as far as I could tell, was that the faux face cut into stone that had been stolen from Chatsworth Antiques wasn't among the boxes. I should have mentioned it before. "Did you see a face carved in stone in the house?"

They looked at me as if I had lost my mind.

"That's what was stolen from the antiques store."

"Oh, I see." Wanda sounded grim. "I didn't notice anything like that. Did either of you?"

"I didn't have that in mind," said Nina. "But I can't say I noticed it. Is it valuable?"

"Apparently, it's worthless. According to Reba, mock artifacts are a decorating trend right now."

Griselda began putting the boxes back into the bag. "The way I see it is we take these back to the store. Then we tell the cops that we made a mistake and nothing was stolen, so they'll close the case. And we never mention it to Natasha."

"Never mention it?" Nina screeched. "How can you do that? Don't you want to know why on earth she would steal this stuff in the middle of the night?"

"I *am* curious." Wanda helped toss the small boxes into the bag. "But I don't see how any good can come from confronting Natasha. We know the truth now. She dressed up like a thief and stole these in the middle of the night. At least we now know that we don't have to worry about a stranger having broken into our store."

"We should pay attention to whether she's coughing," added Griselda.

"I don't mean to encroach on your kind, motherly sweeping of this under the rug, but you have a problem on your hands. What if she does this to some other store? They'll press charges. I think you need to nip this in the bud while it's all in the family." I pulled the strings on the bag tight, so the contents wouldn't fall out.

"Sophie is right, Wanda." Griselda sighed. "Natasha is an adult and whatever her reason was for doing this, we have to call her on it before she does it to someone else and there are significant consequences."

"She's been so emotional." Wanda looked as if she might cry. "I never expected Orson's death to have such an impact on her. First her father, and now Orson—"

"Wanda! The exact same man left my daughter, Charlene, but you don't see her running around breaking into stores. Honey, I am sorry to say this, but you have let Natasha milk being abandoned by her father for far too long. Plenty of girls and boys grow up with one parent and you don't hear them whining about it."

As she spoke, it dawned on me that I might have been right about Orson looking for his other daughter after all. Joan Jankowski grew up without a dad. So did Bonnie Shergold, Riley Hooper, Doreen Donahue, and Cheryl Mancini. None of the women on the board in Orson's secret office grew up with a father. I was almost certain I was on the right track in believing that Orson wasn't some kind of pervert, he was looking for his missing daughter. There must have been some reason he thought she was being raised by a single mother and was now living in Old Town. I was itching to get into the secret office again. I knew there wasn't anything different there. But I wanted to look at the pictures. I would have to wait until Ian and Reba had left for the day, though. "Wanda, did Orson ever tell you about his life before he came to Old Town?"

"You mean like college?"

"Yes. About his youth and before he married Myra."

"Nothing special. He had some cute stories as everyone does. It sounded as if he was a good student. He came from a small town a lot like where we're from, only it was in Maryland. He was a banker for a while, but found antiques more interesting. I remember him saying that every piece he bought had a history and that, if furniture could talk, they would all have fascinating stories to tell."

"Was he married before Myra?"

Nina flashed a look at me.

Wanda was taken aback. "Not that I'm aware of. Why on earth would you think that?"

I smiled and gently said, "I'm trying to learn more about him. I don't have a handle on who murdered him yet." I gestured toward the bag. "What should I do with this?"

"Darlin', please put it back just the way you found it." Wanda held up her palm to stop Griselda's protests. "Natasha has that big deal on Friday. I don't want to upset her now. But on Saturday, we'll sit her down and have a good, kind talk with her."

Griselda rolled her eyes. "I'm going to hold you to that, Wanda."

Chapter 31

Dear Natasha,
My sister-in-law said she's making a candy charcu-
terie board. Duh! Charcuterie means meat. I think
it's a major oxymoron. We have a bet riding on
this, and you are calling the winner. Who is right?
                    I Speak French in French, Minnesota

Dear I Speak French,
I believe you may have an unfair advantage. You
win, unless she's planning to make a board with
candied bacon.

                                        Natasha

That evening, I walked Daisy after dark. I needed to get out of the house. Thoughts about Orson and his missing daughter, not to mention his murderer, swirled through my head. What had happened to Orson's other daughter? Why hadn't Myra told us about seeing Orson the night before his death? Who had broken into the antiques store and why? So many questions and yet, so few answers.

I tried to shake the thoughts out of my head and concentrate on the beauty of Old Town. But when I looked across the street, I realized that we had walked to Karl's store. The windows in the showroom and upstairs above them were dark. We crossed the street and walked along the side of the building. The lot was bigger than I had imagined. An alley ran along the backs of the buildings. Daisy and I turned into the alley.

No light shone in the windows there, either. Karl must be out somewhere. A parking pad filled half of the yard in the back. The other half was being used for poorly tended raised bed gardens. A couple vines of beans grew up a discarded mattress spring. It was a unique use of the spring, but from the look of the garden, I wondered if the beans had grown from beans that had fallen in the soil the year before. Nothing appeared to be planned or taken care of. Carrots grew along the side of the raised bed. At the end closest to the alley, it appeared that some had already been dug up. There were no tomatoes or peppers at all. Maybe Karl only liked carrots and beans.

Overall, the garden was a bit shabby, but Karl got a pass on that from me. Weeds sprouted faster than I could keep up with them.

We walked back to the street and turned right on the next block, slowly making our way back to our own neighborhood. But two blocks later, Daisy stopped at the opening to an alley.

"Come on, Daisy." She'd probably picked up the scent of a squirrel or another dog.

She paid no attention to me at all and tugged against the leash, which wasn't like her. I turned on the light in my phone again. The beam didn't go very far, but part of the way down the alley, I could see a lump of something. A bag of trash, maybe? It was too dark to tell from this distance. I acquiesced but held the leash firmly. She continued to tug in her eagerness to get close to the lump.

And then I heard something. I stopped and listened.

A moan. A deep, rumbling sound, like a person in pain.

We approached slowly. Daisy desperately wanted to move faster, but I was cautious.

In a few steps we were upon the thing I had thought was a trash bag. A man lay facedown on the rough alleyway. "Hello? Hello? Do you need help?"

I thought he might be drunk. But when I shone my light along his body, I saw his shirt and trousers had been torn and he was bleeding. He'd been in a fight. "Hi! Can you get up? Should I call an ambulance?"

He still didn't respond. But I could see his chest moving with each breath, so he was definitely alive. I called 911 and asked for an ambulance.

While we waited, I kneeled next to him. "Hi," I said softly. "Can you hear me?"

He grunted.

"An ambulance is on the way. Can you turn over or sit up? Is there something I can do to help you?"

He tried to move. His hands shook and his body twisted slightly. And then he screamed in pain.

I could hear sirens in the distance.

His shirtsleeve was torn, and his arm bled profusely. I ripped off a piece of the fabric and wrapped the part that bled, putting as much pressure on it as I could. And as I did so, I saw the shadow of a missing watch on his wrist.

"Jordan?"

I leaned down as far as I could and trained the light on him. His eyes were almost swollen shut. In spite of the swelling on his face, there was no doubt about his identity. It was definitely Jordan St. James.

"Who did this to you?"

He didn't respond. As far as I could tell, he had passed out.

I was extremely relieved when the ambulance arrived. I

told them what had happened and heard one of them say, "He took a good beating."

They fastened him to a stretcher, and when they lifted it, something tumbled to the ground. They placed him in the ambulance, and it pulled away.

I trained my light on the stones and dirt of the alley. Two pieces of a concrete-type material didn't fit. I picked them up. When I turned them over, I recognized the crude eyes, nose, and mouth Reba had drawn. I held them together where the piece had broken. They formed a roughly triangular shape just as she had described.

But why did it turn up here? Had someone thrown it out in the alley? Had Jordan had it in his possession? I didn't know what to make of it.

I debated whether to call Stella. But in the end, I thought she would be upset if I knew about Jordan's injuries and didn't tell her. For all I knew, he might have the children the next day and she would wonder why he didn't show up.

I phoned and told her what little I knew.

Stella was shocked. She thanked me for calling and hung up right away.

I didn't mention the faux antiquity to her. She had enough on her mind. But there were two other things that I wondered about. What had happened to his watch and why did he have a cut on his arm earlier that day? Those questions plagued me as I went up to bed.

Stella phoned when I was eating breakfast. "Sophie, I'm sorry I didn't call you back last night to thank you for letting me know about Jordan. It was very late when I came home and I didn't want to wake you."

"How's he doing?"

"He's a mess. He has several broken ribs, a punctured lung, and a broken leg." She paused for a moment and then said softly, "There may be a brain injury, too."

"Did he say anything? Was he able to talk?"

"No. He's been going in and out of consciousness, not making sense. They tell me that happens with brain injuries."

"Stella, who would do that to Jordan?"

"I have no idea! I called Ronin right away. I'm scared to death the police will think that *I* did it! They already think I killed Joan and my father. Sophie, every time I turn around, I'm in deeper trouble. But I didn't do *any* of these things."

"I know you didn't." At least I didn't think so. "I wish I could figure out what happened. Hey, did you ever talk to Jordan about antiquities?"

"Antiquities? Hah! As if Jordan would have had an interest in something like that. Dad had some at the store. Is that why you're asking about them?"

"I found one where Jordan was lying. It's a fake and I believe it was missing from the store."

"You think Jordan took it?"

"Not necessarily. It could have been tossed there by someone else."

"Well, for what little it's worth, I don't think Jordan knew beans about antiquities. He certainly didn't know anything about antiques."

"Are you going to see him this morning?"

"I'm on my way there now. I left the kids at the sitter's house. Wolf made an appointment to see my mom. I promised I would be there with her. He makes her so nervous!"

Had Wolf discovered something that implicated Myra in Orson's murder? "Good luck to your mom. If Jordan comes around, tell him I wish him a speedy recovery."

"Will do! Bye, Sophie!"

She disconnected the call. I placed the pieces of the triangular head in freezer bags and packed them into a tote to take to the store. When the store opened, I called to be certain Reba was there. Ian assured me she was. This time I asked what they would like me to bring for them to drink. Armed with their beverage preferences, I set out for a local café to buy their drinks and some croissants. When I was approaching the café, Jordan's car pulled into an empty parking space.

I did a double take. How could that be? It had to be someone else's car. I stopped and watched as the driver stepped out. She looked up at me.

"Hi, Sophie!" Doreen Donahue approached me. "Are you buying me croissants?"

"Good morning!" The sun glinted on the car. I walked toward it and looked more closely. A tiny window in the front of the driver's side had been broken out. I peered inside the best I could for anything that would identify it as Jordan's car. A blue baby blanket lay on the back seat.

"Come on! I'm starving," said Doreen.

Meanwhile I was thinking I should call Wong. "Just a second." I walked to the back of the car. Sure enough, the license plate read *SAINT*.

"Where did you get this car?"

"The owner lets me drive it."

How many women had Jordan been seeing? Had Orson put together the corkboard of women who were involved with Jordan? I shuddered to think about it. Poor Stella. I gazed at Doreen in ripped short shorts with a pink top that resembled a shaggy bathroom mat and was short enough to display her midriff when she moved. But Doreen was the princess of con artists. Two could play this game. I called her bluff. "So you're a friend of Wolf's?"

Her smile faded. She walked over to the car and kicked it. "I knew I should have burned the thing. That's the only way to keep my nose clean. But I was planning to use it after I got a latte." She said the last part in a whining Valley Girl tone as if begging my permission to continue using someone else's car.

"Where did you get the car?"

Doreen shrugged.

I followed her into the café and bought her a latte and a croissant. And then I texted Wong. I sat down at a table with her, just to keep her there until Wong arrived.

"C'mon, Doreen. Where did you steal the car?"

Chapter 32

Dear Sophie,
I'm supposed to avoid mayo. What can I use to
give some life to a sandwich?
                    Too Dry in Sandwich, Massachusetts

Dear Too Dry,
Iceberg lettuce and a slice of tomato usually help.
But an onion confit or avocado spread would also
add moisture and more flavor as well.
                                        Sophie

"I don't steal cars, I borrow them."

"Do you always return them?" I knew she didn't.

"It depends. A girl has to cover her tracks." She bit into the croissant. "Mmm. Yummy!"

"Have you ever burned a car?"

"Oh, sure. That's really the best thing to do. Nobody wants it or cares about it after that. And the owner gets a brand spanking new car so they're happy, too. You're kidding me about that being Wolf's car, right? 'Cause I don't mess with him. I'd have to burn it for sure if that were the case. They can't charge you for anything if it doesn't exist anymore, you know."

I stared at her in amazement. Surely she didn't think that was true. "Where did you hear that?"

"It's the law. Everybody knows it. You seem pretty smart. I'm surprised you don't know."

"Doreen, I hate to break this to you, but getting rid of the object of a crime does not mean you can't be charged."

She laughed out loud. "You're so silly. Hey, do you need a ride somewhere? I can give you one before I set the car on fire."

With any luck, Wong would be here shortly, and Jordan's car would not be torched. I suspected that Doreen would be going for a ride to the police station for questioning about the attack on Jordan.

"Sure," I lied. "Did you have fun with Jordan last night?"

"Jordan? I don't know what you're talking about." She gulped her latte.

What was taking Wong so long? "Jordan St. James."

"Oh. Him. He's kind of cute, but I didn't see him last night. The club was really crowded, though. I might have missed him."

"Then where did you find his car?"

She studied me. "I thought you said it belonged to Wolf."

"It's Jordan's car. That's why it says *SAINT* on the license plate."

She grinned. "You have a lot of potential, Sophie. I bought it when you said it was Wolf's. Very well done. I think we could be good friends."

Just the thought of wearing bathroom rugs, stealing cars, and dancing in crowded clubs made me laugh.

"Doreen, did you know your father?"

"Nope. He checked out before I was born."

"I'm sorry to hear that."

She shrugged. "You don't miss what you never had."

I thought otherwise. I wasn't a shrink, but she made it her business to seek out sugar daddies. "What happened to him?"

"My mom and him tried to hold up a jewelry store. But neither one of them anticipated that the owner had a gun. He shot my dad dead, and I was born in prison."

"That's very sad. I'm sorry, Doreen."

"It's not so bad. Mom will be out in two years."

"She's still in prison?"

"Not for that. This last time it was for embezzling money."

It was a horrible story. No wonder Doreen turned out the way she had. Of course, it might not be true, but given what Bernie had heard about Doreen's mother, it could be.

Through the window, I could see Wong behind the car, checking out the license plate. She spoke into her radio before entering the café.

"Good morning!" She sat down at the table with us.

"Doreen Donahue, this is Officer Wong."

Doreen's smile faded. "We've met."

"Do you know who parked the white car in front of the café?"

Doreen didn't even flinch. "Not a clue."

"Really? We've been looking all over for it because it was involved in a crime last night."

Shoot. I was hoping I might be able to bring the baby blanket back to Stella. But not if it was evidence.

"A crime? Like what?"

"Let's talk about that down at the station."

"I don't know anything about a crime. I have to be going now." Doreen stood up.

"Let me give you a ride." Wong stood as well.

"Wait! I want to know one thing. Did you set Orson's car on fire?" I asked.

Doreen didn't hide her surprise. "How did you know about that?" she whispered.

"I was there."

She smiled. "See? I told you. They can't charge you for anything if the car is gone." She winked at me and walked out with Wong.

I bought the requested lattes along with croissants. When I left the café, the car was being towed away, probably to the police lot.

I hurried to the store. Reba and Ian were beaming when I walked in. Something was different. I gazed around and realized that the expensive chandelier was gone.

"You sold it?" I asked.

They high-fived me, bubbling with enthusiasm.

"The lady said you opened the store for her when it was closed," said Reba in her soft voice.

"She brought her husband to see it yesterday. Reba and I hoped they would come back. Sure enough, she was waiting for us to open up this morning and had made arrangements for someone to transport it to her house." Ian accepted a latte and the bag of croissants.

"Fantastic! You two are the best!"

Reba took her latte. "This is a nice reward."

"I brought something else for you to look at." I took the pieces of the face out of the bag and unwrapped them. I hadn't even set them together when Reba gasped. "It's the faux antiquity!"

"They must make a lot of these," I said. To be honest, I didn't find it particularly beautiful. Had it been real, then I would have appreciated it for its historical significance.

Ian nodded. "There are probably thousands."

"But I haven't seen any other ones like it in Old Town," Reba pointed out. "Where did you find it?"

"In an alley. Someone had been beaten and this was where he lay."

"It was broken, like this?" asked Reba.

"Yes."

"Perhaps that person stole it and tried to pass it off as authentic," suggested Reba.

I nodded. "That's what I'm afraid of. It could be a coincidence, though. It could have fallen there and broken and wasn't connected to the man at all, but I have a sneaking suspicion that he was our burglar."

While I was fairly certain that no one would be asking for the mock antiquity, I wrapped it up and put it back in my tote. Maybe the police would want fingerprints to find the people who attacked Jordan.

I stayed a while to celebrate with Ian and Reba before I walked home.

As I neared my house, I spied Wolf's car parked on my block and Nina talking with him.

Something was up. I waved at them, and they strode across the street. Wolf carried a file and a huge bag that looked suspiciously like takeout.

I opened the kitchen door to let Daisy out. "Hello!" I called.

"I have news," said Wolf, raising the file. "And I brought lunch. I figure I owe you a meal."

"Perfect timing. Please come in."

Wolf placed everything on the table. "Chinese takeout. Shrimp lo mein, those duck pancakes that you like so much, Szechuan green beans, egg rolls for Nina, lemon chicken, and moo shu pork. I brought extra because I never know who might be here."

I fed Daisy and Mochie a snack and then poured iced tea for the three of us before joining Wolf and Nina around the banquette.

Wolf sipped his tea. "Man, do I need this! It's hot out

there. So I spoke with a cop from Baltimore yesterday. When I phoned the Baltimore police, no one remembered much about this case. But one guy put me in touch with a retired detective, Nathan Long, who was always disturbed by the murder of Mrs. Harris and the abduction of her children. There are cases that bother cops, especially when they're unsolved. He had two little girls himself at the time and related to the case, particularly because the Harris girls were abducted."

"Great! So what did he say?" Nina bit into an eggroll.

"The basics are the same. There were definitely *two* young girls. Sisters. The important thing, though, is that there was a witness. A neighbor who is no longer living. He unmistakably saw Mr. Harris loading one of the girls into his car in a panic. 'In a big hurry' he said, and then Harris drove away, and the neighbor never saw Harris or the girls again."

"He saw *one* of the girls or both of them?" asked Nina.

Wolf nodded. "One of the girls. No one knows if the other girl was already in the car, or left in the house, or what happened to her. He sent me some old photos of Mr. Harris."

Wolf opened the folder and slid copies of photographs toward us. The ones of Mr. Harris weren't close-up, but he had been a handsome man. Next to those, Wolf placed photos of Orson.

"Wow. This is like those age progressions they do of missing people," said Nina.

"They're clearly the same person," I breathed.

"Looks like it." Wolf sighed. "I met with Myra and Stella this morning. It was hard news to break."

"Oh no! They must have been in tears!" I said.

"A lot of emotions. A lot of questions. You can imagine."

"So does Stella know now that Myra isn't her birth mother?" I asked.

Wolf grimaced. "Myra told her before I arrived. Normally, I wouldn't be here telling you this, but I have a feeling Stella will pay you a visit."

"Is she angry with us?" Nina stopped eating and held her chopsticks in the air.

"I don't think so. But she has a lot of questions. We all do." Wolf rolled up a pancake with duck in it. "I didn't want you to be blindsided. Thanks for finding the photographs. They were a huge help."

"So what happens now?" I asked. "Closing the case because Mr. Harris aka Orson is dead would mean they accept that he killed his wife and abducted their children," I protested. "What about the possibility that he ran from a dangerous man?"

"Orson is gone. Stella doesn't remember anything. Even if you found her sister, she wouldn't remember anything, either. The odds of finding anyone who knows what happened are a very long shot."

I toyed with my duck pancake. That wasn't fair to Orson. Of course, there was always the possibility that he did kill his first wife. But I didn't believe it.

"Don't look so dejected. You did a good thing, Soph." Wolf smiled at me.

"All I did was cause Stella and Myra heartbreak. Nothing is resolved. Now Stella will go through life wondering what happened to her sister," I groused. "By the way, did Stella mention how Jordan is doing?"

"Jordan? What happened to him?" asked Nina.

"Someone beat him up and left him in an alley," I said. "He's in the hospital. I have something for you," I said to Wolf, fetching the tote where I had stashed the antiquity.

I slid it out and placed the two halves on the table. "This is a mock antiquity. Apparently, they're all the rage in decorating. As you recall, someone broke into Chatsworth Antiques by breaking the glass in the front door.

Now that the employees are back, one of them was able to identify this item, which was one whole piece at the time, as missing. I showed it to her today and she confirmed that this is the item. However, it is mass produced, so there are probably lots of them. Last night when they lifted Jordan to place him in the ambulance, this tumbled on the ground. I can't say for certain that it was connected to Jordan, but everyone has confirmed that he had a big debt to pay. I think he may have thought this was genuine and tried to pass it off as a valuable antiquity in lieu of payment. I haven't let anyone touch it. Except me, of course, because I picked it up and carried it home, but I thought you might want to fingerprint it."

"It looks like a rough surface," said Nina. "Can something like that be fingerprinted?"

"Oh, sure. You can fingerprint a brick. It's not the best, but they have some interesting methods to try. Thanks, Sophie."

Chapter 33

Dear Sophie,
My doctor suggested using avocados in place of
mayonnaise, but they are always hard as a rock.
How can I tell when an avocado is ripe?
*   It's Not the Same in Mayo, South Carolina*

Dear It's Not the Same,
Gently press the avocado. It should yield slightly.
Some people say an avocado is ripe when the tiny
stem at the top comes off easily.

*   Sophie*

After Wolf left, Nina lingered to help me clean up.
"Poor Stella," I said. "I can't imagine learning something like this. Her mother isn't her birth mother and the
father, whom she loved, may have murdered her birth
mother. It has to be a terrible blow for her."

"And her husband is in the hospital. I bet you're right
about him trying to pass off that thing as valuable."

"I saw Doreen this morning. I think we can strike her

off the list as Stella's sister. Her dad was shot and killed while trying to rob a jewelry store."

"That's terrible!"

"What some people go through."

"I thought I might visit with each of the women on Orson's corkboard. The easiest way to find out which one, if any of them, is Stella's sister would be to do DNA tests, but it's not like I can ask them all for DNA swabs."

"That would be awkward."

I pulled out my phone. "I'm texting Mars. I'd like to talk with Cheryl Mancini." He replied almost instantly. "Looks like she works at a plant nursery. The one out near Sweet Jimmy's."

"I'll tag along."

Mochie and Daisy were snoozing, and it was too hot for them to be out and about anyway. We quietly walked out to the garage.

"How are you coming with a home for Rosebud?"

Nina groaned. "Not as well as I'd like. But she seems happy with us, so there's no big rush."

Russos' Nursery was larger than I expected. The name led me to believe that it was a family affair. Business was slow when we arrived, which wasn't terribly surprising. It was too late to plant vegetables and flowers for the summer. I guessed there must be a lull in between summer and fall items.

I had shopped there before, but had dealt with an elderly man. "Look for Cheryl," I whispered to Nina.

It didn't take us long to recognize her chestnut hair, which she had pulled up in a bun on the top of her head. She wore an apron with the Russos' logo of a hand trowel and a flower on it.

She pulled on gloves and took a plant from a woman.

"If you have any more of these, you need to dispose of them. They're very poisonous."

"But they look just like carrots," insisted the woman. "It's just when I pull them up there's no carrot. I'm sure I bought the seeds from you."

"I certainly hope not! This is poison hemlock. You shouldn't even touch it." Cheryl dumped the plant into a large trash bag and pulled the ties tight. "Honestly, I can't emphasize this enough. It's a deadly weed."

"Nonsense. I just don't understand why the carrots aren't growing," insisted the woman.

"These are in your garden?"

"Yes! That's what I'm trying to tell you. I planted the carrot seeds on the west side of the garden, but these came up on the east side and without carrots. I waited and waited for the little orange top they develop that lets you know when they're ready to eat, but all I got were these scraggly white roots."

Cheryl sucked in a deep breath. "I'll tell you what. Why don't I give you a gift certificate for the price of the seeds. You can spend it on whatever you want here."

"That's nice of you. I still won't have any carrots unless these things finally start to produce them."

Cheryl gestured to the elderly man I had dealt with. "This nice lady brought in poison hemlock, which she thinks she grew from seeds she bought here. I have offered her a gift certificate for the price of the seeds, but I don't seem to be able to convince her that she needs to get rid of these plants."

The man was tall and gaunt with a full head of white hair. His smile lit up his face. "How do you do? I am Marcello Russo."

The woman seemed enchanted. "Betty Hornsbill."

Cheryl turned away, rolled her eyes, and took a deep breath.

"It can be hard dealing with the public," I whispered to her.

Cheryl shook her head. "My grandfather is like a genius with them. I learned a long time ago to bring them to him. I'm worried sick that she'll eat one of those plants! How can I help you?"

I introduced myself and Nina. "We're friends of Mars Winston. He spoke to you the other day about Orson Chatsworth."

She placed her hand over her heart. "That was so sad. How awful for his bride-to-be. I will miss him forever. He and my grandfather were like fathers to me. I don't know how Stella will manage without him."

"Mars mentioned that you lost your father at an early age. We're looking for a woman about your age who lost her father. . . ."

Nina quickly jumped in. "Under unusual circumstances."

"Oh. Well, I don't know how unusual my father's death was. He was in the military and died in a helicopter crash. My mom has the American flag they gave her at the funeral and everything."

"I'm so sorry. It must have been hard on you."

"I never knew him. I was six months old when it happened. My mom and I went to live with my grandparents, and like I said, my grandfather filled in very much like a father. I always liked to imagine that my dad would have been like Orson. He was so much fun! He was always watching us, but from a distance."

"So then, Orson would have known how your father died," said Nina.

"I don't know if he knew or not. My mom was the only one who talked with me about my dad." Cheryl smiled.

"She always told me he was sitting on my shoulder, looking out for me."

We thanked her and I found a pretty blue pot to buy as thanks.

On the drive home, Nina said, "I hate to tell you this, but I think Cheryl just proved your theory wrong about Orson looking for his other daughter. If he lived across the street from the Mancini/Russos, then wouldn't he know about Cheryl's father dying in the military?"

"Probably," I admitted reluctantly. "But I don't know anything about your husband's family, except that they expect you to cook. I don't know if the father-in-law who visits you is his birth father, adoptive father, or a second or third husband of his mother. I know that Bernie's mother married seven times or more, but I don't know anything about the parents of the people across the street from Bernie and Mars."

Nina nodded. "That's true enough. So if we accept what Cheryl said, then we can cross her off the list. Two down, three to go."

"Do you think Joan and Tripp would have talked about their families?"

"Maybe. It's worth a shot."

I parked the car in my garage, and we walked down to the art gallery. It was blissfully cool inside. Music played softly in the background. Tripp was discussing a painting of a mother seated on a bench with her two children, each one leaning against her. Superimposed over them was the cloudy, transparent face of a man. Given our reason for being here, the painting sent shivers up my arms.

The woman decided to think about it and left the store.

"She'll be back," Tripp said to us confidently. "I can always tell."

"How?" asked Nina.

"It's a sixth sense or something. I can tell whether the painting stirs emotion in a person. Like Sophie, just now with that painting."

I supposed it would be rude to tell him that I was definitely not going to buy it because it gave me the creeps. I smiled. "I hope she comes back for it. Did her husband pass away?"

Tripp nodded sagely. "I think so. What can I do for you two?"

"We were wondering if you knew anything about Joan's background. Did she ever mention her parents?"

"Why would you want to know that?"

It was a good question. "We're looking for a long-lost daughter." It was true.

"Oh. Well, I hate to be the one to burst your bubble, but I don't think she's the one. Her birth father died of hemophilia when she was very young. She was afraid she might be a carrier because it's hereditary. Her mother remarried when Joan was about five years old. I met that man and he seemed very nice. Of course, you never know what people are really like when you only meet them socially. Right? He might be an awful man!"

"How are you making out without Joan around here?" asked Nina.

"We have a new employee, Will, who is not only stinking good looking, but the man could sell dirty old shoes to people."

We thanked him for his assistance.

As we walked out the door, Nina said, "That leaves Riley Hooper and Bonnie Shergold. If one of them isn't Stella's sister, then we'll have to rethink Orson's intentions with that corkboard."

I hated to agree, but she was right. My theory was falling flat on its face.

We went home. Nina had to pick up her husband at the airport. Her husband, a forensic pathologist, was in great demand and traveled constantly.

Back in the quiet of my kitchen, I was feeling like our search for Stella's sister was futile.

I was reaching for a box of crackers when I spied a box of vanilla wafers. It dawned on me then that there was one other person who had known Orson in his younger years. A person who despised Orson and possibly me, too.

But he had loved my banana pudding with salted caramel, and it wasn't difficult to make. I set to work locating a disposable container that I could leave with him. In less than an hour, I was layering the vanilla wafers, pudding, and salted caramel into the bowl. I popped it in the fridge to set a little.

But while I had cooked the pudding, it occurred to me that I should probably take someone with me. After all, he was still a suspect, at least in my mind if not anyone else's. Nina was busy with her husband. Bernie was in the middle of dinner service at the Laughing Hound, but Mars might be available.

I called him and was pleased that he was up for a walk. I got out a tote bag and slid the banana pudding inside to make it easier to carry.

I planned to take a secret weapon with me, too. I would bet anything that the little boy jumping off a pier in the picture I had seen at Karl Roth's house had a dog.

The sun was setting by the time Mars, Daisy, and I struck out for Karl's home. We walked leisurely as the air cooled just enough to feel wonderful, like a warm hug. On the way, I brought Mars up to date on everything that had happened.

This time the lights were on in the back windows. I wasn't sure whether to knock on the store door or the back one.

After a brief discussion, Mars and I decided on the store door because the back might be too personal.

I rapped on the door. And again. Finally, the door to his kitchen opened.

"We're closed! Come back tomorrow!"

"It's Sophie, Karl. I brought you something!"

He lumbered toward the door. It was the first time I had seen him when he was not wearing a suit. The short-sleeved golf shirt and seersucker shorts looked more comfortable and most certainly cooler.

He opened the door. "I said we're closed."

Chapter 34

Dear Sophie,
We're trying to cut back on butter, but my family loves butter boards. Are there any similar alternatives we could try?
Crossing My Fingers in Hopeful, Alabama

Dear Crossing My Fingers,
There are alternatives to butter boards, and they're very tasty. Try a hummus board or a cream cheese board!
Sophie

I opened my tote bag, removed the container inside, and held it out to him. "I think we got off on the wrong foot, Karl. I brought you some of my banana pudding as an apology."

He couldn't have been more shocked. "You didn't have to do that."

"I wanted to."

"Thank you very much. I'm forgetting my manners. Won't you come in?"

"Thanks, this is Mars Winston."

Mars shook Karl's hand and apologized for barging in on him in such a gracious manner that I was doubly glad I had asked him along. I could see Karl's expression changing. First the gift of a yummy dessert and now southern graciousness.

I heard the lock clink in place behind us, which made me a little bit nervous, but I reminded myself that I always locked the door when I was alone in Orson's store.

"Now, who is this?" He stroked Daisy's head. "She looks like a hunting dog."

"This is Daisy. Did you grow up with dogs?"

He opened the door to his kitchen and invited us inside. "Oh my, yes. I lived on a farm as a child. We had all kinds of dogs over the years, but my favorite was an Irish setter. We did everything together. Fish, swim in the pond, muck out horse stalls, sleep outdoors in the summertime. He was a wonderful friend to me."

"I'm surprised that you don't have a dog now."

"You know, I really ought to get one."

"My friend, Nina Reid Norwood, works at the shelter. I'm sure she would be happy to help you find the right one."

"I might just call her tomorrow."

"We got Daisy through Nina," Mars said.

"I hope you don't mind us intruding on you so late in the day."

"Not at all. This is a most pleasant surprise."

"I've been checking into Orson's background, and it occurred to me that you have known him as long as Myra, maybe longer."

He nodded. "That's true. We go way back. Doesn't make me like him any better, but in the beginning we got on pretty well."

"Did you know him before he married Myra?"

"Yes. I remember their wedding. It wasn't anything fancy. None of us had much money back in those days. But Myra wore a pretty white dress with lace on it. Stella was a cute little girl. She stole the show. I believe Myra's mother and sister cooked all the food. We ate outside in her mother's backyard. I helped them shove together some long tables and carry a neighbor's folding chairs to their yard. It was nothing like the weddings you see today. But it was one of the warmest and friendliest weddings I've ever been to."

"Do you remember Orson having another daughter?" asked Mars.

I knew Karl had the ability to hide his feelings, but the surprised look on his face seemed genuine. "No. Was there another child?"

"We don't know," I said, quickly getting his mind off it by asking, "What do you know about Stella's mother?"

Karl's lips pulled tight. "Do you remember when I told you Orson had deep, dark secrets?"

"I do."

"He told me that her mother had passed away. But I didn't believe him." Karl leaned toward us and spoke in a hushed voice as though he didn't want anyone else to hear. "Not one family member of Orson's came to the wedding. Not a one!" He held up his forefinger as emphasis. "Who does that? We weren't youngsters at the time, but he didn't have a sister or a brother or any parents living? Not a cousin or a grandparent? Seemed very suspicious to me." Karl sat up straight. "No, ma'am. He was hiding something. And now that he's dead, all his deep dark secrets will come tumbling out into the daylight."

"Did he ever talk about his youth?" asked Mars.

Karl sucked in a deep breath of air. "Not much." Then

he snapped his fingers. "Here's something else. He didn't have a single picture of his mom or dad. Now don't you think that's odd? That's something that happens when you take off in a hurry and there's no time to pack. Nope, I always knew there was something terrible in his past. I hope you're not going to tell me that he murdered someone. You think somebody finally caught up to him and killed him for revenge?"

There was an awkward moment while I pondered how to respond. "Anything is possible. There seems to be some confusion about his early years. Thank you for taking the time to talk with us."

"Most certainly. I appreciate the banana pudding."

"I saw your bean crop and carrots in the back. I guess you still do some gardening."

He swiped his hand through the air. "I swear those are magic beans. I planted them seven years ago and every single year, they come back on their own. When they're young, they're nice green beans. Let 'em grow a little longer and they get delicious beans inside the pods. I'll save you some this year if you like. Just stick those dry beans in the dirt and they'll pop right up. But I don't have any carrots. Wish I did."

"Are you sure? I thought I saw some."

Karl switched on a light in the back of his building and opened the door for us. We filed outside.

"Right there." I pointed at the lush carrot greens.

"Those aren't carrots. They're poison hemlock! Sure look like carrot greens, don't they?"

"They're poisonous?" Mars pulled Daisy closer to him.

"They're noxious weeds but very poisonous. The flowers look like Queen Anne's lace. My daddy always warned us against touching them. It's amazing that they even grow here in the city," said Karl. "I'll have to pull them tomorrow."

Mars quickly took a picture of them. The flash on his phone caught on something shiny.

Trying to act casual, I aimed the light on my phone in that direction. It looked a lot like Audrey's cast aluminum trowel. Clearly, everyone was onto the new trend and tired of rusted garden tools. Even a man who sold rusted items in his store.

"Now what was that for?" Karl asked Mars, sounding a lot less friendly.

"I'd like to show it to my friend Bernie to make sure we don't have any of this in our yard."

Karl seemed agreeable about that. We thanked him again and walked out to the alley.

"What do you think?" I asked Mars.

"I think he knew perfectly well that he had poison hemlock growing in the back of his house. Somebody obviously pulled some out." Mars held up his phone and showed me the picture. There was no mistake that the soil had been disturbed in two places.

It was getting past the time for phone calls when Mars escorted Daisy and me to the kitchen door.

"Want me to make sure no one is hiding in your house?"

I laughed at him. "Don't be silly."

"Sophie, I'm not sure what to make of Karl. He seemed friendly enough, but that poisonous weed was very suspicious."

"He could have simply agreed that it was a carrot plant if he was trying to hide the fact that it was poisonous."

"Not everyone thinks fast on their feet. Don't forget that someone clobbered Jordon. Somebody is out there, and if you get too close to figuring out who it is, he might come after you."

I unlocked the door and opened it. "Okay, fine."

Mars ran through the house while I stashed away the tote bag and fed Mochie a bedtime snack. I looked at the clock. It was too late to call Wolf. But maybe not too late to send a text.

Has the lab tested Orson for poison hemlock?

Mars bounded up the stairs from the basement. "All clear."

"Thanks, Mars. And for going with me, too."

"It was more interesting than sitting around watching TV. Keep me posted?"

"Will do."

I locked the door behind him and went up to bed.

The phone woke me early the next morning. I rolled over in bed and stretched to reach it. "Hello?" I croaked.

"What's this with the poison hemlock?"

I forced myself out of bed and walked barefoot down the stairs to put on the kettle for tea. "Mars and I were at Karl Roth's house last night. It's growing in his backyard."

"That doesn't mean anything."

"Mars got a photo. It's very clear that someone yanked out two plants beside it."

"That doesn't mean anything, either. How do you know those plants that were pulled weren't some other kind of weed, like dandelions?"

"I don't, which is exactly why you should have the lab test for it." I looked it up on my phone while I spoke. "Here, it's called coniine. It's a poisonous chemical compound. An alkaloid."

"Sophie, I appreciate your efforts, but that's not much to go on."

"Wolf, do you know what caused Orson's respiratory failure?"

"No."

"Then what's the harm in testing for coniine?"

I could hear him sighing. "Okay, okay. I hoped you had something more concrete. Thanks, Sophie." He disconnected the call.

Feeling as if someone had pricked a hole in my balloon, I let Daisy out and drank my tea. I was still in my nightshirt when I rinsed my cup and looked out the window over the sink.

Tripp Fogarty was walking by carrying a bird cage. I caught a glimpse of bright yellow inside the white cage.

I ran upstairs and changed clothes as fast as I could. I peeked out of the window and saw him cross the street.

I hurried down the stairs, grabbed my keys and Daisy's halter, and ran outside. "Daisy!" I hissed. "Daisy!"

I locked the door, and she came running from the backyard. I slid the halter over her head, latched it, and the two of us ran to the corner where I had last seen Tripp.

He had passed my house and turned right. Daisy tried to run and I did my best to keep up with her, grateful for the cool morning air. Fortunately, we spotted him. I slowed down and kept well in back of him so he wouldn't see us.

It was silly of me to follow him. But when I saw the yellow bird, all I could think of was James Bond, Audrey's blue parakeet who needed a friend. There was no reason in the world that Tripp couldn't know or be friends with Audrey. But each of them had been especially close to one of the people who had been murdered. It was a hunch, one that I hadn't thought through very well before I ran out of my house. Now, as I followed him down the street, I thought I was being ridiculous, reaching out for any clue, stretching unimportant connections into sinister relationships.

I wasn't far from the store. No one would be there yet, so it would be a good time to sneak into Orson's secret room and reconsider those photographs.

Mindlessly, I followed Tripp when he turned onto another block. The block where Audrey lived.

Chapter 35

Dear Sophie,
I'm buying my first board, but I'm so confused.
What size should it be? My cutting boards aren't
very pretty and they're way too small.
                Ready to Buy in Board Tree, Kentucky

Dear Ready to Buy,
Twenty inches to twenty-four inches in diameter is
a good starter size. It's tempting to go bigger, but
don't forget that you'll probably have to carry it
somewhere when it's full of food. If you prefer
something rectangular, twenty-four inches is a good
starter length with a width of twelve to sixteen
inches.

                                    Sophie

Maybe I wasn't crazy after all. I slowed to a crawl and
stopped Daisy behind a large tree on the opposite
site of the street.

Tripp rapped on Audrey's door. She opened it and, thank

heaven, was focused on the bird. I didn't think she noticed us at all.

Audrey took the cage from Tripp, and then he turned around and glanced up and down the street before stepping inside and closing the door behind him.

It sent shivers up my spine. Who did that? Who was he looking for? Had he stolen the bird?

The door closed.

I was fairly certain that they would be fussing about the bird and not looking out the windows, but to be on the safe side, Daisy and I did an about-face and went back to the end of the block so they wouldn't notice us walking by.

As expected, Chatsworth Antiques was a quiet oasis in the morning rush that had begun. Still, we had plenty of time before anyone arrived to work. I filled a bowl of water for Daisy and opened the bookshelves that led to Orson's secret room. I gazed at the pictures of the five women.

My first instinct was to remove Cheryl, Doreen, and Joan. We knew something about their fathers, and unless they had lied, it didn't seem likely that Orson was their biological father.

That left Bonnie Shergold and Riley Hooper. There were two other possibilities. I searched the desk for a sheet of paper and cut it to the size of the photos, then pinned it on the board to represent the first possibility—that Orson's other daughter was dead or alive but wasn't one of these women. If that was the case, then the only hope Stella had to find her was DNA registries. That would be up to her. Stella might not want to know. Everyone was different.

The second possibility, which in my opinion was far the worst, was that I was wrong, and that my first instinct had been correct. That these women represented something that he found attractive. They were all lovely and I simply could not accept that Orson had been such a doting father to Stella while having some kind of private perversion.

His words echoed in my head. "Tell Stella . . . Tell Stella . . ." There were a thousand things he could have been trying to say. Tell Stella I love her. Tell Stella she has a sister. Tell Stella to beware of Jordan. Tell Stella to take care of Rosebud. Tell Stella to look behind the picture of her in my bedroom. Tell Stella the painting of a cow in the antiques store is worth millions.

I walked out of the secret room and looked at the paintings. I still hadn't brought anyone in to look at them and give me an assessment of their values. I returned to the public office. He probably kept a ledger of some sort with the prices of everything. His accountant would need to know how much he paid for them.

Checking the time, I closed the secret room, put away Daisy's water bowl, and locked up the store. We strolled toward the hardware store where I looked at their display of trowels.

"Hi, Ed," I said to the man restocking shelves. "I don't see the cast aluminum trowels."

"That's because we can't keep them in stock. They're a hot item! Should I put you on the waiting list? I can give you a call when they come in."

"Yes, please."

"Do you want the set of three? That's a cultivator, a digging trowel, and a scoop trowel. You can order them separately, but that ends up being more expensive. We just ordered a digging trowel for Tripp Fogarty and he's paying a lot more for just the one item, so I recommend buying all three at once."

"The whole set, please. I didn't know Tripp was into gardening."

Ed looked up at me. "Me either. I think Joan was the

one who liked to garden. She painted those beautiful vines on our display right there. Of course, now that she's gone, we appreciate it even more. Such a sad thing. Tripp is just devastated."

"Devastated? I mean it's very sad, but—"

Ed grinned at me. "Oh, the things that do go on in this town. I guess when you work together, romance can bloom." He looked over at his coworker Garrett, who was snapping gum and scratching his overall-clad belly. "Now, maybe if I worked with Bonnie Shergold . . ."

I smiled at him. "You really think Tripp and Joan were a couple?"

"Think? I know! I saw them smooching with my own two eyes. Not that it's any of my business, but it's not like I was peeping in their windows. I figure if people are silly enough to kiss behind the stores where I park, then they should expect to be seen. Right?"

A customer lined up behind me.

"I'll call you when they come in."

"Thanks, Ed." I got out of the way fast, thinking about Tripp and Joan as I left the store.

"Good morning, Sophie!" Bonnie Shergold said.

She was putting up a sandwich board outside with a photograph of Colin Warren's new event room on it.

"Hi, Bonnie."

"And my favorite dog!" She mock-whispered to Daisy, "Let's not tell the other dogs. Okay? They might get jealous."

"Bonnie, did you ever hear anything about Tripp and Joan being involved?"

"Romantically? Good grief, no. Joan"—Bonnie sighed—"well, she's gone now, so I guess there's no harm in telling you that she was crazy for Jordan. I told her not to date a man whose divorce wasn't final yet, but she just laughed at me. I'm sorry to say that didn't endear her to me. Stella is my friend, and I just couldn't imagine dating her husband, even if they were separated. Jordan isn't my type, but if he were, I would never have done that to Stella."

I understood completely. I wouldn't have done it, either.

"Come on in. I have dog cookies!" Bonnie sang.

Daisy's ears perked at the magic word, and she followed Bonnie.

A woman stood behind the counter, arranging flowers in a huge vase.

"Sophie, this is my mom, Sharon."

We exchanged greetings.

"I see you're helping advertise Colin's new event space," I said.

"It's amazing. Have you seen it yet? Oh, that's right. You put Colin in touch with Natasha. He was so grateful." She handed Daisy a dog cookie. "We're hoping to make it a one-stop deal for weddings and celebrations. Colin can host the event and I can do the flowers. It will be a family affair."

"Family?"

"Colin is my uncle. My mother's brother. Can you imagine? There were four rowdy brothers and only one girl."

Sharon laughed. "It was a crazy, noisy household. But as the only girl, I had princess status. They knew better than to mess with me!"

"So, then your father was a Shergold."

"My adoptive father was a Shergold and I took his name," said Bonnie.

I could hardly believe what I was hearing. I tried to remain calm. "I didn't know that you were adopted."

"It's a complicated story and sort of romantic."

"Oh, Bonnie," said her mother.

"Mom! It's not as socially unacceptable as it was back then."

A blush rose on Sharon's neck.

"My mom fell for this very handsome young man from France. He was a musician and a singer for a rock and roll group. He had an enticing French accent and everything. Isn't that cool?"

Sharon rolled her eyes.

"But it turned out that he was married."

"Which he had not told me," Sharon protested.

"And then he went back home to France. *Pierre Martin*," Bonnie said in a mock French accent. "Anyway"— she held up her palms—"ta da! Here came Bonnie! When I was five, Mom married Eddie Shergold, who adopted me, and I took his name."

"Did you ever meet Pierre?"

"No. I've looked for him online. I found an obituary notice that sounds like it was probably him. He's been dead for years now, but that's all right. Eddie has been a wonderful dad to me."

Sharon smiled at her daughter. "He really has."

"He's over at the event space helping get it ready for the grand opening tomorrow. I hope you'll come! You can meet the whole family," said Bonnie.

"I already met your Uncle Terry. I guess he's your uncle, Bonnie. Probably one of your brothers, Sharon?"

Sharon nodded. "The whole crew will be here. It's their dream come true. They always wanted to own an event hall, but money was tight, and loans weren't easy to get when you came from a big, poor family. We're very proud of Colin."

"I'm looking forward to it. I'll see you tomorrow then."

I walked home thinking there was only one possibility left now—Riley Hooper. Besides the chestnut hair and blue eyes, every single one of the women on Orson's board had lost her father at a young age. Orson must have known that. I was more convinced than ever that he was looking for his other daughter, Callie. Maybe he had given her up for adoption because he couldn't handle an infant. Whatever the reason, he thought she was alive and he was looking for her.

I tried to put the women out of my mind for the time being so I could focus on BabyFest, my next convention. It would be starting in nine days, and I had plenty of work to do to make sure it came off without a hitch. Stella was my biggest concern. The cocktail reception on Sunday afternoon, when everyone would be arriving and checking into the host hotel, was a very big order. I had hired her to make baby gender reveal boards as examples of what could be done. I didn't know if she was up to it, with Orson's death, moving, and the stress of being on the police radar.

If I phoned her, she would tell me she was on track. I thought I might pay her a visit instead. There were a lot of different components to BabyFest and I didn't want any of them to fall through. The boards were a big order for one person to handle.

I took a walk over to Stella's new house. When I banged the door knocker, Myra answered.

"Good grief. Not you again. Haven't you caused enough trouble already?"

"I'm sorry, Myra. I never saw all this coming."

"If you had just left everything alone."

"Who is it, Mom?" called Stella.

"It's Sophie."

"Send her back here."

Myra grudgingly allowed me to enter the house. "She's in the kitchen."

I found Stella putting together butter boards. "Hi," she said wearily.

"How are you doing?" I asked.

She sighed. "Nothing will ever be the same. Wolf and

Mom showed me the pictures of my birth mother and baby sister. It's inconceivable to me that Dad would have murdered my mom and my sister. Why not me? Why let me live?"

"I don't think he killed them."

She turned weary eyes toward me. "But that's what the cops think."

"I know. I think your sister might be alive."

Myra magically appeared in the doorway. "Don't do that to her. Don't raise false hopes. Stella has been through enough."

But Stella didn't take her eyes off me. "Really?"

I had no hope to give her. "I have trouble imagining that your father was that evil. He told you," I said, gesturing at Myra, "that someone else killed his wife. Someone he was afraid would come back and kill Stella and him, too."

Myra nodded. "Someone with brothers. I remember that part. Like if one was dead, the other would come after him. But people lie, Sophie. That could have just been a cover."

"You must have believed him, or you would have left him."

"You see?" said Stella. "These are the thoughts running through my head. Between settling in, and Jordan in the hospital, and the divorce and custody problems, not to mention work, I feel like a zombie. Like this isn't my life anymore."

"That's actually why I came over here. BabyFest will be starting a week from tomorrow. Are you up to providing all those boards? It's a big order."

"Yes. Oh my gosh. Yes, I can do it. Mom will help me. Right, Mom?"

If you asked me, Mom didn't look at all enthused about

it. But she said, "I'm here for you, Stella. Whatever you need."

Stella rose from her chair and hugged her mom. "I don't know where I would be without you."

"How's Jordan?"

"It's touch and go. He's under heavy sedation."

"If you see him, give him my best."

Stella nodded. I said good-bye and let myself out.

Chapter 36

Dear Sophie,
I am sick and tired of my friends taking phone calls when we eat out. It's just awful. Everyone stops talking. That person leaves the table. It's terrible manners. We always talk about "no phones," but invariably someone has a call they just have to take. Help!
> *I Love My Phone But . . . in Phoneton, Ohio*

Dear I Love My Phone But . . . ,
You might try this simple trick. When you sit down, everyone places their phones in the middle of the table. The first one to reach for his phone pays the tab for everyone at the table!
> *Sophie*

That afternoon, I roamed my closet in search of semi-formal nautical. Luckily, I often needed formal and semiformal attire for my job. A navy blue linen dress that was fitted in the waist and had a flare skirt down to my knees was just the ticket. I pulled my hair up in a loose twist to keep cool and added white faux pearls and matching earrings. There wasn't anything particularly anchors-away about it, but low white wedges with a sprinkling of rhinestones seemed to help.

I fed Daisy and Mochie an early dinner, tucked the invitation into a navy clutch, and strolled down to the waterfront. The other guests were immediately recognizable by their blue and white attire. There were so many people wearing navy and white stripes that it was a little dizzying.

Natasha reminded me of Morticia Addams in her long, slinky, navy dress with oversize flowing cuffs and a matching ruffle on her very low-cut V-neck. Nearly all the gentlemen wore navy blazers with white trousers.

I showed my invitation and stepped on board. The yacht was huge. A large robin's-egg-blue sign greeted everyone, WELCOME TO NATASHA STYLE.

Natasha hurried over to me and air-kissed me on both sides. "I'm so glad you could come. Especially since you gave me the idea for this."

"I don't think that's possible because I don't know what this is."

"It's everything I am. You'll see a selection on each of the levels. I can Natasha Style your house. Or your wardrobe, which you really could use. Or I can Natasha Style your food, your party, or even your life. It's the ultimate dream of everyone to live Natasha Style."

"I'm eager to see everything."

"I must greet other people—mingle, Sophie."

I recognized many of them. Myra in a navy and white caftan, Karl in a navy and white seersucker suit with a bow tie that sported mini sailboats, Audrey in a chic white dress with navy trim and gold buttons. As I drifted along, it dawned on me that everyone was single. A server approached me holding a tray of red drinks garnished with a tiny flag that said *Natasha Style*. "Natasha Style River Breeze?" he asked.

I accepted one of the drinks, which was pleasantly icy and fruity with a vodka kick. I recognized Stella's boards in the middle of the mess hall. Around the entire room were large boards with photographs and sales pitches for Natasha Style and the various services she offered. I nibbled on charcuterie and helped myself to delicious compounded butter from butter boards that I smeared on baguette slices.

When I emerged, Natasha called me over to her. "Sophie Winston, have you met Joe Bulfin?"

"Yes, of course." How could I forget the homely professor who was taken in by Doreen's scam?

"Why don't you get to know one another better? I'll be back, I have more people to introduce. This is my matchmaking service, Love, Natasha Style."

Joe looked as green and uncomfortable as I felt. I burst out laughing and Joe joined me.

"Sorry about that," I said.

"I have to hand it to her, Natasha is creative."

"Have you found the food yet? It's right in there," I said.

"Great. I'm starved." He headed for the mess hall.

My phone dinged and I took a second to look at it. Uh oh. A text from Wolf. It was very brief: **Coniine present.**

So it *was* Karl who murdered Orson with the poisonous hemlock in his backyard! A flush of heat wafted through me as I considered what might have happened if I hadn't taken Mars with me to see Karl.

Natasha sidled up to me. "No phones, Sophie. That's so rude!" She snatched my phone from my hand. "Honestly, I thought you had better manners than that!"

Sirens wailed on shore. Three police cars drove toward the pier. Officers jumped out and ran toward the yacht.

And Karl, with menacing eyes, flaring nostrils, and a grimace worthy of a gargoyle, launched himself toward me. "You! You reported me to the police."

I sidestepped him and, as the yacht lurched, his outstretched arms caught Natasha and the two of them tumbled overboard.

Chapter 37

Dear Natasha,
What can I serve on a board for dinner?
No Time to Cook in Cooke City, Montana

Dear No Time to Cook,
You could eat charcuterie, cheeses, fruits, and veggies from a board. And you could serve a butter board with warm bread with it. But if you're planning to make a hamburger board or a chili board, then you might as well just order takeout if you're pressed for time.

Natasha

For a moment, everyone fell silent. Then Natasha's screams could be heard below mixed with the heavy pounding of police running on board.

Natasha's dress was seriously tight and midi length. There was no way she could swim or kick her legs. Not unlike a mermaid, I thought. I looked around for a life buoy. Happily, one was close by. Hoping I wouldn't hit her on the head, I yelled, "Natasha! Grab this!" I tossed it overboard and watched it splash into the water. Good grief, she couldn't reach it.

Karl, who could have helped her, was churning away from the yacht as fast as he could go.

There wasn't time to give it much thought. I grabbed another life buoy, kicked off my shoes, and jumped.

Amazingly, the water was very cold. Because I held onto the life buoy, I didn't go down far. I surfaced and looked around for Natasha, who thankfully had managed to keep her head above water, but was struggling. I swam toward her and handed the life buoy to her.

"Hold on to this."

Natasha clutched it, her breath coming hard.

"It's okay," I said. "Don't try to swim, just hold on."

She nodded. I held on to it, too, and sidestroked toward the other life buoy. Once I had it in hand, I kicked our way to the pier.

Hands reached for us. I pushed Natasha in front of me. She was coughing and needed to be pulled out first.

When she was safely on the pier, I accepted help getting out of the water.

For once I welcomed the summertime heat and humidity. I doubted that even the best dry cleaner could rescue my dress, but it didn't matter. The important thing was that we were safe.

"Where's Karl?" I asked.

A police officer said, "In custody. They pulled him out of the river." He pointed and I could see the boat that had picked him up.

"Is he under arrest?"

"I would think so."

I watched as they transferred him to a squad car, and it drove away.

"This is all your fault," Natasha murmured.

I turned toward her. "Are you okay? It seemed like you swallowed some water."

"I am never inviting you to anything again. I'm so embarrassed that I just want to die."

"Please don't do that."

"It's all these murder cases that you're always pursuing. It's not ladylike. Look what a mess I am. This was supposed to be the best day of my life! Sophie, we are no longer friends."

"Karl is the one who poisoned Orson and killed him."

"What? They must be wrong."

"Nope. He used poison hemlock."

"But he dresses so well."

"I guess we should learn something from that."

"I invited a killer to my party?"

A van from the local news station pulled up. "Go fix your hair. I see a reporter coming."

She gasped and got to her feet. "Is my makeup running?"

"Yup."

Barefooted, Natasha ran along the pier and onto the boat.

"Are you all right?" I knew it was Wolf without looking.

"I'm fine."

"Are your shoes in the river?"

"They would be on the boat."

Wolf tilted his head, and an officer went to look for them.

Another officer approached him. "Sir, the press is here. Do you want to speak to them?"

Wolf squatted next to me. "Do you want to talk to the press?"

"No. That's Natasha's thing. Maybe she can turn this into a Natasha Style moment."

The officer returned with my shoes. Wolf held them out to me.

"Thanks!" I said to the officer who had fetched them.

"I'll give you a ride home." Wolf stood up and held his hand out to me.

When he left, I took a long, hot shower. I could hear my landline ringing, but I didn't get out to answer the phone. It was probably the press.

I stepped out and wrapped myself in a warm, cozy bathrobe. But I heard voices. Daisy and Mochie weren't anywhere to be seen.

I listened. There were two or three of them. And then I heard Nina yell, "Where is she?"

"I'm up here." I ran down the stairs. "What's going on?"

"We were worried about you when you didn't answer your cell phone."

"Ah. I believe it's at the bottom of the Potomac River."

Nina turned on the TV in my kitchen. Mars put on the kettle.

Bernie hugged me. "I'm glad you're all right."

Natasha spoke on TV in a soaking wet dress that looked even more like Morticia Addams's gown than before. It clung to her.

"I couldn't let a murderer escape. I simply had to stop him, so I jumped in after him," said Natasha.

"Natasha actually jumped in the Potomac voluntarily?" asked Mars. "That's hard to believe."

Wasn't it, though? I started laughing. "She wanted attention and she's getting it now. I guess her party worked to her benefit after all."

"Who is the murderer?" asked Mars.

"Karl Roth."

"No kidding?"

"I suggested that they test Orson for coniine which is in poison hemlock, which looks like carrots when it's growing. They found it in his system. Karl is Orson's killer."

Bernie sat down next to me, and Mars brought me a steaming cup of tea.

"But why?" asked Nina. "Just some old grudge? Why wouldn't he be able to get over it?"

I shrugged. "Envy? Old grudges?"

"I guess we're lucky he didn't offer us food or drinks last night," said Mars. "Close call."

Bernie ordered takeout from the Laughing Hound for dinner. As we ate, I brought them all up to speed about the women on the corkboard. "Our last hope is Riley Hooper."

Before they left, we agreed to go to the grand opening of Colin Warren's event space the next evening. I stashed the leftovers in the fridge, left the dirty dishes soaking in the sink, and took my laptop upstairs to bed.

I Googled *Maryland Warren family*. Most of the hits were about the new event space. Colin was getting a lot of publicity. Unfortunately, there were a lot of people named Warren. But as I continued, I found an article about Sharon Warren Shergold, who had cancer as a child back in the days when only 10 percent of children survived. The main gist of the article was how far treatments had come. The photos that accompanied it showed a skinny little girl wearing a flower headband on her bald head. It was heartbreaking. But the picture of a healthy Sharon next to it was wonderful to see.

Late the next afternoon, Mars, Bernie, Nina, and I walked over to the new event space. It was every bit as glamorous as I had hoped. Bonnie and her mom, Sharon, had outdone themselves with floral arrangements. They were gigantic and vibrant. The railing in the ballroom had been completed. People stood on the upper balcony that led around the room. Servers mingled with trays of drinks.

Tables had been set up with charcuterie boards and butter boards. A round table showed off a chocolate fountain.

Someone arrived with a media entourage. Everyone was whispering about who it could be. A senator? The mayor? When the media pulled away a hair, I realized it was Natasha. She had a cameraman filming her, probably for her TV show on Monday.

Everyone attended. It seemed as if the entire town had turned out for the event.

Colin's uncle Terry gave me a curt nod. This time I approached him. "Colin said you were the best at building. This is beautiful. Very well done."

"Thank you, ma'am."

"Is the rest of the family here?"

He pointed. "Over there, my sister and three brothers."

"There's a family resemblance."

"We all look like Warrens. Always have." He rubbed his nose with his forefinger. His hand was black and blue. And his suit jacket and shirtsleeve were pulled back just far enough for me to see a Rolex on his wrist. One with a navy blue face and bezel.

"Ouch!" I said. "What happened there?"

"Aw, it's nothing. I was lifting a heavy beam and the rascal got away from me."

"It looks very painful."

"I've had worse. I believe they're calling me."

They were lining up for a family photo.

Behind me, a woman said in a low voice, "Will you look at that? To see them now, it's hard to believe my dad forbade my brothers from hanging out with the Warren boys."

A second woman said, "My father did, too. Those boys were a handful!"

"And will you look at little Bonnie. Didn't she turn out pretty? Doesn't look a thing like them, though."

The woman was right. The Warren family members did look alike, except for Bonnie.

"Sharon looks so healthy! It's amazing after what she went through. She was the sickliest little girl I ever knew. All that chemo and radiation."

"I remember when she lost her hair, bless her. No wonder those boys ran wild. Their parents had to be focused on Sharon."

"Remember how they said she wouldn't be able to have children? I tell people that all the time when they get bad news from a doctor. Doctors don't know everything. Though I never did buy that story about the French boy."

"I was skeptical about that, too. I always thought it was a local boy, but Sharon knew if she said who he was that her brothers would beat the you-know-what out of him."

I desperately wanted to ask them questions, but I was afraid they would clam up. They started to drift away! I turned quickly. "Excuse me. Did you know the Warrens growing up?"

"Why yes," said the one with a white streak in her hair. "We live in Old Town now, so we wanted to show our support."

"That's very kind of you. It's a beautiful place. Um, if you don't mind, you were saying something about Sharon?"

The two women exchanged a look.

The one with the white streak said, "Sharon had cancer when she was young. She had to go through chemo and radiation, and thank goodness it worked! Look at her today."

The other woman whispered, "The treatments saved her life, but they *said* she was infertile. She couldn't have children. It was tragic. Sharon loved kids. So everyone was a little bit surprised when she turned up with a baby. No one could remember seeing her pregnant. I know some women can hide it well for a while. Heaven knows I never could."

"But Sharon is an amazing seamstress. You would not believe what she can sew. We thought maybe she had made some clothes for herself that were structured to hide the belly."

"It was the talk of the town. Didn't they say that Bonnie was very premature and had to stay in the hospital for a few months? I think that was it. The baby probably wasn't full term when Sharon delivered."

"I see. They're a lovely family."

"Nice meeting you," they said as they hit the charcuterie boards.

So Orson had been on to something with Bonnie after all. I hoped she might be Stella's missing sister, Callie. Only DNA could prove that, and it wasn't as though I could ask Bonnie.

And now I couldn't help wondering about her uncle Terry. I didn't believe for a minute that he lost control of a beam that somehow managed to fall on his hand. But I suspected that whoever beat the pulp out of Jordan probably had a hand or two that looked like Terry's right now.

But how would the fake artifact fit in? Terry didn't seem like the kind of guy who would be interested in antiquities and artifacts. I could follow up with Wolf. He probably had a bead on Terry Warren by now. I stepped into the lobby and texted Wolf: **Meet me at the store tomorrow morning? 8 a.m.?**

Chapter 38

Dear Natasha,
My little boy would like a doughnut board instead
of a cake for his birthday party! I'm happy to do
that for him, but how?
    Proud Mommy in Round Bay, Maryland

Dear Proud Mommy,
Buy or bake a variety of doughnuts with different
toppings. Be sure some have sprinkles! Place them
on a large board and add small cookies and the
birthday boy's favorite candies in between them.
    Natasha

I stopped on my way to the store to pick up bagels and lox, and lattes. Wolf waited at the door when I arrived. He carried lattes and Krispy Kreme doughnuts, my favorite.

The two of us laughed as I unlocked the door. I turned off the alarm and promptly locked the door behind us. And then I turned the alarm on again.

I opened the bookshelves that led to Orson's secret room.

"We're eating back here?" Wolf asked.

I nodded. He wore shorts and a golf shirt. "Is it your day off?"

"I'm planning to play golf today unless you have earth-shaking information."

"I'm sorry. You deserve time off. Want me to tell you tomorrow instead?"

"Aww, you're kidding!"

I shook my head, sipped a mocha latte, and unpinned the picture of Riley Hooper, which left the photo of Bonnie Shergold.

"Really?" he asked. "This should be interesting."

"You may recall that Orson told Myra he found his wife dead and took off with Stella because he knew who killed her and that he would be back to kill Orson and Stella. Myra tells me Orson specifically said the guy had brothers."

Wolf smeared cream cheese on his bagel and layered lox on it while he listened.

"Terry Warren—do you know who I'm talking about?"

"Alas, yes. Colin's uncle."

"Terry Warren has brothers. Apparently, they were a wild bunch. And they had a sister named Sharon, who had cancer as a child and was very sick. The story was that she couldn't have children because of all the treatments. She showed up one day with a baby girl, whom you know as Bonnie Sherwood."

"She's very nice. That's where I buy flowers for my wife."

"Bonnie thinks her father was a French rock and roller, who is now deceased. Two women who knew the family said they can't remember Sharon being pregnant, and there was a story about the baby being premature and kept at the hospital for months. I think Bonnie is Callie Chatsworth, the daughter Orson was looking for."

"Rumor and gossip is hardly enough to go on. Fortunately, there is an easy test to find out for sure. Wow! That's going to come as a big blow to Bonnie."

"That's not all."

Wolf had started on the second half of his bagel.

"Jordan St. James had a big loan to pay off. Stella was concerned about it because she couldn't see a bank giving Jordan a loan, which meant he must have gotten a private loan from someone."

Wolf nodded.

"Jordan also had a very flashy Rolex with a vibrant navy blue face and bezel. Hard to miss. But the last time I saw him, he wasn't wearing it. He has a spot on his arm that isn't suntanned where he used to wear it."

"Pawned."

"Possibly. Last night at the grand opening of the Warrens' new event space, the whole family was present, including Terry. His right hand was black and blue, like he'd been punching someone."

"Jordan?"

"That's who I suspect. And he wore a Rolex on his wrist with a vibrant navy blue face and bezel."

"So Terry gave Jordan a loan. When Jordan didn't have the money to pay him back, he gave Terry his Rolex."

"But it wasn't enough to cover the loan, so when Orson died, Jordan broke into the store and stole the mock antiquity that went missing from the store and I found in the alley after the ambulance left with Jordan.

"Which was why Terry beat up Jordan. And if Terry really was the man who shot Orson's wife, he might also have murdered Orson."

"And it was probably Terry who was following Orson around."

"Why wouldn't Orson have mentioned him in the letter he left for you?"

"I think he didn't get around to it. We all put things off. That's why he didn't mention the photos of the girls. He thought he would be the one figuring out if one of them was his missing daughter. Terry hasn't been here long, so maybe Orson didn't even realize that Terry was in town. It's been decades. They might not even have recognized one another right away. The Warrens have a strong family resemblance, but age changes us."

I finished my latte and nibbled on a bagel with salmon.

"That's quite a recitation. Congratulations. You have ruined my golf plans."

"Can you take tomorrow off instead?"

"I always plan to, but it never works out that way. I hope we can get Terry to talk."

"If I'm right about this, then Karl will be very happy."

Wolf eyed me. "Poisoning doesn't sound like it's something Terry would do. He'd more likely shoot someone or mess with the brakes in a person's car."

"Or beat them up," I said. "But he had a very big motive. And none of my other suspects have had as great a motive."

"The size of the motive is within the killer. Some people kill for relatively minor matters, but they feel like they're huge."

Chapter 39

Dear Natasha,
I love your new Natasha Style business. I never miss your show and I have styled myself to be as much like you as possible. Could you do a column on how you dress and your favorite makeup products?

Huge Fan in Wears Valley, Tennessee

Dear Huge Fan,
I would love to do that. How would you like to come to Old Town for a visit? Maybe we can do a Natasha Style makeover for you on my TV show!

Natasha

After Wolf left, I indulged in a chocolate-iced Krispy Kreme doughnut and sat back, looking at the photo of Bonnie. I took a deep breath, feeling as if I had accomplished what Orson wanted. I had found Stella's sister. At least I hoped so!

But Wolf's words troubled me. He was right. It wasn't like Terry Warren to poison someone. Everyone had a style, and poisoning was not Terry's style. I chuckled, thinking of Natasha. Maybe she was right—everyone had a style, even if it was how they committed murder.

I pulled out paper and a pen. Which of the possible murder suspects would not be likely to use poison?

Myra? Yes. But it would have to be neat and easily available. I couldn't imagine her picking poison hemlock. She was more likely to overdose someone with pills.

Jordan? I didn't think he had the patience to prepare a poison. Did he cook at all? He might have chopped up hemlock greens and scattered them on a butter board. But if he had done that, other people would have died. I had my doubts that he would use poison.

Stella definitely cooked. I could see her plucking a poisonous plant and making a stew with it. Or using the hemlock greens in a salad or as a garnish. But I didn't think she had a motive. She loved her father.

Audrey! Poisoning fit her perfectly. She was a nurse. She probably knew a lot about poisons and medicines. She probably hadn't baked the pastries she served us, but she had made a special drink. And she gardened! I had to reconsider Audrey.

Karl might cook. He was raised in the country and probably learned a thing or two about cooking. And he had poison hemlock in his backyard. He had plenty of old pots where he could have brewed the hemlock.

But Karl had now moved into the number two position in my mind, even though he'd been arrested and was out on bond.

Audrey had been dumped by Orson. What was that saying? Hell hath no fury like a woman scorned. That was the kind of motive Wolf was talking about. It might not seem like a motive for murder to most of us. But it was a big deal for Audrey. Even her parakeet, James Bond, had asked, "Howww could he?"

But the bigger question in my mind was—how had she poisoned him? We knew that she used poison hemlock. She had likely made a brew of some sort and used it in a drink or a meal. But he had died at the party, which was catered.

How could I have been so stupid? Tripp Fogarty had worked the party as a server. Nothing would have been easier than for him to slip poison into Orson's drink. He would have been in a perfect position to do that.

He'd brought Audrey that yellow bird. They were definitely acquainted. She had mentioned a nephew who lived with her. Was it possible that Tripp was that nephew?

By now, Audrey must have heard that the police arrested Karl. Everyone in town was probably talking about Natasha going into the Potomac after him. Even if that wasn't exactly how it happened. So if I was right about Audrey being the person who murdered Orson, she was probably feeling pretty good right now. The police had a suspect and the suspect had the poison that had killed Orson.

What would I do in her situation? She was probably lying low. Keeping her nose down. And then she might go on a vacation. Get out of town while the case cooled off.

I was tempted to peek in her backyard to see if that cast aluminum trowel was still missing. Was she the one who dug up the poison hemlock in Karl's garden? Had she been spooked by Karl or afraid he might catch her and left her trowel there? Was that why Tripp had ordered another one?

It was Sunday morning, which was brunch day. She might choose to stay home and work in her garden, but it was getting fairly hot for that already. Maybe I would follow her.

I phoned Nina. "How would you feel about tailing someone?"

"I would love to do that! But I have to drop my husband off at the airport first. We're nearly there. I'll text you on my way back and meet you wherever you are."

That sounded good to me. I was afraid my remaining doughnuts would not appreciate the heat, so I left them in the secret room, closed the bookshelves, set the alarm, and left, taking care to lock the front door.

I strolled toward Audrey's house, but spied her at an outdoor table on the terrace of The Laughing Hound, Bernie's restaurant. Fortunately, I knew my way around there. I entered through the main door, but waved away the hostess and walked through the kitchen to a back door that led to the outdoor fire-cooking addition at the back of the terrace. If I played my cards right, she might not even notice me. I was close enough that I might even hear what she was saying if she made a phone call, or someone joined her.

Having had enough lattes for one morning, I ordered iced tea and pretended to consult the menu while I was actually watching Audrey.

"I have someone coming to join me," she said. "He's running late, so I'll go ahead and order two Eggs Benedicts, please."

Wonderful! I could hear her well.

My phone peeped with a text coming in: **The eagle is waiting to take flight.**

No wonder Nina was my friend. I laughed at her silly message. Unless there was a lot of traffic, she should join me shortly. I texted her back. **The falcon and mouse are at The Laughing Hound. Go through the kitchen to the fire-cooking grills.**

When I looked up, Audrey was thanking the server for the additional water glass he had brought.

I lowered the menu and pretended to be looking at my phone as if I was bored. She was seated at a slight angle, and I was able to photograph her easily. I doubted that she would do anything in a public restaurant, but you just never knew.

I felt a hand on my shoulder and nearly squealed.

Nina eased into the chair next to me. "Who are we watching?"

I pointed in the direction of Audrey.

Nina gave me a thumbs-up.

Our server returned to take our orders. I had already eaten breakfast and a doughnut, so in a very hushed voice, I ordered something called the Fruit Board.

Nina ordered a cheese omelet with hash browns and coffee.

"What happened?" whispered Nina.

"Long story," I whispered back.

"At least there will be food. Beats sitting in a car."

The server brought Audrey two plates of Eggs Benedict.

Audrey sipped her coffee and gazed around. Then she withdrew a small jar from her purse.

Nina elbowed me.

I nodded.

Audrey used her fork to lift the eggs and shook a powder on the Canadian bacon.

I snapped a photo. What if it was poison hemlock?

She screwed the top back on and placed it in her purse again.

Tripp ambled in, causing Nina and me to raise our menus to cover our faces.

"Hello, dear. Was traffic bad?" asked Audrey.

"Isn't it always?" said Tripp.

"I went ahead and ordered. We usually get the same thing anyway and I know how you love Eggs Benedict."

"Great. I ordered you a replacement trowel."

"You what?"

She lowered her voice and I had to lean closer to hear her.

"You idiot! I told you to go back and get it. Our fingerprints are all over that thing!" she whispered.

I peeked around my menu and realized that Audrey had swapped seats. It was a four-sided table, and they were sitting next to each other as opposed to across from each other. Audrey's back was to us now. But Tripp would notice us if he turned his head to the right far enough.

"She swapped seats," I mouthed.

"Did she take her plate?" Nina whispered.

I shrugged. Some spies we were.

"How do we stop him from eating it?"

"Stand up and spill something on him."

Tripp was already starting to eat. I did what Nina suggested. I picked up my water glass and rose, then pretended to stagger, and leaned over to pour the water directly onto Tripp's Eggs Benedict.

He yelped and shoved his chair back.

"Oh, I'm so sorry!" I said.

But Audrey was eyeing me. I had a bad feeling she knew that it hadn't been an accident.

"Sophie! I'm all wet."

A slight exaggeration, although some of the water had missed the plate and spilled on his trousers.

"Gosh, Tripp. I'm sorry. Let me order you another one."

I grabbed a cloth napkin so I wouldn't get poison on my hands and used it to pick up his plate and move it to our table.

"Hey! What are you doing?" asked Tripp.

He reached over and grabbed one of the Eggs Benedicts with his bare hand and wolfed it down.

"No!" I yelled. "No! Don't swallow. Spit it out!"

By now everyone on the terrace was watching.

"What is wrong with you?" asked Tripp.

Our food arrived. Before Nina dug into her omelet, I grabbed her plate and shoved it in front of Tripp. "Here, eat this. At least it will dilute whatever was on your Eggs Benedict."

Tripp put his hand to his throat. "Uh oh. Peanuts."

"That can't be, darling," said Audrey, sweet as sugar. "There aren't any peanuts in Eggs Benedict."

"Throat closing," gasped Tripp. He stood up and wobbled.

"Stay calm. Where's your EpiPen?" asked Audrey.

Tripp waved his hands in a weird and frantic gesture that I guessed meant he didn't have one on him.

I ran into the kitchen. "Do you keep an EpiPen somewhere?"

One of the line cooks yelled, "Bernie! EpiPen!"

Bernie came charging through the kitchen, grabbed an EpiPen from a drawer, and then saw me. "You don't have a food allergy."

"Outside."

He followed me.

Tripp was already on the stone floor. Everyone had stopped eating and now watched.

Bernie administered the EpiPen, while I called for an ambulance.

I texted Wolf: **The Laughing Hound. Outside terrace. Now!**

I could picture Wolf groaning.

Wong came running from the indoor part of the restaurant. "What happened?"

While Audrey explained about Tripp's peanut allergy, I moved Tripp's plate out of Audrey's reach.

Audrey shouted, "What are you doing?"

"I don't want it to fall and break."

Nina nodded. "Good idea."

Audrey's tone became harsh. "Give me that. It's going to be evidence when we sue this place."

"I think we'll leave it right back here for now. No one will touch it. And Wolf can collect it when he arrives."

"I have to take it with me to the hospital. It will be confused with the other plates and thrown out. I must take it," Audrey insisted.

The howl of an ambulance sounded.

"The plate stays here. I'll make sure the cops get it."

"It's not your place to make those decisions. Oh, I get it. Bernie is your friend. A special friend, perhaps?"

"He is a very special friend, and I don't like what you're insinuating. And why are you arguing with me over a plate when your nephew is writhing on the floor? Shouldn't you be a wee bit concerned about him?"

Thankfully, EMTs ran in. I knew one thing. That plate wasn't going anywhere except to the police.

Bernie backed up toward Nina and me to make more room. The diners spoke softly, and we only heard the rare hiss of a whisper or clink of flatware.

The EMTs were, as always, quick and efficient. I gathered that Tripp's condition was of grave concern and that they wanted to get him to the emergency room pronto. He was carried out on a stretcher and relief among those on the patio was obvious.

Audrey stood firm. "If Tripp dies, make no mistake, I will sue this restaurant for so much money you will have to shut down. The hospital lab needs to know what was in his food so they can treat him appropriately. Listen to me. I'm a nurse. I *know* what I'm talking about."

"You put something in his food," I said.

Bernie shot me a wide-eyed look. "I'll be happy to hand it over to Wong or Wolf. One of them can deliver it to the hospital."

Audrey spun around. In a very loud voice, she said, "Do you hear that? You're my witnesses." She pointed at people. "All of you see that they refuse to give me the plate, so we'll know what was in my nephew's food."

Bernie kept an eye on her. "Kaylee," he said to one of his servers, "please fetch some plastic wrap from the kitchen."

She reached for the plate.

"No," I said. "Leave that out here where everyone can see it. I don't want anyone claiming that you substituted a different plate."

Kaylee hurried into the kitchen. She was back in a flash and handed the plastic wrap to Bernie.

"Thanks, Kaylee."

Bernie wrapped the entire plate with the food on it in front of everyone. "Wong, would you like to take this to the hospital?"

At that moment, Wolf walked through the door. Wong quickly explained the situation to him. He walked over to Audrey. "What happened?"

"There were peanuts in my nephew's meal. He's having a terrible reaction. But they won't give me the food so I can take it to the hospital. The doctors will need to know what was in it. I'm a nurse. I know what will happen if they don't have it, but they won't let me take it with me."

"She sprinkled something under the egg on the Canadian bacon," I blurted. "It's in her purse."

Audrey snatched her purse and clutched it under her arm. "That's nonsense. I did no such thing."

"We both saw you, Audrey," said Nina. "And then you switched seats so that would be Tripp's plate."

I could hear other diners gasping.

"All right," said Wolf. "Wong, you take the plate. I'll give Audrey a ride to the hospital."

"Am I under arrest?" Audrey asked in horror.

"No, ma'am. I'm giving you a ride as a courtesy. Shall we get going? I'm sure your nephew will feel better knowing you're there with him."

She gave me a nasty look before she walked out with Wolf. We could hear her saying, "You can't look in my purse without a warrant. I know my rights!"

Wong collected the plate. "Are the stars in a weird alignment or something? Did she really try to kill her own nephew?"

"I think so!"

"But why?" asked Wong.

It was a very good question. But maybe the better question was—why now?

Chapter 40

Dear Sophie,
What's the difference between a fruit plate and a
fruit board?
   Gone Fruity in Peach Bottom, Pennsylvania

Dear Gone Fruity,
The biggest difference is the surface on which the
fruit sits. It's mostly a presentation thing. The
board is more likely to contain small bowls with a
dipping sauces and may be larger to feed more than
one person.
         Sophie

Unless I missed my guess, Audrey would be tied up at the hospital and the police station for some time. I was very tempted to peek in her garden to see if her trowel was there. But she could have taken it indoors, and I didn't want to leave my fingerprints anywhere or mess up her home or garden, which would be thoroughly searched once they found the peanut powder in her purse.

Instead, Nina accompanied me to Chatsworth Antiques,

where I bought a painting and took merciless kidding from everyone because I insisted on paying for it, when technically, it all belonged to me anyway.

The next morning, Wolf stopped by when Nina, Mars, Bernie, and I were eating waffles in my garden. I retrieved a plate, napkin, and a mug of coffee for Wolf, who promptly helped himself to a waffle and topped it with butter, maple syrup, and raspberries.

"After all the digging you did," he said, "I thought the four of you deserved to know what was happening. First of all, we did find peanut powder in Audrey's purse as well as on the Canadian bacon, just as Sophie said. It was a lucky thing that you happened to be there watching." Wolf shot me a look that meant he wasn't happy about the fact that we were spying on Audrey.

"Tripp felt pretty lousy and started spilling information fast. It happens sometimes when a person is sick. He, um, didn't want us to let his aunt anywhere near him. It took a while to get the story out of the two of them. It seems that Audrey wanted to poison Wanda, not Orson. As she put it, she needed to keep Orson and his money alive. To do that, she had to get rid of Wanda. She cooked up the hemlock in a sugar syrup, and Tripp, who was serving at the engagement party, was supposed to put it in Wanda's glass, but he goofed and gave that glass to Orson. Audrey was devastated. Tripp had ruined all her dreams for her future."

"Wanda! That was a close call," said Nina, exchanging horrified glances with me.

Audrey had noticed the poison hemlock growing behind Karl's building. She figured he wouldn't notice if they took some. So she sent Tripp over to dig it up and bring it to her. But Tripp accidentally left Audrey's trowel there, which worried her.

"Audrey was suspicious when Joan died suddenly. From

everything she could glean, Jordan had an alibi. She was convinced that Tripp was getting too bold. Taking too many chances, and he had to be eliminated. She called him 'a loose cannon who was going to take her down with him.' He has a pretty lengthy record of crimes in Kentucky where he was living before he moved here."

"Will he be okay?"

"The doctors think so. But he'll likely go from the hospital to the jail."

"Why did he kill Joan?" asked Bernie.

Wolf shook his head. "He hasn't admitted to that yet, but he was on our radar for that crime."

"I think I know," I said. "Scuttlebutt has it that Joan was seeing Tripp and then it sounds like she threw him over for Jordan," I said. "Both relationships were supposed to be hush-hush, but I guess they weren't."

"Speaking of Jordan, did you question Terry about him?" I asked.

Wolf nodded. "Your buddy Terry was bailed out of jail by his brothers. You were right, Sophie. Terry made a loan to Jordan. Jordan didn't have the money to pay it, so he gave Terry his Rolex. But that wasn't enough, so when Orson died, Jordan broke into Chatsworth Antiques and stole what he thought was an antiquity to give to Terry for the remainder of the loan. But Terry took it to an antiques dealer in town who laughed in his face and told him it was probably made last year in China along with ten thousand more."

"That was when Terry beat Jordan and left him in the alley. It was Jordan who broke into Orson's house, too, wasn't it?" I asked.

"How'd you know that?" asked Mars.

"The same day, Nina and I had lunch with Jordan, and he had an injury on his arm. I didn't think it was a coincidence. Whoever broke in would have had to reach inside through the broken glass to unlock the door."

"What about Stella? Is Bonnie her sister?" asked Nina.

Wolf smiled. "Turns out that Orson told Myra the truth. Terry was a tough nut to crack, but he made a deal with us. I think he knew the murder of Stella's mother had finally caught up to him. So he agreed to tell all if we didn't prosecute Sharon. She was terrified. According to her, Terry walked in one day and handed her a baby girl. He told her that the child's father had killed her mother, then he ran off with the other child, leaving this baby without any parents. She read the accounts of the crime in the newspaper, and they verified what Terry told her. She desperately wanted a baby. She thought about turning the baby over to the authorities, but she just couldn't bring herself to do it."

"Was Terry having an affair with Stella's mother?" asked Nina.

"No. He wanted to build houses, but he needed a loan to get going. He and his brothers already had a rough reputation, and they were all broke with no collateral. Orson was the banker who turned him down. Terry was so outraged that he wanted to hurt Orson. He went to Orson's house intending to kill Orson, but he wasn't home. He shot Orson's wife instead. Stella was screaming. He didn't want her, but when he saw the baby, he thought of Sharon and took the baby with him. Given Terry's history, I think Orson may have been right when he thought Terry would come back to finish the job by killing Orson and Stella, too.

"But why wouldn't Orson have gone to the police?" asked Mars. "That's what I would have done."

"Because if Orson turned Terry in, one of Terry's brothers would have murdered Orson or Orson could have ended up in the slammer for the murder of his wife and he would never find Callie," I said. "Saving Stella and finding Callie became Orson's lifelong mission."

One week later, I made an appointment with Ronin. It turned out that I could do exactly what I had hoped with Chatsworth Antiques. Even better, he was able to confirm that Bonnie's DNA matched Stella's, proving that they were sisters.

I thought a party might be the best way to tell everyone my plans. Then I went shopping for a very specific blue baby blanket.

On Friday evening, I hosted a barbecue in my backyard. Stella provided the charcuterie boards and butter boards that served as appetizers. They were gorgeous, laden with meats, cheeses, crackers, olives, pickles, and fruits. We heated loaves of bread on the grill to use on the butter boards. My favorite was the one with onions and garlic.

Natasha, Wanda, and Griselda came together. Francie and her dog, Duke, arrived via the gate between our properties. Nina brought summer drinks with and without alcohol that we set up outside in tubs of ice. She brought along little Muppet and Orson's dog, Rosebud.

Wolf shook his head at me when he saw Ronin arrive. I just smiled and introduced him to everyone, including Wong, who I thought looked particularly fetching that night.

Bernie and Mars manned the barbecue grills. Myra insisted on bringing Mochie outside in his harness and leash. He was fascinated by Myra. She was certain he could tell she was a cat person, but I suspected he was more interested in the cat smells on her flowing caftan.

I invited all of the employees of Chatsworth Antiques. Ian and Reba were thrilled to see Rosebud again.

Jordan had been released from the hospital, but wasn't

ready to party yet. I debated inviting Karl, and decided it was time to make amends. After all, I was sort of responsible for the trouble he landed in. But honestly, if he hadn't jumped off the yacht and tried to swim away from the police, he wouldn't have seemed so guilty.

Bonnie and her mom, Sharon, arrived, looking tentative. I steered them over to Myra. After all, Sharon and Myra were going through similar emotional states. Both of them had raised a spectacular daughter to whom they hadn't given birth. In spite of the way they had become mothers, they were real moms to their daughters in every way.

We were a noisy, happy bunch. There were a lot of toasts, and even more laughter.

I had baked lemon meringue pies for dessert. After the tea, coffee, and after-dinner drinks had been poured, but before the pies had been sliced, I clinked my fork against my glass and stood up.

"Thank you all for coming. You're such a wonderful group of people and I hope you'll forge some new bonds as a good result of all the tragedies you've been through. When Orson announced that he had left Chatsworth Antiques to me, I was shocked, as were many of you."

That brought on some chuckles.

"But I understood that he must have had a reason for doing that. I just didn't know what it was. The only instruction he gave me was 'you'll know what to do.' In a way, Orson was right about that because I was intent on discovering that reason. And I found it. It took me a while to understand that Orson had been searching for his daughter. When he lay dying, he said to me, 'Tell Stella . . .' I thought perhaps he wanted to say, 'Tell Stella that I love her.' Because he really did. Everyone told me what a wonderful father he was and how he doted on Stella. But I came to realize that he was trying to say, 'Tell Stella she has a sister.'"

I glanced over at them sitting side by side. It was such a sad time for them, yet something good had come of all the sorrow. "So, I feel like my job is done now. Consequently, I am going to disclaim my inheritance of Chatsworth Antiques. Ronin has assured me that by doing so, according to Orson's will, the store and everything in it as of now will be part of a trust for the benefit of his surviving children, Stella Chatsworth and Bonnie Shergold." After a long moment of silence, everyone spoke at once.

I interrupted. "A couple more things. First . . ." I pulled out the baby blanket that was identical to the one Jordan had taken. I walked over and handed it to Stella. "Maybe Olly will think it's the same one."

Then I walked over to a covered item that I had set out earlier. "I bought this item from the store because I knew it meant a lot to Myra. I think if Orson knew she wanted it, he would have left it to her." I whisked a cover off a painting of a mother cat and her kittens. Myra began to cry.

Nina popped up. "Just a minute. I think this would be the appropriate time to announce where Rosebud is going to live. I have to tell you, I love Rosebud and considered keeping her myself. But I think she'll be happiest with Ian and Reba, who are planning to share custody of her. They'll be taking her to work at Chatsworth Antiques, just like Orson did."

Reba and Ian fussed over Rosebud and thanked Nina.

Myra hurried over to admire her painting. She gave me a hug. "I don't think for one minute that Orson would have given this to me, but it means the world that you did. And that you brought light to something dark and horrible. It hasn't been easy, but you did the right thing."

As the sun went down, Mars turned on the outdoor string lights. They added a glowing ambiance to the party.

Stella and Bonnie approached me.

"We can't believe you would do this," said Stella. "Are you sure?"

"One hundred percent! That's why your dad set up the documents to include his living children. He didn't know if or when he would find you, Bonnie. He hoped I would be able to achieve what he hadn't."

"This is amazing," said Bonnie. "A new family, now a store! Good grief, it's overwhelming."

"How is Jordan?" I asked.

Bonnie's lips tightened.

Stella blew air out of her mouth. "He's still in rehab."

Bonnie threw a glance at her. "I'm having a lot of trouble feeling sorry for him. Do you know what he did?"

"I don't think so," I said.

"Stella, you're the one who told me these things. You give him too much slack." Bonnie ticked items off on her fingers as she spoke. "He is the one who called the police hotline and reported Stella for murdering Joan! He is the one who broke into Orson's house and stole the baby blanket. Why? So he could claim that it wasn't a safe environment for the children."

"Well," said Stella, "I'm not sure he meant to steal the baby blanket. It's more like he picked it up to stop the bleeding on his arm where the glass cut him."

"Oh, Stella!" Bonnie slung an arm around her. "Honey, he was doing everything he could to get custody because he hoped to live off the money tied to your children."

"How do you know all this? Did he confess?" I asked.

"The police found his fingerprints on the door where he broke the glass. And then they found his blood on the baby blanket," said Bonnie.

"I bet that's what he used to wrap his hand when he broke the glass in the door of the antiques store. There was a tiny bit of blue fabric that snagged on the glass." I would have to ask Wong or Wolf to compare it with the baby blanket.

"It was Ronin who put it all together and confronted Jordan's lawyer with it," said Stella. "They agreed to give me full custody. But Jordan gets supervised visitation."

"And now," said Bonnie with a big smile, "Stella has a baby sister to watch out for her. I have already told her that I will have to approve of the men in her life, so she won't fall for another guy like Jordan."

Myra and Sharon joined their daughters and my thoughts drifted as they talked about the painting.

Wanda drew me aside and whispered, "Natasha heard you say that daffodils are toxic. She stole the homeopathic meds from our store because she feared I had given Orson some to take and would go to prison for Orson's murder. My wonderful daughter was trying to protect me!" She gave me a hug and returned to Natasha.

Ronin and Wong were seated next to each other, engaged in deep conversation. I liked that! I looked over at Wolf, who shook his head at me, which made me laugh.

Ian sat on the grass holding Rosebud, who was licking his face. Reba stroked Rosebud gently.

Everyone was having a good time. I looked up at the stars and hoped Orson was watching. At long last, his daughters were together again.

Recipes

Avocado and Egg Toast

Makes 2 servings.

Don't worry about doing this the wrong way. It's super easy and there is no wrong way to do it. If you like a little spice, add it at the end. Use whatever seasonings appeal to you.

2 teaspoons extra virgin olive oil
4 eggs
Salt and pepper to taste
Bread
2 avocados

Please note: It's definitely a matter of preference, but be advised that runny yolks may contain salmonella and make you sick.

Preheat the pan briefly on medium to warm it. Add the olive oil and swirl around the pan before adding the eggs. Place a lid on the pan and cook until the very edges of the yolks begin to show some cooked egg white. Salt and pepper to taste. Take them off the heat and set them aside with the lid on to allow the yolks to cook. You may wish to cook the yolks through to avoid salmonella.

Meanwhile, toast the bread.

Cut the avocados in half lengthwise. Using a soup spoon, scoop out the avocado in half-inch thicknesses from the bottom working back. Place the slices on a plate and press them with the back of a fork to flatten or mash them.

Place half an avocado worth of slices on each piece of toast. Top with the cooked eggs. Sprinkle with your favorite seasonings.

Lavender Lemonade

This is a lemonade base with lavender and a spirit, but can be served as a mocktail without the alcohol. The lavender will not have a purple tint after it's steeped, but when the lemon is added, it turns a lovely pink. I found this made about eight servings in coupe glasses. If you need more, simply double the recipe.

1 cup sugar
1 cup water
¼ cup culinary lavender
¾ cup lemon juice
2 additional cups water
¾ cup vodka
Sprigs of fresh lavender or lemon slices for garnish

Make the lavender syrup first because it needs to steep.
Place 1 cup sugar in a small pot. Add 1 cup water and the culinary lavender. Bring to a brief boil, and stir to help the sugar dissolve. Refrigerate to cool and let steep for at least 20 minutes.

Meanwhile, squeeze the lemons. Pour the chilled lavender syrup into a pitcher and add the lemon juice, 2 cups of water, and ¾ cup vodka. Chill before serving. To serve, pour into individual coupe glasses and garnish with a fresh lavender sprig or a lemon slice.

Onion Confit

Onion confit roasts onions over low heat until they cara-melize. Use it as a spread on bread, a topping on burgers, or to accompany meats that you are serving. If you have a mandoline, it will speed things up, but the onions can also be sliced by hand.

½ cup extra virgin olive oil
2 tablespoons butter
3 onions
4 garlic cloves
1 teaspoon thyme
3 tablespoons dark brown sugar
1 tablespoon balsamic vinegar
Salt and pepper to taste

Slice the onions thin. Peel the garlic, smash with the flat side of your knife, and mince. Warm a large sauté pan over medium heat. Pour the olive oil in the pan and add the butter, then the onions and the garlic. Stir to combine and coat the onions with the oil and butter. Add the thyme, dark brown sugar, and balsamic vinegar. Stir the mixture to combine. Adjust the temperature as necessary; the onions should cook slowly but not burn. Cook for 30 min-utes, stirring occasionally. Salt and pepper to taste. Store in the refrigerator.

Avocado Spread

This is a quick and easy spread that works well on toast.

2 ripe avocados
3 garlic cloves
2 teaspoons lemon juice
Salt to taste

Cut the avocados lengthwise. Remove the pit. Scoop out the avocado into a bowl. Mash the avocados with a fork. Peel and crush the garlic cloves. Mince with a knife and add to the avocados. Squeeze two teaspoons of fresh lemon juice into the bowl and mix together. Add salt to taste.

Mars's Favorite Walnut Pesto

3 tablespoons walnuts
3 cups fresh basil leaves
2 teaspoons minced garlic
½ cup extra virgin olive oil
½ cup Parmesan cheese
Salt and pepper to taste

Chop the walnuts in a small food processor. Add the basil leaves and garlic and pulse. Slowly add the olive oil in a stream while pulsing or add in small amounts and pulse in between. Add the Parmesan cheese and pulse. Add salt and pepper to taste and pulse one last time.

Krista's tip: Plant a couple of basil plants in the spring. They're easy to grow and you'll have plenty of basil leaves to make this dish.

Salted Caramel Banana Pudding

Makes 4 servings.

This is a fun twist on an old favorite. Be generous with the caramel and the salt so they don't disappear in the mix. Table salt will not work here. You will likely have some leftover caramel. Store in the fridge, and microwave to warm, then pour over ice cream!

Shopping List
4 bananas (not green)
Vanilla wafers
Flaky sea salt (like Maldon)
1 egg
2 cups cold skim or nonfat milk
sugar
cornstarch
vanilla
unsalted butter
dark brown sugar
1 pint heavy whipping cream
powdered sugar

Make the pudding:

⅓ cup sugar
¼ cup cornstarch
salt
2 cups cold skim or nonfat milk
1 egg
1 teaspoon vanilla
1 tablespoon butter

Place the cornstarch, sugar, and a dash of salt in a heavy-bottomed saucepan. Using a whisk, mix them together. Pour the milk into the pan and whisk with the dry ingredients to blend. Crack the egg into the empty milk-measuring cup and whisk to break the yolk and combine. Use a fork to whisk if you don't have a mini whisk.

Turn on the burner to medium high. Stir the milk mixture with the whisk to be sure it doesn't burn. You may need to turn the heat back a bit when it begins to bubble. Stirring the whole time, let bubble softly for one minute. Remove from heat.

Drop a few drops of the hot mixture into the egg and whisk. Add a few more drops and whisk again to temper the egg. Add the egg mixture to the milk mixture and whisk to blend. Stirring continuously, bring it back to a gentle boil and cook for one minute.

Remove from heat. Add vanilla and 1 tablespoon butter. Stir to mix.

Make the caramel:

4 tablespoons unsalted butter
1 cup packed dark brown sugar
¼ cup heavy cream

Place 4 tablespoons unsalted butter, 1 cup packed dark brown sugar, and ¼ cup heavy cream in a deep microwave safe dish. (I use a 2-cup Pyrex measuring cup.) Microwave in short bursts, stirring occasionally, until it bubbles up and the sugar is melted.

Assemble:

Cover the bottom of a serving dish or individual bowls or trifle glasses with vanilla wafers. Top with a layer of pudding. Top with sliced bananas and drizzle with caramel sauce. Sprinkle with flaked salt.

Note: Depending on your preference, you can be a little heavy-handed with the caramel sauce and the salt so they are more noticeable.

Add another layer of vanilla wafers, pudding, and bananas and drizzle with caramel sauce. Sprinkle with flaked salt. Repeat until you end with a layer of pudding on top. Refrigerate for at least 4 hours before serving.

Make the whipped cream just before you are ready to serve:

1 cup heavy whipping cream
1 teaspoon vanilla
⅓ cup powdered sugar

Beat 1 cup of heavy cream in a mixer. When it begins to take shape, add 1 teaspoon vanilla and ⅓ cup powdered sugar. Beat until it holds a shape. Spread or pipe over the top level of the vanilla pudding. Store extra for use in coffee or hot chocolate!

Optional: You may wish to drizzle caramel over the whipped cream.

No Cook Version of Banana Pudding with Salted Caramel Sauce

Buy:
vanilla pudding
vanilla wafers
bananas
caramel sauce
flaky salt
whipped cream

Assemble as in recipe above.

Banana Walnut Bread

This is a health-conscious version of banana bread. The walnuts are chopped fine so that they take the place of some flour. In addition, it's made with whole wheat pastry flour!

8-x-4-inch loaf pan
Butter or oil for greasing
1 cup walnuts
4 tablespoons whole wheat pastry flour
3 teaspoons baking powder
4 eggs
½ cup sugar
2 ripe bananas

Preheat oven to 350. Grease and flour an 8-x-4 bread-baking pan.

In a bowl, stir the nuts with the flour and baking powder. In a food processer or blender, mix the sugar with the eggs until smooth. Add the nut mixture and the bananas and blend until mixed. Pour into prepared pan and bake for 1 hour or until a cake tester comes out clean.

Cold Mocha Coffee with Ice Cream

Makes 4.

16 ounces coffee chilled (instant coffee or leftover coffee)
¾ cup cold milk
2 tablespoons sugar
Vanilla ice cream
Chocolate sauce

   Place the coffee, milk, and sugar in a blender. Mix well so it foams a little. Pour into mugs or double old-fashioned size glasses about ¾ full. Add a scoop of ice cream to each glass. Drizzle chocolate sauce over the ice cream and serve with a spoon.

Roasted Potatoes

2 pounds red or yellow potatoes
2 tablespoons extra virgin olive oil
1 teaspoon garlic powder
1 teaspoon paprika
Salt and pepper to taste

Preheat the oven to 425.

Wash the potatoes and remove any eyes or unpleasant spots. Cut the potatoes into roughly 1-inch cubes. Place the potatoes in a large bowl. Add the olive oil and toss the potatoes so they are coated. Add the garlic powder, paprika, salt, and pepper to the bowl. Toss the potatoes to cover them with the seasonings. Spread on a baking sheet. Roast for 35 to 45 minutes. When they are done, a fork should slide into them easily.

For a fun change, try using smoked paprika!

Summer Succotash

Makes 6-8 servings.

Want to make it more irresistible? Crumble in cooked bacon!

Hint: It can sometimes be hard to find fresh lima beans and corn. Happily, they are usually quite abundant in the frozen section of your grocery store. All you have to do is thaw them.

If the corn is on the cob, cut it off.

3 tablespoons unsalted butter
1 large onion
3 garlic cloves (3 teaspoons diced)
1 cup of zucchini
1 red pepper
1 yellow pepper
1 bag frozen lima beans, thawed
1 bag frozen corn, thawed
1½ teaspoons sage
1½ teaspoons thyme
6 cherry tomatoes
Salt and pepper

Dice the onion and mince the garlic. Cut the zucchini and the peppers into small pieces. Melt the butter in a large skillet. Cook the onion over medium high heat until it is tender, stirring as needed. Add the garlic and cook briefly. Add the zucchini, peppers, lima beans, corn, sage, and thyme. Cook until the zucchini and peppers are soft, stirring as needed. Halve the cherry tomatoes and add them. Toss everything together, season with salt and pepper to taste, and serve.

Peach Cake

8-x-8-inch baking dish or 8-inch deep-dish pie pan

1 tablespoon butter and 1 tablespoon flour for greasing
   the pan
For the peaches: 3 to 4 peaches
1 lemon
3 tablespoons unsalted butter
$\frac{2}{3}$ cup sugar
$\frac{1}{4}$ teaspoon nutmeg
1 tablespoon flour

For the cake:

1 cup flour
1 teaspoon baking powder
$\frac{1}{4}$ teaspoon salt
1 egg
$\frac{1}{4}$ cup sugar
1 tablespoon unsalted butter
4-6 tablespoons milk
$\frac{3}{4}$ teaspoon vanilla

Grease the baking dish with butter and dust with flour.
Peel and slice the peaches. Toss with the juice of the
lemon. Melt 3 tablespoons butter. Add the sugar, nutmeg,
1 tablespoon flour, and 3 tablespoons melted butter to the
peaches and toss to coat. Set aside.
Preheat the oven to 425.
Mix together the flour, baking powder, and salt. Beat the
egg with the sugar. Add the milk, 1 tablespoon melted butter, and vanilla and beat. Slowly beat in the flour mixture.
Place the fruit in the baking dish, overlapping the peach
slices in a pleasing pattern. When you have completely

covered the bottom with fruit, pour the remaining liquid over the top of it. Then slowly pour the batter over the fruit in a thin ribbon so that you cover all the fruit as much as possible. There may be a small part along the edges that isn't covered, and that's okay.

Bake at 425 for 30 minutes, or until the fruit bubbles and the top is golden brown.

Do not turn out of the pan! Allow to cool. Cover with aluminum foil and refrigerate overnight. When cold, run a knife around the edges and press gently to loosen. Top with a plate and flip.

Serve with lightly sweetened whipped cream, crème fraiche, or clotted cream.

Bourbon Peach Iced Tea

2 peaches + extra for optional garnish
1½ cups sugar
1 cup + 8 cups water
4 bags of black tea
1 cup bourbon
1 cup peach schnapps

Peel the peaches and cut into pieces. Place them in a heavy-bottomed pan with the sugar and 1 cup water. Cook over medium-high heat until the sugar dissolves. Simmer for an additional 10 minutes.

Set aside to cool. When the mixture has cooled, puree in a blender and refrigerate.

Boil 8 cups of water in a large pot. Add the tea bags and steep. When it cools, add the peach mixture, bourbon, and peach schnapps. Stir and refrigerate. Pour into a pitcher to serve.

Garnish with fresh peach slices.